T0323270

Sisters
OF
Fire
AND
Fury

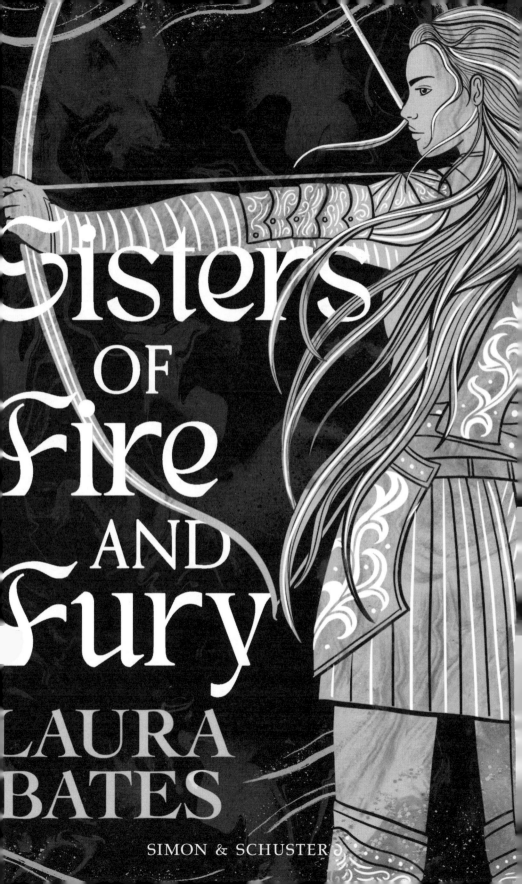

Sisters
OF
Fire
AND
Fury

LAURA
BATES

SIMON & SCHUSTER

First published in Great Britain in 2024 by Simon & Schuster UK Ltd

Text copyright © 2024 Laura Bates

1 3 5 7 9 10 8 6 4 2

Simon & Schuster UK Ltd
1st Floor, 222 Gray's Inn Road
London WC1X 8HB

Simon & Schuster: celebrating 100 years of Publishing in 2024

www.simonandschuster.co.uk
www.simonandschuster.com.au
www.simonandschuster.co.in

Simon & Schuster Australia, Sydney
Simon & Schuster India, New Delhi

A CIP catalogue record for this book is available
from the British Library.

HB ISBN 978-1-3985-1937-4
eBook ISBN 978-1-3985-1938-1
eAudio ISBN 978-1-3985-1939-8

Typeset in the UK by Sorrel Packham

Printed and Bound in the UK using 100%
Renewable Electricity at CPI Group (UK) Ltd

MIX
Paper | Supporting
responsible forestry
FSC
www.fsc.org   FSC® C171272

For Evie and Grace
Sisters are magic

Prologue

The girl knelt in a meadow of wild flowers. A riot of colour danced around her. Cornflowers bent their bright feathered heads in the warm summer breeze, daisies swayed merrily and poppies shone blood red against the long grass. But the girl was quite still. The setting sun gave a golden crown to her bent head of chestnut curls.

Beside her in the long grass a sword lay glinting in the last rays of sunlight. Its silver blade was sharpened to a fierce point, the ruby hilt glowing as if a fire burned inside. Something a little like rust was caked messily along its sharp edge.

The evening was young. Giddy sparrows trilled their sunset farewells as they wheeled and skittered across the meadow and returned to the safety of the trees at the edge of the forest and still the girl knelt, motionless, as if she could not hear their chirping.

Slowly, and without looking at it, she reached out her hand towards the sword. Her outstretched fingers hesitated, frozen for a moment above the handle. Then she gripped it, with a sudden decisive clench of her hand, and it flew to her side as though bidden by her mind. With a single fluid movement, she leaped from her knees to the balls of her feet, crouching.

Faster than should have been possible, the blade flashed through the air in a perfect circle as she spun. The bright flowers bled their blues and reds in an arc of spilled petals and neatly sliced stems as the sun reached the horizon and the meadow was drenched in gold.

Chapter 1

The sun was already high in the sky when Cass awoke. Her mouth was tinder dry and her head ached. When she pushed herself upright it felt as if all the muscles in her body protested, aching as if she had run for miles the day before. She lay there, tensing and untensing her limbs, gently probing how sore they were, watching the dust motes dancing in the light that streamed in through the window, falling on the sheepskin rug that warmed the stone floor. In front of the fireplace, lying where she must have left it last night, though she could not seem to remember coming to bed, was the magnificent sword she had drawn from the stone in the last battle.

Cass was not used to sleeping so late. Usually Sigrid

would have woken her long before this, with demands for her to help her with armour or see to her horse. She stared at the closed door that led into her mistress's chamber. No. Not her mistress, she realized with a sudden start. Not any more. For Sigrid had been banished.

Now she was a servant without a mistress. A squire without a knight. Cass didn't know whether to be more worried about how she herself would cope without Sigrid to guide and train her, or how the sisterhood would cope without Sigrid's fearsome sword in the coming battles.

But Sigrid's was not the only powerful sword. Not any more.

Cass stretched her aching limbs and padded softly across the floor to the fireplace, where she knelt on the hearth, examining the sword she had pulled from the stone. Whenever she drew close to it, she had the strangest feeling that it was vibrating or humming, as if there were some invisible energy reaching out from it towards her, calling irresistibly to her.

Her fingers seemed to tingle as she stretched them towards it, and as she grasped it, she gasped aloud. There was a warmth, a power that flooded her body, rushing up her arm from where she held the sword and then suffusing every part of her, exhilarating her. She felt invincible, as though she could take on any enemy and win any fight.

And when she moved, to draw the sword experimentally through the air and bring it slashing down first to the left, then to the right, a kind of magic happened. She could not explain it, but the blade was somehow guiding her. It didn't take control or pull her against her will, but seemed to know what she wanted to do before she had realized it herself, leaping to action in perfect unison with her body.

The fire in the ruby hilt seemed to leap and flicker, and Cass held it at arm's length for a moment, then relinquished it quickly, laying it back down on the hearth.

Without it she felt cold, her arm heavy and awkward. She was drawn to it: her fingers itched to take it up again, but she backed away, not taking her eyes off the blade, and sat back down on the edge of her straw mattress.

Alys's words rang in her ears as she sat there.

There is a prophecy. Made when I was a child, before the last of the old people had been forced from the forests. A prophecy about a great leader, a light to unite the Britons. A leader who would hold back the darkness. And we would know this leader by the drawing of a sword . . .

Cass shook her head. She felt dazed, there was a slight ringing in her ears. It was preposterous. Arthur was king. And yet . . . her gaze was drawn back magnetically to the sword, as she remembered Alys's words.

This prophecy was made many years before Arthur's

allies chose him as ruler and placed that sword in the churchyard to give their choice the stamp of divine authority. Fate played no hand in what happened that day . . .

Cass baulked, her throat constricting as all the protests she had made to Alys leaped to her tongue just as they had before. She remembered the times she had sat in Alys's hut, bunches of herbs and ingredients hanging from the ceiling, evidence of her wisdom all around, and yet Cass couldn't accept what she seemed to see inside her. Yet Alys's words were as relentless as the elderly woman was stubborn, ringing in her head no matter how she tried to clear it.

The prophecy did not speak of a king. It spoke only of a leader. A leader who would pull a sword from a stone in Gefrin of Northumbria, and become the light to drive out the gathering dark. And we would know them by the sword, with a ruby at its hilt.

The ruby seemed to shine brighter, and Cass could not take her eyes off it. She longed to hold it again, but part of her recoiled even as it seemed to call out to her. She had never intended to draw the sword from the stone. Never tried her hand, straining, like the men she had seen attempt to bluff and bluster their way to claiming it when she had first laid eyes on the sword last Yuletide. Alys must have been confused, or misremembered the prophecy. And what did a prophecy signify anyway? Some old wives' tale passed down and morphed in the retelling through years of gossip and exaggeration? Arthur was king, his accession but a few years old, and it was he who was charged with protecting Britain from the many encroaching forces that threatened it.

Cass shivered a little, though the morning was warm.

Cass was not, *could* not be the great leader Alys had spoken of with such reverence. And she saw Lily for a moment, bursting with laughter so that her dimples flashed and her golden ringlets shook with mirth. *Cass the squire, once and future queen,* she would say, with mock reverence, sweeping a low bow and looking up at Cass, snorting, from beneath those long mischievous eyelashes. Nobody had ever been able to make her laugh as easily as her incorrigible, teasing best friend. And Cass smiled too, though it faded with the image, leaving behind the dull throbbing ache of absence.

She could put the sword back, she thought, and for a moment the idea seemed that it would ease her worries: simply relinquish it back to the stone and be done with it. Leave it for someone else to find, someone else for Alys to badger.

But Alys did not begin talking to you about the prophecy when you drew the sword from the stone, that quiet voice in Cass's mind piped up. *She spoke of it to you earlier, did she not? When she saw your scar and read your tea leaves. She knew there was something inside you, just as Sigrid saw it. And the woman who bowed low to you in the woods outside your home when you were just a child, her golden eyes wide with shock as if she knew you for what you were, she saw it inside you too.*

Cass sighed and closed her eyes, pressing the heels of her hands into her eyelids until the colour exploded. In the day since the battle with Mordaunt, since she had pulled the sword from the stone, she had escaped the heavy sadness of the sisterhood. Kneeling silent in the meadow, the sword beside her, she had been half in a dream, considering this new truth that had been revealed to her. A dream that now she could not quite remember, as it danced just beyond her grasp.

Chapter 2

With a great effort, Cass tore her eyes away from the sword and gave herself a shake. She was suddenly aware of her belly, which was growling and clenching like a ravenous beast, and realized she could not remember the last time she had eaten or washed.

The cold water from the pitcher shocked her awake in a way she hadn't felt in days. Out of habit more than anything else, she stepped into a soft grey silk dress, the feminine clothing the women at the manor had always adopted when they weren't training, to avoid the prying eyes of unexpected visitors. For the first time, as she smoothed down the skirts, and quickly bundled her hair up, it truly hit her that their disguises were no longer necessary. The sisterhood had revealed themselves to the world. The enormity of it struck her like a blow to the stomach. They were free. Free to ride out in their armour, to remove their helmets and openly compete in tournaments and challenges. That was, if any other knight accepted their participation. Or if they weren't hounded back into hiding by shocked men, disapproval fuelling their censure.

Downstairs, Cass found a few of the members of the sisterhood who were well enough to be out of bed clustered round a single table at one end of the hall.

Elaine was there, her long, heavy golden braid swept over her shoulder. Her pregnant belly strained her pale blue silk dress to its limits. Her face was milky pale and her eyebrows drawn together with worry, but Cass's heart leaped with relief to see that she was not hurt. A few other knights and squires were eating quietly, and Cass saw that they all looked as dazed and shocked as she felt.

They had never experienced brutality like it. Never lost so many women all at once.

Cass swallowed hard. It had been the right thing to do. Mordaunt and his men had been terrorizing the region, forcing his tenants into poverty and sowing division and hatred. They'd razed whole settlements, as Cass had seen with her own eyes, brutally killing innocent villagers. She could still see the ruins of the huts, still smell the acrid, stomach-turning smoke. And Angharad had been right: they could never stand together against the threat of outside attack while Mordaunt made unifying the region impossible.

And yet the price they had paid to rid themselves of him . . . Cass watched as little Nell, the youngest squire, sat quietly at the end of the table, pushing her porridge around her bowl. She raised a pink hand and rubbed at swollen eyes.

Cass looked down to the other end of the hall, where Alys had been tending to Mordaunt's injured men. They had been arriving at the manor in twos and threes over the days since Mordaunt's stronghold had fallen and Alys had cleared away the long wooden tables and benches from one end of the hall and laid out straw mattresses and blankets on the floor to tend to them. Many still lay covered with blankets, strangely out of place beneath the beautifully woven tapestries and ornate sconces that lined the walls. Alys moved between the makeshift beds, muttering, dishing out pungent-smelling medicine and changing bandages, shaking her head and tutting.

There were about a dozen men. A few had stayed behind to bury the dead, promising to follow them to the manor, but the rest had fled when their leader had been killed. Still, a dozen of Mordaunt's men to swell their ranks was better than Cass could have hoped. If they could be trusted. They'd need every sword hand they could get if the Saxon war bands were encroaching. But it would take some getting used to the uneasy truce. After long months of keeping men from their door, disguising themselves and hiding their armour and weapons when male visitors arrived, the idea of welcoming them inside the manor was unsettling and strange.

Alys was pouring water from a pitcher for one of the injured knights but when she saw Cass she hurried over, stifling a yawn. 'How do you feel?' she asked tentatively, as if Cass too were recovering from serious wounds.

'How long has it been since you slept?' Cass asked, ignoring the question, taking in the older woman's bandaged wrist, stained apron and tired eyes.

Alys shook her head. 'I don't know. There's too much to do. And I didn't want to take my eyes off them.' She jerked her head towards the remaining invalids, pausing to smooth down a rumpled blanket.

As her hand touched the soft wool, the man lying beneath it reached out and grabbed her wrist in his meaty fist. Cass leaped forward as he struggled to sit up, his breath rattling. But he held up a hand to her, shaking his head as he struggled to speak.

'Thank you,' he wheezed, looking directly into Alys's eyes. 'We are grateful for your skill. And your kindness. When it has not been given in return.'

And as he collapsed back onto the bed, Cass remembered

the day she had gone to Alys's hut to find the door daubed with the word 'witch'. But Alys said nothing, only wiped her hands on her apron, gave the slightest incline of her head and turned back to Cass.

'Where is Rowan?' Cass asked, her eyes raking the empty spaces along the benches. 'And Angharad?'

'Angharad has been busy since the moment we returned, sending out messengers to our allies and those who were aligned with Mordaunt, trying to convince them of the encroaching dangers – trying to unite them. And Rowan –' Alys sighed – 'has not woken yet. She took a nasty blow to the head during the battle and though she made it back here, she fell into a deep sleep and hasn't been roused.' Alys put a soothing hand on Cass's arm as her eyes widened in alarm. 'She lives. But she needs rest. Not just for her body, but her mind as well.'

Cass nodded. 'You should rest. Elaine and I could put Mordaunt's dregs back in their place between us if they try anything.' She eyed the men. 'Not that it looks likely,' she added, flashing Alys a smile. 'I'm all right,' she reassured her. 'Really. And you need sleep.'

Alys gave her a long, searching look and then, seeming satisfied, she nodded, patted Cass on the arm and left the hall without another word.

Cass rubbed a weary hand across her forehead. Then

swallowed and tried to convince herself, as she had Alys, that all was calm. But the turmoil in her stomach, the urgent, relentless call of the sword that tugged always at the edges of her mind, would not be quieted.

Cass joined the other members of the sisterhood, taking her seat on a bench between Iona, the swordsmith, whose long, dark blonde hair was loose around her serious, narrow face, and Susan, a young squire who seemed to have escaped the assault on Mordaunt's manor with only cuts and bruises.

'How's Joan?' Cass asked. She knew Susan and Joan were close, and she had seen Joan badly wounded in the battle.

'It's bad but she'll live,' Susan answered. 'She's hurt worse by Leah's loss than the sword point she took to her stomach.'

There was a moment of sombre silence. Leah, one of the most senior knights of the sisterhood, had perished fighting Mordaunt's men. Joan had been her squire.

Cass had barely reached for a piece of bread when there was an ear-splitting crash and one of the doors burst open. Rowan careered into the hall, her armour half hanging off, her boots caked in mud, the deep brown of her skin weighted with darker circles around her eyes.

She took in the scene and her mouth twisted in disgust as she strode across the floor towards the nearest of Mordaunt's men, and with a jolt Cass realized that she held a blade, that she was swinging it upwards high into the air above the man's bewildered face.

There was a sharp intake of breath from the table of knights, a clatter as another man tried to scramble to his feet and tripped over his blankets, and the pounding of boots racing across the flagstones from behind Cass. As Rowan's sword reached the apex of its arc and began to descend, another flashed up to meet it, straight and sharp, and the two blades came together with a clash and a screech of metal barely a finger's width from the man's face.

There was a moment of pure silence, as Rowan, chest heaving, eyes flashing, glared at Angharad, whose sword was gripped firmly in both hands, her fiery hair loose around her shoulders. Then she lowered her weapon, shoulders slumping, and pandemonium broke out.

Mordaunt's knights rushed forward, shouting angrily, even as Rowan jabbed an accusing finger at them.

'They tried to kill us. And succeeded too, many of them. And you've brought them here, under our roof? Are you mad?'

The other women had joined the scuffle now, Elaine remonstrating passionately with Rowan, Iona arguing with one of Mordaunt's men, and Cass noticed numbly that Nell had started to cry again.

Angharad raised two hands to quell the din. 'ENOUGH!'

'We need each other,' she said firmly, simply. 'We have no quarrel with these men, Rowan. Mordaunt was as merciless to them as he was to his enemies. I promised full clemency to any who would join us and I meant it,' she added, with a meaningful glance towards the angry knights.

'Strange way of showing it,' muttered the man Rowan had attacked, his face sheet white.

'My knights will uphold this truce,' Angharad retorted, her face set, glaring at Rowan, who met her gaze with defiance.

'You would eat here beside Leah's murderer?' she yelled, looking past Angharad at Susan and the other squires.

Susan's lip trembled and she faltered, looking from Rowan to Angharad. 'I would not choose to break bread with them,' she said, and her voice was hoarse, 'but there are bigger battles coming. Leah trusted Angharad. So I do too. You are not well, Rowan, you have been injured.'

'Better to forge uneasy alliances than to die isolated,' Angharad said angrily, two bright red spots burning on her pale cheeks. 'You know this, Rowan. You've heard the scouts. You know the Saxons draw closer by the day. We have no chance without every sword we can muster. And perhaps no chance even then.' She threw up her hands, and Cass could feel her frustration and fear.

Rowan scoffed. 'And you think they will stand alongside us and defend our manor against those forces?' She gestured dismissively towards Mordaunt's knights. 'You do not think they will turn and stab us in our backs the moment someone offers them a greater incentive?'

The knight Rowan had targeted growled indignantly, but another stepped forward. A pleasant-looking, ruddy-cheeked man with a round boyish face and a thatch of thick blonde hair. 'My lady,' he said, nodding to Rowan, who laughed humourlessly.

'Do not call me "lady",' she spat. 'I am no more a lady than you are. I am a knight, and my name is Rowan.'

If the man was taken aback, he did not show it. He simply nodded. 'Rowan, then. I am Sir Bale. I understand your mistrust. Many of our fellows died at your hands also. This isn't easy for any of us. But please understand that many of us did not share Sir Mordaunt's beliefs or his attitudes towards his neighbours. That we are glad of the opportunity to serve a worthier leader.' He gestured towards Angharad. 'We will not betray you. You just need to give us the chance to show it.'

Rowan stared at him sceptically, still breathing heavily. He held out his hand, and she looked at it but did not take it.

The moment was broken by the arrival of a band of exhausted and mud-caked scouts who clattered into the hall, laying down their weapons, and surged immediately towards the remaining food.

'You can speak freely,' Angharad told the scouts, who were gobbling down hunks of bread as if they hadn't eaten for days. Her eyes were still on Rowan, a slight frown line between them.

'The Saxons are massing in the west,' said one of the scouts, who seemed to be the leader of the group, in a low voice. She was a short, stocky girl only a little older than Cass, her face covered in freckles. 'They're gathering a war host, just south of Deva. If they take the settlement and the Roman fort they will have a formidable stronghold from which to invade further.'

Rowan puffed out her cheeks. 'They would have to come through Mercia first before they would reach our borders.'

Cass felt as if a cold hand had clutched her insides. Her family were in Mercia. Her parents and younger siblings, and her beloved sister Mary, with her husband and new baby.

The scout nodded. 'There are more immediate threats. New raiding bands have landed along the coast. If they travel up the Humber, they might penetrate Northumbria from the south. We are tracking their progress.'

Rowan drew breath, but the scout interrupted her.

'But the most urgent risk is closer to home still.'

Nell let out a small whimper and Cass saw Elizabeth, one of the other squires, reach across the table and squeeze her hand. 'We've heard rumours,' the girl began, biting her lip worriedly.

'What rumours?' Elaine asked sharply, and Cass knew she was worrying that her presence at the manor might have been discovered, especially after the part she had played in attacking Mordaunt's stronghold. It had been Elaine who had drawn out his guards, pretending to be in distress, using her pregnancy as a distraction, before the other women swept in behind her.

'I know Arthur has sent knights to look for me at Lancelot's behest,' she gabbled, her voice strained. 'If Lancelot discovers I've fled here to have his child . . . after he told the world I had died for love of him . . .'

'Your baby is safe, my lady,' the squire quickly reassured her.

Elaine, who had half risen from her seat, slumped back down again, relief written all over her face.

'And you will both remain safe, as long as we have anything to do with it,' Rowan added vehemently, glaring at Mordaunt's knights as if to dare them to disagree. 'So what is this threat?'

They all turned back to the scouts expectantly.

The scout's eyes swept the hall, lingering on Mordaunt's remaining men, and she dropped her voice, so that they all had to lean in closer to hear her. 'Mordaunt's defeat has left a power vacuum. His knights left most of the local settlements weakened from hunger and poverty, and now many of the region's fighting men have been called away by King Ceredig and others to help them repel invaders further south.'

She lowered her voice still further and whispered: 'There are those who would like to step into Mordaunt's place. And we are more vulnerable than we have ever been before. Not just because our numbers have dwindled, but because we have revealed ourselves for the first time. Now our neighbours all know the truth. And our display of strength against Mordaunt won't keep them at bay for long. Not if they realize how many sword hands we lost in the fight.'

Susan gasped. 'They'd try to take the manor by force?'

'By force or by marriage,' Angharad answered, and her voice was like ice. 'Little difference in the outcome.'

They were all staring at her, horrified, when the main doors into the hall from the courtyard outside opened.

Instinctively Angharad strode forward, Rowan and Cass immediately flanking her, Rowan's hand leaping back to the handle of her sword.

Still reeling from all the scouts had said, Cass moved in a blind panic, not sure whether the small crowd of people entering were enemies or suitors or both. It wasn't until the intruders stopped directly in front of them, until she was looking straight into the bright hazel eyes beneath those thick dark eyelashes, that she fully registered the group of newcomers and realized they were led by Sir Gamelin.

Cass stopped dead, her hands falling limp at her sides, her heart beginning to race though she tried to keep her expression calm.

'Sir Gamelin.'

She saw him sparring with her in the woods, seizing her from behind, drawing her body close to his chest . . .

'You have come to swear fealty?'

She saw his black tunic and the silver cross emblazoned across it as if for the first time, reliving the lurch in her stomach as she had realized he was one of Mordaunt's men. Automatically her enemy.

'Aye.' The smile lines crinkled at the edges of his eyes as his full lips parted in a genuine smile. 'I come with the remainder of Mordaunt's men and the women of his court. Those not injured or fled.'

Laughing with her at Mordaunt's Yuletide feast, telling her about his rural childhood, how he'd been trained by his uncle and sent to Mordaunt's court when he came of age.

'Your wounded are being well cared for,' she said carefully, courteously.

As the knights behind Sir Gamelin looked cautiously around the hall, Cass noticed a couple of them nudge each other, staring at her and whispering to each other.

His sword flashing as he fought Mordaunt at the battle, begging Cass to believe he'd known nothing of the attacks on the villages, that he was on her side.

'We bring with us some of the ladies of our household, who cannot be left defenceless at a deserted manor house.'

Kissing those soft lips in a moment of impulse, as he yielded his sword to her in the pouring rain on the tournament field. Yielded to protect her secret.

'Of course. You are all welcome here.' It was Angharad, beside her, her voice smooth even as she threw Rowan a warning glance. Rowan's mouth twisted but she said nothing. 'I promised lodging for all those who yielded. We all stand united in defence of our lands. You will all have a place here in my household.'

But Cass hardly heard over the buzzing sound in her ears. Gamelin nodded courteously but his eyes did not leave Cass's face. She stepped towards him, and it was as if there were nobody else in the hall except the two of them. No other knights, no squires, no injured men. He was here at the manor. No longer a guilty secret to be kept from Rowan, Angharad and the others. No longer bound to a master who was her greatest enemy.

He took a step towards her too, and the morning light seemed to burst in through the windows and bathe the hall in gold as she reached out her hands towards him.

He took one more step but his hands did not meet hers. He reached behind him and drew forward one of the ladies. A slender birdlike woman perhaps a few years older than Cass, with an intelligent narrow face, dressed in a simple dark woollen tunic, her wide-set blue eyes filled with gratitude and eager friendship.

'My betrothed,' he said with a strange, forced nod, and suddenly his eyes were elsewhere, resting anywhere but on her. 'Lady Anne of Camulodunum.'

'Of course,' Cass said lightly, while her feet froze in place and her heart hammered in her chest. 'A pleasure to meet you, Lady Anne.' She said it as if the words didn't smart like a freshly skinned knee.

Lady Anne took them all in, her dark hair falling forward as she nodded with genuine enthusiasm. 'I have heard much of your strength and valour,' she said, turning to Angharad.

'I would not be suited to taking up a sword or a bow. I do not have it in me,' she said quickly, glancing at the small knot of five or six expensively dressed women behind her. Several of them nodded their agreement nervously, though some seemed less sure. Cass saw one, a younger woman with olive skin and dark plaits hanging on either side of an oval face, look at Angharad's sword with open curiosity.

'You might be surprised to discover what you have in you,' Angharad replied lightly with a smile towards her squires. 'Many of the other women who have taken refuge here have been.'

Lady Anne did not seem convinced. 'We are more than willing to contribute in other ways,' she said, looking around. 'We are content to do whatever is required to help in the running of the household in return for your allegiance and protection.' She gave Cass a tentative smile, as if to promise friendship as well as honest work.

And a field in the pouring rain flashed in front of Cass's eyes as she smiled back.

Chapter 3

There was enough to do with finding rooms for the new arrivals and helping them to settle in at the manor to cover Cass's lack of composure, and she threw herself into the work gratefully.

Her mind whirled as she and Blyth lugged extra bales of straw up into Leah's old chambers, covering them with sheets and sheepskins for the women of Mordaunt's court.

There were Saxons massing, raiders advancing. Local noblemen greedily eyeing the lands Mordaunt had controlled. And always beneath it all the awareness of the newly expanded power that had awakened inside her with the drawing of the sword. The words of the prophecy. The weight of what it might mean and the hot pit of fear it sparked in her stomach. She pummelled the straw, pushing the mattresses into position beneath the sheet. Betrothed. His betrothed.

'Cass, are you all right?'

'Me?' she panted, lugging another mattress across the floor. 'Absolutely. Fine.'

'Mmm.' Blyth raised an eyebrow but didn't probe any further.

If only Sigrid were here, she could ask her what to do. Whether to embrace the strange new force that seemed to throb beneath her skin or to push it down inside. Whether to trust Mordaunt's men or keep them at arm's length. But Sigrid, with whom she might have discussed such things, was gone. Banished by Angharad because she had slain Mordaunt to avenge the death of her brother. Angharad had craved unity, Cass knew, but she understood Sigrid's actions too. Mordaunt and his closest circle of men had been responsible for Lily's murder. Lily, the one person she might have trusted with the unpredictable flickers in her chest when she caught sight of Sir Gamelin. The one person she might have talked to openly about the power that surged in her breast when she held the new sword. Gone. And Cass had never felt so alone.

The manor seemed suddenly to bristle with eyes and ears. So many of the sisterhood lost. So many newcomers in their place. They crowded the kitchens, taking over food preparation, churning and baking. Their horses chuffed and stamped in the cramped stables. Their chatter filled the hall. And in spite of Angharad's promise of pardons, in spite of the fact that a good number of them remained splinted and bandaged, Cass had to admit it was hard to trust those who had so recently drawn swords against them in Mordaunt's defence.

She knew that the most brutal of Mordaunt's men had fled, that those who had come to swear allegiance to Angharad had been, like Gamelin, uneasy at their former master's cruelty. And yet it was hard to breathe, hard to relax, when she risked bumping into an unfamiliar man round every corner. And it didn't help that she had the uncomfortable feeling many of them seemed to be watching her, looking up sharply when she entered a room and seeming to mutter among themselves as she passed.

'If the scouts were right,' Rowan said grimly, as she and Cass met in the meadow in the early morning a few days later, 'then there is grave danger on our doorstep, and we must act quickly.'

'What do you suggest?'

'We move immediately against the landowners who threaten us. If they see us as a vulnerable group of women, we will prove them wrong, and make the mistake a fatal one for them.'

Cass sighed. 'Our forces are at their lowest ebb. Even those fighters we have not lost are still recovering from their wounds. We are in no state to attack, and even if we were, it would likely only create more violence. Angharad was clear, the region must unite if we are to have any hope of holding off bigger threats.' And her stomach clenched as she thought of the massing Saxons and pictured the raiders advancing stealthily along the waterways. 'We need allies, not more enemies.'

Rowan's hand clenched round the handle of the sword slung at her belt and for a moment Cass thought she would draw it, but she nodded slowly. 'Then we unite. Let us call a witan and invite everybody who will come. Our neighbours, those who consider us friends and those who do not.'

'And we make a pact to stand together in the face of the approaching threats?'

Rowan nodded again, more decisively this time. 'And swear to respect each other's sovereignty over our individual lands in the meantime,' she added, her mouth tightening into a grim line. 'Or face the consequences.'

It was easier than Cass had expected to persuade Angharad to agree. She and Rowan visited her chambers that evening, where a flickering fire danced merrily in the grate, throwing shadows across the intricately carved wooden screens that edged the room. Sheaves of papers were spread across Angharad's desk, and Cass's eye fell on a piece of crumpled parchment which had been smoothed out carefully, weighted down with a delicate silver dagger.

It was the final message Vivian had sent to her lover before she rode to her death, sacrificing herself to protect Angharad and the sisterhood from being exposed.

What we have built is worth saving. You are worth saving. The cost is not too high. I love you.

She swallowed through the pain in her throat, and the flash of Vivian's long silver hair in the sunlight as she drilled Cass and the other squires relentlessly seemed to hover for a moment before her eyes.

Angharad's gaze seemed very far away, and Cass wondered if she, too, was seeing Vivian, the woman who had loved Angharad so deeply she had murdered the husband who had abused her and stayed by her side unflinching through every battle that came after. Until the one battle came that she knew they could not win. And in death Vivian had chosen Angharad, as she always had in life. 'Very well.'

She did not know if it was Vivian's last message to her or a desire to placate Rowan that led Angharad to agree so quickly to the suggestion of a witan, but she had barely heard their suggestion when there came a banging at the door that made Mason the dog growl and raise his hackles from his spot on a rug next to the hearth.

The door burst open as a tangle of people tumbled through it, several of them holding unsheathed weapons. Loud panting and angry raised voices rang off the stone walls.

'OUR weapons—'

'Left defenceless—'

'Could have taken my arm off—'

'Silence!' Angharad's voice was cold with anger.

Cass saw Iona and Susan, red-faced and sweaty, and noticed with a shock that Susan's eye was swollen and oozing. Three of Mordaunt's men were behind them, one a skinny man with a ratty, pointed face and a cut on his lip, whose hair was dishevelled, another behind him who looked ashamed and, at the back, Sir Bale, his brow creased in consternation.

'They broke into the armoury,' Iona burst out, her cheeks burning, glaring accusingly at the pinch-faced knight. 'I caught them in the act, looting our weapons.' She gestured angrily to the front two knights. 'Susan was with me, and when she tried to stop them stealing . . .' She pointed to Susan's face.

'Not stealing,' the skinny man said in a nasal voice, 'just preparing ourselves for potential intruders given the news imparted by your scouts the other day. And I apologize,' he muttered rather unconvincingly in Susan's direction, 'but I reacted out of habit when attacked.'

'Preparing yourselves is a nice way to describe stealing,' Susan retorted, cautiously dabbing her eye on her sleeve and wincing.

'Some of us have no weapons,' the second knight whinged, looking accusingly at Angharad. 'Not since you relieved us of them during your attack. It is us who should be suspicious of you, not the other way round,' he huffed at Susan.

'Tell that to my best friend's mistress,' Susan replied, looking towards Rowan for support. 'Except you can't, because she is dead.'

Rowan drew breath but before she could add her voice to the fray Sir Bale stepped forward, curtly rebuking the other two knights. 'If we are in need of resources, we will ask for them,' he snapped. 'It can do nobody any good to break the fragile trust we are trying to build here.'

He stared down the other two men until they sheepishly handed the blades they were carrying to Iona, who tucked them under her arm.

'These are designed for women,' she said sulkily, clearly aware of her Aunt Angharad's glare. 'I could make some better suited to you if you come to the armoury tomorrow and let me take your measurements.'

Susan looked ready to mutiny but said nothing. The men shuffled out, Iona following them, but Rowan laid a hand on Susan's shoulder as she turned to leave, and though

Angharad was out of earshot, bending over the papers on her desk again, Cass heard what Rowan whispered to the younger girl.

'We bide our time. But, believe me, if they lay a finger on one of our people, they'll die for it, orders be damned.'

Chapter 4

The witan was very different from the ones Cass had attended before.

All morning they arrived, dozens of local landowners and nobles, some of them with bands of their closest knights, some with their wives or sons, many alone. They filed into the hall, where the floor had been cleared and benches arranged around the walls, as the chandeliers blazed with candles overhead and the fire roared despite the warmth of the day outside.

'Angharad is making a point,' Rowan muttered to Cass, as they entered the hall and noted the splendour. The tapestries twinkled in the golden light and tables on either side of the fireplace were laden with the best of their silverware, flagons of ale and mead, platters of delicate spiced cakes and meat pies. 'It's a show of strength.'

When Angharad strode into the room, her presence instantly silenced the murmur of chatter. She was fully armed, her intricately carved leather breastplate gleaming like a freshly dropped chestnut, her flame-red hair bound into a tight coil at the base of her neck, her shoulders broadened by the solid pauldrons that encased them, her hand resting lightly on the shining hilt of her sword.

Cass and Rowan, who had dressed in their usual silk, more motivated by the force of habit when meeting outsiders than anything else, watched as their neighbours' mouths fell open and an audible gasp swept the room.

'But they already knew,' Cass whispered, confused. 'After we took Mordaunt's stronghold, everybody knew, surely?'

'There's something different about seeing it for yourself,' Rowan replied, as two portly men seated beside each other on the furthest bench frowned and began to whisper to each other. 'Let's see them write us off as a bunch of weak and defenceless women now.'

Angharad swept to the centre of the room, standing with the fire behind her so that it threw her defiant figure into sharp relief. Her feet were wide, her hands on her hips, and Mason, her faithful hound, prowled round her feet. Cass saw how totally different she must have looked to the assembled men compared with the demure, mild-mannered widow they had last seen at the Yuletide festivities held at Mordaunt's manor.

'We are all here because we have a common problem,' Angharad began, her voice ringing out around the hall. 'Raiders and Saxon invaders advance across the country and while King Ceredig and others are gathering forces to meet them further south, we cannot be certain we will not come under attack from individual bands closer to home.'

There was an increase of muttering, and Cass saw some of the nobles looking suspicious and others shaking their heads disbelievingly. She recognized Sir Albinor from the Yuletide celebrations: a tall frail man, whose elderly wife clutched his hand tightly. Next to him was a thin man Cass did not recognize, with pocked scarring on his cheeks and heavy dark eyebrows. But it was the woman sitting next to him that drew Cass's attention; she was young, perhaps as young as Cass, and her catlike eyes were narrowed in on Angharad as if she were preparing to pounce.

'Do not think we are safe and far from the conflict here,' Angharad continued, seeming to recognize the scepticism with which her words were being met. 'Our scouts have seen worrying signs of invaders from more than one direction. And we were attacked last year by a band of Saxon raiders who tried to take this manor.' She slammed her open hand down on the mantlepiece. The hum of conversation intensified.

'Why did we not know of this?' a thin man with heavy eyebrows demanded.

'We dispatched them, Sir Aran,' Angharad answered coolly, and Cass saw the man's gaze slide down towards Angharad's sword and then round at the other women of the sisterhood who were gathered in twos and threes.

'As you have no doubt already heard,' Angharad continued, 'my women and I live here as a sisterhood. Just as you each have your strongholds, your manors and your knights, we are no different. We are trained and armed to fight when we need to. We follow the codes of chivalric conduct and seek to uphold fairness and justice. We protect what is ours.'

An unpleasant sneering laugh sounded from the back of the hall and a short ruddy-cheeked man with sparse gingery hair and matching whiskers rose to his feet and sauntered towards Angharad. She stood her ground as he advanced, though Cass could have sworn she heard Rowan growl low in her throat, her muscles tensed, her eyes not leaving him for a second.

'Lord Murgatroyd.' Angharad nodded, her voice pleasant.

The man ignored her, walking beyond her to examine the silverware on the tables piled with food, his footsteps echoing in the expectant hush, then leaning arrogantly against the mantle that spanned the length of the fireplace.

He took his time, looking around the hall, elongating the silence to emphasize how easy it was, how immediately the gathered crowd granted him authority in Angharad's home. Cass's lips tightened angrily.

'My dear,' he spoke slowly, his voice dripping with condescension, 'do you really expect us to yield to your wishes as some kind of proxy for Mordaunt? To take this –' he gestured at her clothing and gave a snort – 'dressing-up game seriously?'

He looked round at the gathered crowd, raising his eyebrows, addressing them directly as if Angharad were not present. 'It is an insult to the memory of her husband, who you all knew as a strong and decent man. This outlandish charade degrades his household. And there is no part of me that believes for one moment these lasses can safely steer us to any kind of strategic—'

He was interrupted by a flash, a whispering swish of a noise and then a thunk.

Lord Murgatroyd stopped talking very suddenly and looked down at the floor. His long straggly ginger moustache lay limp at his feet like some kind of vermin that had been dragged in by a cat. And Angharad's silver dagger quivered in the mantle next to him, its blade buried almost up to the hilt.

'My husband,' Angharad said softly, and all trace of

pleasantness was gone from her voice, 'was not a decent man. And if you have any doubt about how seriously to take my women, perhaps you might take a look at the freshly dug graves outside Lord Mordaunt's manor.' She turned to the gathered landowners and raised her voice. 'I do not seek to give you orders, nor to take Mordaunt's place. I simply called you here so that we might unite behind a common purpose. To join together and care for our community, not divided and cowed as Mordaunt would have had it, but in trust and friendship.'

There was a long silence and a log fell into the fire with a hiss.

'I stand with you,' came a reedy voice. Sir Albinor had risen to his feet, supported by his wife.

'And I,' said a younger man, with a kind round face.

Angharad nodded. 'Thank you, Sir Prior.'

There were murmurs of agreement from around the room, though Cass noticed that the portly men who had been whispering to one another earlier did not speak.

'As do we,' said a low steady voice, and Sir Gamelin walked through the hall to stand shoulder to shoulder with Angharad, the dozen or more of Mordaunt's men who were strong enough to be out of bed behind him. Cass noticed that Lady Anne rose and stood by him, saying nothing but staring steadily at Murgatroyd and the others. A dull ache started up in Cass's stomach instantly and she rubbed at it absently.

'Angharad and her knights defeated Sir Mordaunt in combat,' Gamelin was saying, 'and we have sworn fealty to her as custom dictates. Any who seek to encroach on her lands will answer to our swords as well as her own.'

'Very well,' said Angharad briskly after a brief silence, which she was clearly taking as assent. 'We will need to discuss raising a fyrd. All those of fighting age and strength will need to join together if—'

One of the ruddy-faced men interrupted her curtly, with a smile that was clearly supposed to be apologetic but had a little of a triumphant smirk to it. 'You have not heard. There can be no fyrd, no great fighting force of Northumbria to do your will, lady. King Ceredig has called for aid – and most Northumbrian men will answer his call. They well remember how he and his forces came at our summons when the Picts threatened our borders some years back, during the unrest that preceded Arthur's kingship. We march south in days.'

'It was not a total loss,' Rowan pointed out, a few hours later, as they sat round the table, picking at the remainder of the spread they had prepared for the witan. 'At least that snivelling Murgatroyd will think carefully before underestimating us again.'

Angharad inclined her head with a faint smile that did not reach her eyes.

'And those pompous asses will not quickly try to exploit the villages Mordaunt had crippled with his tithe demands,' Susan added, chewing a bite of pork pie. 'Nor likely attack us here, now they have seen how Gamelin and the others have reinforced our numbers.'

They all looked up as Alys entered the room, supporting Elaine, who was shuffling slowly, one hand on the curve of her stomach, one on Alys's shoulder. 'You needn't quiet on my account.' She laughed, wincing slightly as she eased her weight into a chair. 'It is only a child, not a terrible illness.'

Her laugh was warm, but Cass caught Alys's eye and knew there was something Elaine was not saying.

'We held the witan,' Cass told them, understanding that Elaine did not want to be treated like an invalid or excluded, especially since she had played such a crucial role in the battle against Mordaunt. 'And Angharad bared her teeth and warned our neighbours off our territory. But we cannot raise a fyrd to meet the Saxons. The men leave within days to join King Ceredig.'

'Cannot raise a fyrd?' Elaine asked, and her eyes were dancing. 'Why ever not?'

'I told you,' Cass repeated. 'Those of fighting age will be gone before the week is out.'

Elaine shook her head slowly. 'No. The *men* of fighting age will be gone.'

Angharad's head snapped up and her eyes met Elaine's across the table.

'The men will be gone,' she repeated, and when she smiled Cass felt as if she were seeing their leader again for the first time in days. 'Then let them go. And when they are gone, we will train the women.'

Chapter 5

Angharad thought it was best to wait until the menfolk had all left before making their move, but nobody at the manor was idle. Over the next few days, they settled into a new rhythm. Rowan had moved into Sigrid's old room, so that several of the men of Mordaunt's court could be quartered in the chambers she and Vivian had once occupied. An extra mattress was brought into Cass's room, where Susan now slept. She was an earnest, hardworking squire who rose at dawn to begin her duties, and so Cass still had the chamber to herself much of the time.

Blyth, who preferred to work alone, and who had kept largely to the stables since the influx of new people, could be seen beavering away at the edge of the meadow from morning until night, putting up new fencing to create stalls for the new knights' horses. In the milder weather they would not need covered shelter overnight, and by the time winter came . . .

Cass tried not to think too far ahead. As soon as she allowed herself to imagine what might happen next she descended into strange and troubling daydreams full of white-hot power that made her fingertips itch and faceless enemies. The silver locket her mother gave her was a constant weight at the base of her throat, causing her to rub at her collarbone when she jerked herself out of the reverie.

She was brushing down her black pony, Pebble, one morning in the stables after a ride when she was pulled out of another daydream by a soft snort behind her. She turned to see Lord Gamelin saddling his horse, a piebald mare with soft brown eyes.

'I did not mean to startle you,' he began apologetically, and Cass felt the same twinge that had twisted her stomach when he had introduced her to Lady Anne.

'You did not startle me,' she said a little stiffly, returning her attention to Pebble's flank.

'No longer the nameless knight,' he said lightly, but when she looked up his smile was tinged with sadness. 'It was not until I saw you fighting that day that I could be sure I had successfully put all the parts of the story together. The youth in the forest, the victor at the tournament, the young lady at the ball –' he inclined his head to her – 'the warrior.'

'Cass,' she said simply, and he nodded.

'It is nice to make your acquaintance at last, Lady Cass.'

'Thank you,' she said quietly, without pausing the long slow strokes of her brush while Pebble huffed happily. 'For yielding to protect my identity at the tournament, and for intervening at the feast.' Her face flushed and her fingers tightened on the brush in spite of herself. A boorish knight of Mordaunt's court had cornered her in the courtyard that night and if Gamelin had not happened upon them . . .

'It was, in both cases, the right thing to do.' He shrugged. 'And you nearly had me at the tournament. We were evenly matched.'

'You do not find it strange? That we bear arms?'

Gamelin thought for a moment. 'I have a sister. Janet. As a child, she was three times as brave as me and far quicker with her fists. One day, when we were herding the cattle to milking, a fence broke and one of the bulls charged towards us, practically shaking the ground. He must have been twice the size of your little horse, and his horns were the length of three handspans.' He chuckled. 'I was rooted to the spot, trembling with terror. But Janet leaped in front of it and began to whirl her arms above her head and shriek like a mad thing. She was fearless. And that bull took one look at her, stopped dead in its tracks and shambled off back in the direction it had come.' He smiled at Cass. 'It always seemed odd to me that I was the one sent to learn the arts of knightly combat with our uncle while she remained at home preparing for a life of boiling potatoes and washing sheets.' He patted his horse and tightened one of the saddle buckles.

'Your sword—' He turned to Cass curiously, hesitating as if he was not sure how to word the question.

Cass's hand flew instinctively to the empty belt at her waist, where she had always worn her old sword until the battle at Mordaunt's manor. Since they had returned, since that strange dreamlike first day when she had drawn the new weapon from the stone, held it and felt its power, she had not allowed herself to touch it again. It lay under her bed in the dust, as if removing it from her sight could somehow silence the feelings that roiled within her. The uncertainty about who she was and what she was supposed to do, about whether the other-worldly energy that overcame her when she held it was to be greeted with celebration or fear.

She shook her head, then quickly bent down, pretending to check one of Pebble's hooves, hiding her face.

'It is the sword from the stone, is it not?' he asked from above her. And when she did not answer he added, 'We all saw you draw it, lady. And none who had tried before had ever been able to move it.'

Cass reluctantly rose to face him. 'I did not mean to,' she said quietly. 'I felt around for a weapon in desperation and it seemed to jump into my hand. I did not realize it was the sword from the stone until afterwards. If you seek to claim it as Mordaunt's property—'

'No,' he interrupted, holding up his hands. 'It is rightfully yours. And seeing you draw it was one of the reasons so many of Mordaunt's men came here to swear fealty. But it is not too heavy for you?'

Cass frowned. Truthfully, the sword had felt light, weightless even, every time she had held it, but she thought this would sound strange and so she kept it to herself. 'I have built up strength in my arms, I suppose, these past months.'

And he nodded and seemed to accept her explanation, though his eyes followed her curiously as she returned to Pebble's grooming. 'My lady,' he said quietly, and his voice was so gentle she did not quite trust herself to turn round and remained with her face half buried in Pebble's soft mane. 'I did not know . . . about Anne.'

Cass felt her breath catch in her throat and a weightless feeling in her stomach, but she could not think of what to say.

'I did not know about the betrothal,' he continued slightly awkwardly, 'until she arrived at the manor just a few weeks ago, sent by my uncle. He had arranged the match and sent her to Mordaunt's court to be married.'

Still Cass said nothing. She could feel the steady beat of Pebble's pulse under her fingers and she tried to slow her breathing in time with it, as if it would help her to ground herself.

'It would not have been my choice,' Gamelin whispered with an urgency in his tone that compelled her to turn round and meet his eyes, which were searching for hers. They had darkened to an intense golden brown that threatened to melt her resolve to remain impassive, to keep him at a distance. But she could not bring herself to look away, as he continued. 'But now she is here, and to send her back home unmarried –' he spread his hands helplessly – 'it would badly affect her reputation.'

'Yes,' Cass said quietly, trying to keep her voice steady. 'Of course.'

'But I want you to know that if things were different—' He stopped suddenly, as Blyth bustled into the stall, pitching a bale of hay into Pebble's manger.

'But they are not different—' Cass began, wishing her throat would not ache so, wishing her traitorous eyes would stay dry, that she could present the cool, unflushed face she wanted him to see.

Before she could finish, there was an ear-splitting crash

and splintering of wood as the manor gates in the courtyard outside burst open. Together she and Gamelin leaped to the stable door, just in time to see armed men spilling through the jagged edges of the broken gate.

Meeting each other's eyes for one burning moment, they ran side by side towards the screaming lookouts, who had been taken by surprise and were now clambering down from the ramparts above the gate, drawing their swords. Gamelin drew his blade as he ran, engaging the largest of the armoured men immediately, but Cass felt panic constrict her chest as she scrabbled at her belt and remembered there was no weapon there.

Then Iona was behind her, bursting out of the forge, throwing her a sword, and Cass caught it and whirled to pursue a man who was striding across the courtyard, making for the doors to the great hall. She sliced out wildly, sick with fear that he would reach those doors and burst in upon the unarmed women within. The blade caught him from behind, cutting across his thigh in the unprotected space between the cuisses and the breastplate, and a fountain of blood spurted across the cobbles as he fell with a cry, clutching at his leg.

Two more descended on her fast, and suddenly Sir Gamelin was there, the body of the man he had been engaged with slumped motionless against the gate. Wordlessly they pressed their backs together, each facing off against one of the attackers. The man squaring up to Cass was stocky, with a grizzled matted beard that descended beneath his round metal helmet. His face was pock-marked and puce-coloured, and he spat derisively on the floor as if the idea of fighting a woman disgusted him.

Cass felt a surge of anger rise up inside her. How dare he crash in here, into the sanctuary they had created, and then look at her as if she was not even worthy of defending it? These men were always harrying and chafing at the edges of the life she wanted for herself and the women around her. The frustration and the fury and the unfairness of it all burst out of her, and she ran at him, smashing into his bulk with her shoulder, sending him reeling backwards in surprise. Then she kicked out, anger driving her boot into his groin, and he grunted and recoiled, doubled over.

She heard a sharp intake of breath behind her and turned to see Gamelin stagger off balance, clutching at his side, where a ruddy bloom was spreading across his tunic. She gasped and leaped in front of him, bringing her sword up to meet the blade of the enormous man moving in to strike a fatal blow. She parried it, using both hands to grip the handle of her weapon, but the sheer force of the man brought her to her knees. Before she could regain her footing he had kicked her in the shoulder, sending her sprawling backwards onto the cobbles as pain exploded down her left arm.

As she looked up at him, her fingers scrabbling for her sword, he bore down upon her, his lips curling in a victorious snarl, then his eyes suddenly widened in shock as a heavy blow struck him on the back of the head and he collapsed next to Cass. She looked up, panting, to see Sir Bale nod briefly at her before he ran forward, followed by several of his men emerging from the hall, to meet the rest of the intruders.

There were around a dozen of them. As Bale and the others engaged them, Angharad and yet more women emerged, and the attackers were soon surrounded and subdued. As it became clear that they were no match for the men and women within the manor walls, the last of them, a scrawny man with a helmet too big for his head, turned and fled, swiftly pursued by Rowan.

Others had spilled out into the courtyard by now, and Cass sat, slightly dazed, wincing as she rotated her shoulder painfully, and watched Alys examining Sir Gamelin's wound. His lean muscular torso was sticky with blood.

'It's a scratch,' he wheezed, wiping sweat out of his eyes. 'Check on the others.'

'It's more than a scratch,' Alys retorted, pressing rags to the wound. 'But you'll live. You were lucky it wasn't deeper.'

At that moment Rowan returned, her face grim, a smear of blood across her cheek.

'I caught the man fleeing,' she told Angharad, as she caught her breath. 'And he was not alone.' And behind her, through what was left of the gate hanging off its hinges, she roughly pulled the woman with the catlike eyes from the witan.

'Lady Aran,' Angharad greeted her, and her voice was like ice. 'You brought armed intruders to my door.'

Lady Aran tossed her dark head, her heavy-lidded almond-shaped eyes narrowed in arrogant defiance. 'Did you think we would all quietly submit to your will, *my lady*?' she asked, her words dripping with sarcasm as she took in Angharad's masculine clothing, the weapon in her hand and the hair bundled unceremoniously upon her head.

'No.' Angharad sighed heavily. 'But I had hoped that you would realize my suggestion was in everybody's best interests, including yours and your husband's.'

'If you kill me,' Lady Aran whispered defiantly, 'others will come.'

'Others are coming already, you fool,' Rowan retorted, twisting Lady Aran's arm behind her back so that she jerked her chin upwards and gasped. 'And you would rather welcome them into our midst than stand against them together? What did you think those men would have done next, had they taken the manor? Thanked you kindly and then left your own property and lands alone?'

'Did your husband know of this?' Angharad asked in a low voice, her eyes appraising the other woman with distaste.

'No.' Lady Aran tossed her head. 'He is indecisive and weak. He could not see that he was the natural successor to Lord Mordaunt's power. I did what needed to be done for both of us. And for the sake of our young sons.'

'Then he will not know if your body is found with the corpses of these men –' Angharad gestured coldly towards the motionless attackers slumped around the courtyard – 'that you did not die at their hands.'.

A long moment passed while the two women gazed at each other, and nobody spoke. Then Rowan released the woman's wrists and stepped towards Angharad.

'But with all the men dead too,' she said, looking around, 'it would not make sense that they had killed her. And if Aran found out . . .'

Angharad nodded slowly, never taking her eyes off the woman's face.

'There would be no end to the infighting it would spark,' Rowan finished heavily and she slowly sheathed her sword.

Angharad's shoulders sagged a little, as if a great tension had suddenly left her body, and Cass, watching, thought that it was not acceptance but relief. And the relief had nothing to do with Lady Aran or her fate, but more to do with the willowy young woman who turned away from their traitorous neighbour and strode back into the hall without a backwards glance.

*

Cass sat for a long time that night in her chamber, staring at the sword with the ruby hilt and wondering if the battle might have gone differently if she had not left it to gather dust beneath her bed. She turned over the events of the afternoon in her mind. The knife-sharp questioning with which Angharad had determined what had happened. How Lady Aran had admitted the Saxon raiders that had approached her manor and saved herself with the promise of a richer prize. She had been dismissed by Angharad and allowed to retreat to her manor with her tail between her legs. How Rowan had shifted along the bench that night at supper when Sir Bale and Sir Gamelin had entered the hall so that they might sit alongside the women and eat together for the first time since their arrival. How she had seen Angharad eat a full meal and smile.

Still her mind came back to the fight. To the sharp shock of the pain in her shoulder and the brutal ache of her winded lungs as she fell backwards. The cold dull weight of the sword in her hand had lacked the warm rush of power she had felt with her own sword. It felt as though she had turned her back on her destiny, but still she shoved the sword away beneath the mattress before she blew out the tapers and climbed into bed.

Chapter 6

They were lucky the group had been small. But Cass knew Angharad was acutely aware they might not fight off a bigger attacking force next time. They needed to train more sword hands, and quickly. But the recruitment did not go exactly as they had planned.

They rode out together: Angharad, Rowan, Cass and a small group of other squires, Elizabeth and Susan amongst them. The woods were bursting with the colours of summer. Vivid purple foxgloves lifted their delicate necks to flaunt their mottled throats, half-open white hellebore flowers swayed as they passed and little pale pink herb Robert flowers clustered like stars at the base of the trees.

Cass felt her spirits lifting as Pebble trotted happily along the path, tossing her messy black mane in exhilaration. The sweet scent of lily of the valley filled the warm air and the sun filtered down through the canopy of leaves above in flickering golden shafts.

First, they rode towards Elsdon, a small village Cass had not visited before. 'There are about forty dwellings,' Rowan told her, as Angharad cantered ahead, hair streaming out behind her, catching the sunlight like flames. 'Perhaps a dozen or so women of fighting age without very young children to tether them.'

Cass watched Angharad, her straight, proud back encased in leather armour, her sword hanging ready at her side, and felt how strange and unnatural it seemed to be riding out in these woods without any disguise. No face coverings, no riding demurely in side-saddle in their long dresses – just freely wearing their armour and carrying their weapons, unafraid of exposure now that the worst had already happened. It was exhilarating almost to the point of intoxication. She half hoped for some bandit or enemy to intercept them, so great was the burning desire to fight fully in her own right for the first time, but the ride was pleasant and uneventful as Pebble trotted quietly after the others.

The village was quiet, too, when they arrived, with only a few chickens scratching in the open square at the centre of the dwellings and a handful of grubby children playing hopscotch, stopping to gawk shamelessly at the riders as they dismounted and led their horses to the drinking trough.

'We are here to offer an invitation,' Angharad began warmly, as the village women straggled out of their houses in twos and threes, clearly interrupted from their daily tasks, some wiping their hands on their aprons, others with smudges of flour on their cheeks.

'An invitation and an opportunity,' Rowan added. 'To learn to defend yourself and your neighbours if the worst should happen.'

A faint whispering ran around the group but nobody stepped forward. Cass's eye was caught by a young woman a little apart from the others, with a bucket of freshly drawn water. She was perhaps fifteen or sixteen, with large dark eyes set in a pale oval face and straight dark hair tied at the nape of her neck so that it hung in a long tail over one shoulder.

'To come under our protection in the case of any attack by Saxons or raiding bands,' Angharad continued, frowning slightly at the village women, who stood quiet and still, watching her. 'And to stand with us in protecting others and their lands nearby.' She stopped, clearly expecting some kind of response, if not a rush of new recruits hastening to join them. She turned a baffled face to Cass, who took up the task.

'We will teach you to ride and to fight,' Cass explained, drawing her sword. 'Provide you with weapons and train you to use them to defend yourselves.

'There was an attack on our manor yesterday,' Rowan added, exasperated. 'These are not imaginary threats.'

From a dark doorway behind a group of young women came a wizened old man, balding and stooped, leaning heavily on a wooden crutch.

'You have already outstayed your welcome,' he told them, his voice raised harshly, and Cass noticed that the dark-haired young woman flinched and slopped some of the water out of her bucket. 'You can see there are none here tempestuous or foolish enough to run and join your dangerous games. You'd do well to return to your homes and leave it to the menfolk who have gone to risk their lives to keep us safe.'

There was a murmuring of assent amongst the other villagers, and a little boy picked up a stone and threw it in their direction before disappearing behind his mother's skirts. The stone landed at Pebble's feet and she reared backwards skittishly, so it was all Cass could do to hold on and to try to calm her.

'We will not stay where we are not wanted,' Angharad said, her voice strained. 'But you know where to find us, should any of you change your minds.' And she looked not at the old man but at the women, who turned back to their chores without meeting her eye.

They were well on the road to the next village when the sound of hooves came clattering along the path behind them and they turned to see the girl Cass had noticed hurrying to catch up. They reined in their horses to wait for her.

'I am Edith,' she said, when she reached them. 'I will join you if you will have me. I can ride and cook and –' she took a deep breath and suddenly burst out in a rush – 'and I will not wait quietly at home while my father and brother risk their lives when I have two perfectly good arms to wield a sword or bow and could probably aim just as well if I was taught how.'

She stopped, breathless, looking quite taken aback at her own boldness, but Angharad was smiling. 'Then we will teach you how.'

But it was a small and quiet group that rode back to the manor late that afternoon, after experiencing the same subdued reception at several more villages, and Edith was the only rider who had not left the gates with them that morning.

'It'll take time for them to get used to the idea,' Cass said gently to Angharad as she dismounted and led her horse Star to the stables. 'It was a shock to me too, when I first arrived. But in time they'll come to see that joining us is their best chance at defence.'

'Time we do not have,' Angharad snapped, as she thrust her roan mare's reins into Blyth's startled hands and turned on her heel. 'If we cannot raise a fyrd before the Saxons arrive,' she called hotly over her shoulder, 'there will be nothing left to defend.' And she slammed open the great doors and disappeared inside, leaving Cass in the courtyard with Pebble.

Cass took her time stabling the little cob, brushing her down carefully and feeding her an unripe green apple she'd plucked as they'd ridden and kept in her pocket. Pebble grounded her in a way that nothing else had since Lily had gone. There had been moments, with Lily, when she had been able to laugh and relax and talk of things that did not matter. Moments that had taken her back to days climbing trees and picking apples with her sister on the farm where she had grown up. Carefree days unburdened by fears about raiding bands and hostile neighbours and the ever-present nagging enormity of the power that surged in her when she held her new sword. Now that the manor was bursting with strange faces and Lily was no longer there to sneak off into the meadow with her to gossip and eat honeyed pastries, it was only with Pebble that she could find that calm place again.

She lost herself in the rhythmic sweeping motion of the brush, in the sweet, honest smell of the freshly cut hay, the buzzing of the flies that Pebble flicked away with the swinging swish of her tail. In these snatched periods of rare solitude with Pebble, she sometimes allowed herself to take out the grief she tried to keep carefully locked away and pushed down deep inside her. As the brush slipped through Pebble's coarse black hair, she allowed herself to examine her pain, turning it over gently. She let the heat of it burn until it threatened to engulf her, before pushing it back inside again and wiping away the wetness from her cheeks as she waited for the heaving in her chest to subside.

When she finally emerged reluctantly, back into the courtyard, Elaine was waiting for her, leaning against the wall, her hand shielding her eyes from the lowering rays of the early-evening sun.

Cass took a swift step towards her, fear lurching in her stomach. 'Are you—'

'I am well; the babe is fine.' She waved a hand dismissively and patted her protruding stomach. 'But it is you I am concerned with.' She took Cass's arm and led her not through the main doors that led to the great hall but round the side of the building instead and through the small postern door that led to the meadow. She looked intently at the girl, taking in the telltale redness around her eyes.

'You're going to have to face it sooner or later, Cass,' she said frankly, and Cass cringed. That was Elaine. Always so direct and forthright, like nobody else she had ever known.

'You cannot run from who you are.'

Cass said nothing but she felt her blood rise in frustration. How easy for Elaine, who had seemed utterly fearless from the moment she had ridden into the manor, heavy with child and furious with Lancelot who had abandoned her. How easy for her, always completely certain of herself and her decisions, to tell Cass to embrace her destiny. But how could she embrace who she was when she had no idea? The farm girl who skinned her knees three times a week and could never quite smooth her hair or keep her shoes clean like her elder sister could? The novice knight-in-training now rudderless without her mistress? The girl left broken-hearted by the loss of her best friend? The true owner of the sword in the stone? Her heart skipped a beat and she shook her head.

'It's all right,' Elaine told her. 'I'll not force you to speak of it if you don't wish to. But there are battles ahead and if you won't discuss them, then at least I can play a part in preparing you for them.' And she handed Cass a polished ash bow and a quiver of arrows.

Cass raised an enquiring eyebrow and Elaine gave her ready warm laugh.

'Growing a child does not render me utterly useless, you know. I do still have some knowledge to share.'

'But I already know how to shoot,' Cass began.

'Standing still, yes. And Sigrid trained you in hand-to-hand combat and jousting. But none of these skills will be of much use to you in the type of fighting I fear may be ahead. It will be horseback archery – being able to ride fast and shoot accurately at the same time – that will be of most use when you are pursuing enemies in wooded terrain.'

Cass swallowed hard. She'd worked hard to master the art of riding, and she was competent at archery now, even if Rowan's skill with a bow far surpassed hers, but combining the two? With one hand to hold the bow steady and one to pull back the string it seemed to Cass that there was one glaring problem.

'How do you hold on to the horse?' she asked, and Elaine laughed again.

'Don't worry about that just yet,' she said reassuringly, and she strode across the meadow to where her horse was waiting patiently, harnessed to a small cart. Cass watched as Elaine clambered into the saddle with considerable difficulty, sensing that she would not welcome an offer of help. And it was only when Elaine set off at a smart trot and the cart began to rumble along behind her that Cass saw the target tied onto it with a rope, facing towards her.

'Let's start with a moving target,' Elaine called determinedly, and Cass set her jaw and nocked the first arrow to her bow.

Chapter 7

The next few days passed in a pleasant lull and it would almost have been possible to believe that things were back to normal, if it weren't for the fact that Angharad was striding around the manor like a dog with a thorn in its paw, or that their usual quiet mealtimes were punctuated by occasional roars of laughter from Mordaunt's knights, who still kept a wary distance. Cass could not help noticing that Sir Gamelin was carefully polite when he encountered Lady Anne but that they did not seem to spend any time alone together.

With each day that went by the likelihood of any women from the towns and villages they had visited arriving at the manor dwindled further, and the cloud that seemed to hang over Angharad's head darkened. But Cass escaped into the meadow each morning with Edith, who proved to be a quick learner and a natural with a sword. She and Rowan took it in turns to coach the girl, and a strange satisfying feeling took Cass by surprise when she found herself teaching Edith the basic skills she herself had learned from Sigrid the year before.

'Focus on parrying the blow first, before you attempt a strike,' she explained, after she had easily sidestepped one of Edith's wild attempts at a stabbing motion with the wooden batons they used for practice. 'There's no use planning a killer blow if you're already skewered on your opponent's sword.' Edith gave a frustrated sigh and Cass, remembering her own impatience with Sigrid, grinned at her. 'Be patient and practise. It will come.'

In the long golden afternoons she saddled Pebble and went to train with Elaine, painstakingly relearning how to ride using only the strength of her thighs to keep her in the saddle and the movement of her calves to communicate with her horse.

'Feel the rhythm of the horse,' Elaine called after her, exasperated, as Cass attempted to master a running trot without using her hands for what felt like the hundredth time and lurched wildly to the side, almost losing her balance altogether. 'You will not be able to keep your bow steady unless you can keep the ride smooth, and the only way to do that is to move your body up and down in time with the horse's gait.' And she demonstrated the upwards thrusting motion with her pelvis, which only made Cass dissolve into peals of laughter because the action looked so odd with Elaine's enormous pregnant belly protruding as she gyrated her hips. Elaine laughed too, but they both stopped suddenly when a pair of Mordaunt's knights emerged from the manor to practise sparring, each trying to regain their composure and avoiding the other's eye for fear it would set them off again.

On the third day, Elaine decided that Cass had mastered the separate skills of shooting an arrow at a moving target and riding Pebble with no hands and was ready to attempt combining the two.

'When you are cantering through the trees in pursuit of a moving enemy, timing will be everything,' she told Cass, 'so we minimize the time taken at each step of the process.' She showed Cass how to tuck her arrows into her belt for quicker, easier access and how to slide her fingers quickly up the shaft of the arrow to find the fletched end point without taking her eyes off the enemy.

'Usually you would draw back the bowstring using your fingers, but when you are on horseback it is quicker to curl your fingers into your fist and use just your thumb instead.'

Cass tried it, her arrow flying wildly off to the side.

'You'll get used to it.' Elaine took Cass's arm, indicating the three targets she had set up along each long edge of the meadow. 'You'll ride down the centre, firing three arrows as you go, one for each target. Then turn and ride back this way, shooting at the targets on the other side as you return.'

Cass mounted and took a deep breath. She could ride confidently now, even without holding the reins or the pommel of her saddle. She could hit close to the centre of the target three times out of four. How difficult could it be to do both at the same time?

They set off, Pebble trotting gamely forward, Cass relying on her thighs to keep herself in the saddle, trying to remember the rising and falling rhythm Elaine had taught her.

She whispered under her breath, each word forced jerkily out of her lungs by the jolting of the horse's gait: '*Draw – arrow – push – forward – pinch – nock – slot – on – draw – string*—' But before she could get as far as *aim* and *release* she had fumbled the arrow, losing her rhythm and sitting down hard when she should have risen up, and it had fallen uselessly into the buttercup-strewn grass as they passed the first target.

'That's all right,' Elaine shouted from the end of the meadow. 'Keep going. Fit another arrow!'

So Cass did, this time managing to pull back the bowstring without losing it, but the target was already zooming past and she aimed wildly, shooting so wide that her arrow landed closer to the first target than the one she had actually been aiming at.

'Never mind, on to the next,' Elaine urged.

'Right elbow up, pull the string back, don't push the bow forward!'

Turning to focus on the opposite row of targets, Cass began. The first arrow soared high over the target, the second lodged in the ground a horse's length in front, but the final shot hit the very edge of the board with a satisfying hollow *thunk* and Cass felt a burst of pride even though it was nowhere near the centre of the target.

'Not bad for a trot.' Elaine smiled, her eyes twinkling mischievously at Cass. 'Now let's see you gallop.'

By the end of the afternoon Cass's thighs were burning, the tips of her fingers were sore and her arms were as heavy as lead. But she felt exhilarated and energetic, and as she walked off the field it occurred to her how different the feeling was from the nerves and fear she had felt in her first training sessions all those months ago.

She trudged back into the manor, ravenous and aching all over, past Alys, who was fixing rowan branches and sprigs of rosemary and sage round the doorway.

'We're going to need all the protection we can get,' she muttered darkly, as Cass gave her a questioning look. 'Especially if we're going to be trying to hold most of Northumbria with a handful of Mordaunt's leftovers and barely half our usual number of knights.'

Cass glanced at Angharad, who was sitting proud and tall in her usual carved chair at the head of one of the tables in the hall. Outwardly she was listening politely to something Edith was saying, but Cass knew from the way her fingers gripped the arm of her chair and the slight tightening at the corners of her mouth that she was holding the same fears just under the surface.

There had been a time when the gentle pressure of Vivian's hand on her shoulder would have calmed her and loosened those tight lines into a smile. But without Vivian, who had known Angharad so well and been unafraid to confront her when she was in a stubborn rage . . . Cass thought it was like being in a boat with only one oar: untethered and spinning hopelessly out of control.

The mood that evening was subdued. There had been no further news from the scouts in the two weeks since their last visit, so they had no way of knowing if the threat remained at a distance or crept ever closer to their doorstep. Angharad was stubbornly refusing to discuss their failure to attract new recruits to the manor and looked expectantly towards the door every time it opened, though it was only Blyth coming in to fetch a box of carrots for the horses. And as long as she maintained the pretence of expecting newcomers at any moment, it was too awkward for anyone else to confront the reality that they needed a new plan.

Chapter 8

Cass slept fitfully, plagued with dreams of shadowy figures moving through the forest, swarming towards the manor, and of powerful fists banging at the gates, demanding to be let in. She tossed and turned, her sheets damp with sweat. 'Go away,' she murmured, but the pounding only intensified.

Suddenly she was awake, sitting up in the dark with the bedsheets gathered tightly to her chest, heart pounding, as somebody continued to bang at the chamber door.

'Cass?' Susan's voice sounded small and panicked in the dark.

Cass leaped out of bed, grabbing the sword that always lay within reach, and swung open the door swiftly, the blade up and ready to strike.

'Wait!' Sir Gamelin held up one hand in a panicked gesture, his eyes wide as Cass's blade flashed in the flickering light of the candle he held in his other hand.

Cass lowered her sword, her heart hammering in her chest. She was acutely aware of the flimsiness of her cotton nightgown, and perhaps Gamelin was too, because he seemed to look anywhere except directly at her.

'There has been an attack at Elsdon. Raiders. A young boy from the village rode to ask for help but we do not know if we will be too late.'

Cass nodded and turned to wrestle on her breastplate and boots, as Gamelin strode away to pound on the next door. 'No time,' she gasped out, as Susan held up her pauldrons, looking terrified. She automatically caught up her shield and for a moment, without thinking, she thrust her spare hand under her bed towards the new blade with the ruby hilt that seemed to sing and thrum as her fingers touched it. But Cass recoiled from the vibrations she felt already beginning to answer in her own fingers, the way her blood pulled towards the weapon. She shoved it unceremoniously aside and slid the older sword into her scabbard instead, trying to ignore its dull cold weight as it hung at her belt.

Lastly, as she ran from the room, she remembered Elaine's

words and slung her bow over her shoulder before racing down to the stables.

Blyth was awake, having been roused by Gamelin and some of the other knights who had still been awake, playing cards in the hall, when the messenger had arrived. Half the horses were already saddled, including Pebble and Angharad's roan mare Star, who was stamping her front hoof in excitement at the prospect of a nocturnal adventure. Angharad came flying out of the manor as Cass mounted, an emerald-green cloak hastily thrown over her shoulders. Like Cass, she had only paused to don the most essential pieces of her armour. Wordlessly they left the stable together, passing through the open manor gates and streaking away into the woods.

They rode fast, Cass leaning forward and urging Pebble onwards, trying not to think about what they might find when they reached Elsdon. She remembered the horror of seeing the aftermath of another village sacked just months previously, the gut-churning image of bodies crumpled on the floor that had seared itself into her brain, the silent scream that pierced her like a knife when she saw Lily's lifeless body. Bile rose up, burning her throat, and she swallowed hard and hastened onwards across the dappled moonlight that carpeted the forest floor.

They were almost at the outskirts of the village when

Rowan caught up with them, just as the sound of shouting and the clash of weapons floated towards them on the fragrant night air, making Cass feel as if a large cold stone had fallen into her stomach.

'You two distract them,' Angharad hissed urgently, as they approached the first of the buildings, 'and I will ride round the perimeter and surprise them from behind. The others shouldn't be too far behind us; we will have reinforcements before long.'

There was no time to argue. Angharad was swallowed by the night, her cloak billowing briefly behind her, and Cass drew her bow and nocked an arrow as she and Rowan galloped onwards towards the centre of the village.

They had arrived just in time.

There were no corpses yet, no smouldering ruins of buildings; instead, as they approached the open space at the centre of the village, they could see by the light of the moon in the clear sky that the villagers had been lined up against the walls of their houses, shivering and cringing in their night clothes, children crying and cowering behind their mothers. Cass and Rowan reined in their horses, hanging back behind a small cluster of wooden huts. Peering round the side of one of the buildings, Cass saw the elderly man with the balding head sitting dazed on the cobblestones, his wooden crutch snapped in half a short distance away.

And facing the straggling, wretched line of villagers, laughing and trading gruff remarks in a rich guttural language Cass didn't recognize, was a band of around a dozen men, most of them tall and broad-shouldered. They wore long woollen tunics under a mixture of leather and chainmail armour, and helmets the like of which she had never seen before. The dull bronze-coloured metal arched from straight cheek protectors over the men's eyebrows, then descended sharply with a long flat strip that bisected their faces, covering their noses and upper lips.

'Too many of them to take in single combat,' Rowan whispered, her mouth close to Cass's ear so that her warm breath tickled her neck. 'Our best chance is to pick them off one by one from a distance. But we will have to keep moving, or they'll be upon us in an instant.'

'You mean—'

Rowan nodded briskly. 'Good job you brought your bow.'

Cass felt the panic rising in her, clawing up from her stomach towards her throat, threatening to suffocate her. 'But I have only just started—'

'Even if your arrows do not find their targets, they will add to the general confusion and help to split their attention.' Rowan gave her a look that clearly forbade any further argument and touched her heels to her horse's sides, racing away towards the next cluster of buildings. She hissed over her shoulder as she went and Cass looked up from the arrows she was hastily shoving into her belt: 'Just try not to hit the villagers.'

And the parting jibe was so typical of their daily sparring sessions that in spite of everything, in spite of the sense that this was not real, Cass felt a grin split her face as she raised her bow.

Her first arrow flew so far short of its target that it landed, feathered end quivering, at the raiders' feet, but the effect was just as Rowan had predicted. The nearest men jumped backwards, swearing, and they began to shout in alarm, twisting their necks to try to see the source of the attack. Before they could spot Cass, another arrow whizzed across the marketplace, and she knew Rowan had found her target when she heard a wet thud and one of the men cried out in pain.

The villagers were starting to stumble around in panic, tripping over each other, uncertain if the arrows were fired by friends or more foes, blindly pushing and shoving as they scrambled to find shelter.

Cass paused between two buildings, glancing down to try to find the notch to nock her second arrow, and her hesitation betrayed her. There was a yell and she looked up to see one of the tallest of the men lumbering furiously towards her, helmet down, like a charging bull. Cursing herself for not heeding Elaine and Rowan's instructions to keep moving, she hurriedly kicked Pebble into a gallop, retreating a little way and then doubling back between another set of huts to come out behind the attacker. He was just a few yards away, turning, seeing her, reaching for his sword, and Cass knew that if this arrow did not find its target he would be upon her before she could draw her bowstring back again.

As the great mountain of a man bellowed and lunged towards her, Cass tried to freeze time, tried to leave the heat and the speed and the chaos of the moment, with Pebble's eyes rolling to the whites in fear and spittle flying from the man's mouth and her thighs screaming in protest as she stood high in the saddle. She took herself back to the meadow, to the golden light and the buttercups and Elaine's laughter. And she heard Elaine's voice, as if she were standing right beside her. *Run your fingers down the shaft – pull back the bowstring with your thumb – curl your fingers into your palm – never take your eyes off the target –* And the arrow seemed to loose itself, streaking through the air and burying itself with a smack in the man's forehead. His momentum sent him toppling grotesquely forward, his eyes unfocused and mouth slack, and Pebble screamed and reared up to avoid the body that had fallen at her feet.

Another man was upon her before she had taken her eyes off the twitching body, his sword too close, too fast for her to reach for another arrow. She drew her sword, the sword she had used to fight alongside Lily, had used to train with Sigrid, and felt it lifeless and strange in her hand. She turned, almost in a daze, as the man threw himself towards her, and almost by accident the blade plunged into his stomach, so that his face seemed to split open in shock and he crumpled. Cass looked down at the sword and felt the urge to throw it far from her horse, to discard it in disgust. Bile rose in the back of her throat.

And then there were other screams and the moment was broken. Cass thrust the sword back into her belt and turned in the saddle to see Angharad riding into the open space of the marketplace from behind the group of remaining men who were still straining to locate the source of the arrows. Star reared, and Angharad was upon them before they even had time to turn. With one clean sweep of her sword, two of them fell in the mud before the third and fourth had managed to draw their swords. As the next one engaged Angharad, who swung herself down out of the saddle to meet him, Cass saw another fall and knew that Rowan had found her mark again. Quickly, with fingers that trembled and shook so the arrow clattered against the bow, Cass let another arrow fly, and then another, aiming for the men at the edge of the group, for fear she might otherwise accidentally hit Angharad. And though her strikes served mainly to distract the men while Rowan dispatched them, by the time her quiver was empty there was just one man left standing, locked in single combat with Angharad, his height and weight advantage allowing him to force her backwards towards the huddle of terrified villagers. Then there was a blur of something flying through the air and a sickening crack, as the old man's wooden crutch took the tall invader out at the knees. And Angharad lost no time in running her sword smoothly through his throat so that he fell backwards, gurgling quietly.

With the last dregs of his energy, he reached for the edge of Angharad's cloak, pulling her towards him, and gave an obscene smile, his teeth shining with fresh blood. 'This is just the beginning,' he croaked hoarsely in heavily accented tones, before he shuddered and lay still as his blood ran out onto the cobbles.

By the time Gamelin arrived with a band of Mordaunt's knights and some of the other women from the manor, it was all over. But as the men gazed around them at the carnage the women had wrought on their would-be conquerors, Cass noticed, with a stirring of satisfaction, that they looked back at the members of the sisterhood with something between wariness and a new-found respect.

The sky was stained a dirty pink as they made their way back, hardly talking, feeling as if they were waking from a strange and violent dream. The people of the village had been too shocked to even voice their thanks as they had helped each other to their feet and staggered back into their homes. It was not so different, Cass thought a little bitterly, to when they had competed at tournaments in disguise, with no reward or acknowledgement for their victory.

But she was wrong.

They slept late the next morning, after crawling back into bed as the sun began to rise in earnest, and when the gates to the manor were opened around noon there was a crowd of women some two or three dozen strong waiting there, some carrying bows or daggers, some leading horses.

'We heard your invitation,' said a stout freckled girl with reddish-blonde hair at the front of the crowd, fingering a knife at her belt. 'And we have come to learn to fight.'

Chapter 9

When Cass had first arrived at the manor, she had thought that training as a knight was the hardest thing she had ever done. But within a few short days of the influx of new recruits, she was beginning to think that teaching was far harder.

Cass stood waiting with Angharad, Rowan and a group of other squires as the women trooped nervously into the meadow bright and early on the second morning, one tripping over her shoes and several others skirting, terrified, around the horses Blyth had lined up for them to ride. They weren't the most inspiring group, ranging in age from a skinny girl of about eleven to a slightly stooped but determined-looking woman who must have been seventy, her snow-white hair plaited tightly into a crown across the top of her head. 'I am Martha,' she said stubbornly, when Cass cast her a doubtful look, 'and if you dare tell me I'm too old for this I'll have you over my knee like a bairn and give you a spanking before you know what's hit you.' Cass blinked in surprise, while Susan and some of the other squires dissolved into fits of giggles. 'I've borne seven children, and buried four, I've worked the land my whole life and I'm all muscle and sinew,' Martha continued loudly, holding up her forearm to demonstrate her sun-browned, firm bicep. 'And if you turn me away, I shall turn up again at the gates tomorrow and the next day and the day after that, so you may just as well save the trouble and start training me now.'

'Martha, you are exactly the sort of person we are looking for,' Angharad reassured her, and Martha grinned, revealing several missing teeth, and strode proudly forward amongst the slow-moving crowd.

They were an unimposing group, dressed in an odd array of men's clothes that had clearly been cobbled together from the remnants left behind by the men who had left to fight the invaders further south. Cass tried hard not to imagine the faces of a band of Saxon raiders should they ever be confronted by this ragged crew. The only possible silver lining, she thought grimly, was that they might be laughing too hard to aim their arrows straight.

'Remind me again why we ever thought this was a good idea?' Cass said under her breath to Rowan.

'Because we can't take on any more raiding bands with only a dozen sword hands,' a teasing voice came from behind them, and Cass jumped as if she'd been scalded as Gamelin and a couple of the other knights from Mordaunt's court stepped closer. 'Thought you could use some help,' he smiled, and Cass nodded, flushing, and then, seeing the hostility on Rowan's face, hastily strode forward and clapped her hands before Rowan could reject their offer of aid.

'We will start with basic skills,' she announced, and with Rowan's help she divided the women into six groups of five. She, Rowan and Angharad each took one group to learn basic sword handling, using the wooden batons that Cass had practised with when she first arrived at the manor. At the opposite end of the meadow, Blyth was teaching those who had not previously ridden how to saddle, mount and dismount a horse. And Sir Gamelin and Sir Bale were running drills, building up the new recruits' general fitness with obstacle courses and exercises.

'You couldn't call it an immediate success,' Rowan remarked drily, as one of the women leapt rather too enthusiastically into her horse's saddle and immediately slipped out the other side into the mud. The horse looked down with an expression of bemused surprise and then continued grazing. Meanwhile, two plump women, who looked to be in their thirties, were sitting dazedly at the bottom of a tree having run pell-mell into each other from opposite directions without looking where they were going, and Gamelin was supporting a tall girl with her hair in two plaits as she limped off the field after apparently having twisted her ankle while waiting in the queue for her turn to try sword fighting.

Edith, the dark-haired young woman who had pursued them through the forest, was the only one who seemed to be showing any natural aptitude. Keeping herself slightly apart from the other villagers, she was locked in hand-to-hand combat with Angharad, her wooden baton moving methodically from side to side as she parried, sliced and struck.

'I taught her that,' Rowan said, proudly. 'Just don't look at the other twenty-nine.'

'Was I really this slow and stupid when I first arrived?' Cass asked, gazing around in dismay, and then she caught the glint in Rowan's eye as the taller girl opened her mouth.

'Only when you first arrived?' Rowan queried sweetly, and stepped smartly out of reach as Cass swung a wooden baton in the direction of her backside.

They kept it up all day, breaking only for a brief respite at lunch time, when Alys and Elaine brought out plates of fresh bread and cold meat and baskets piled with sweet red apples. Lady Anne and some of the other women were with them, offering cups of fresh milk from a large pitcher. Cass tried not to notice how Anne smiled shyly up at Sir Gamelin from beneath her fringe and told herself she had imagined the unseemly leap of something like joy in her chest when he nodded politely as he accepted a cup of milk, but quickly turned away and struck up conversation with Sir Bale.

Two of the ladies from Mordaunt's court lingered after the others had returned to the manor; the young woman with the dark, silky plaits and another of about the same age, both of them hesitating awkwardly at the edge of the field, eyeing the others and their weapons with open curiosity.

'Would you like to join us?' Cass asked with a smile, and they nodded eagerly, each pulling down their fashionable dresses to reveal borrowed simple men's clothing underneath. A couple of the village women shouted their approval, and even Rowan's lip twitched with what looked suspiciously close to a smile.

By the time the shadows of the trees began to creep across the meadow and the sun turned deep yellow in the late afternoon, there were exhausted groups of women scattered around the grass, lying down and groaning like the casualties of some great battle. But Cass was relieved that while they seemed completely shattered, they didn't look mutinous. She even had to grudgingly admire the fact that not one of them, from Martha to the eleven-year-old, whose name was Tess, said a single word about giving up. However daunting training was, she suspected it was less terrifying than the memories of their village being attacked by men with swords. 'Just the beginning,' the dying man had crowed, and Cass thought she was not the only one in the meadow who still heard those words ringing in her ears.

After the women had hobbled off towards home, some clutching each other for support, but promising to return the next morning, Angharad retired, leaving Cass and Rowan, Gamelin and Bale and a group of the squires lying in the grass, listening to the melodic song of the woodlarks and soaking up the last warmth of the evening sun.

'Well,' yawned Bale, breaking the silence and voicing what they all were thinking, 'if an attack comes soon at least our defeat will be swift.' And they all let out peals of laughter as the tension dissipated.

'Speak for yourselves,' Rowan rolled over onto her front, propping herself up on one elbow and putting a hand up to shield her eyes as the low sun shone into them. 'We are not the ones who recently yielded our stronghold to a group half the size in both strength and number.'

Gamelin winced, and Bale gave a mock gasp, clutching at his chest as if her words had wounded him.

'Too soon?' Cass threw Rowan a nervous glance.

'Too soon in the morning, it was when you attacked, yes,' Bale retorted, sitting up. 'For we'd have routed you for certain if you had not taken us by surprise, half dressed and half asleep.'

'We would defeat you again any day of the week –' Rowan laughed – 'and in any state of dress or undress.'

'Is that an invitation?' Bale enquired, and now it was Rowan's turn to look flustered, and Cass relished the opportunity to get her own back with a sly look.

'To spar?' Rowan leaped to her feet and grabbed one of the wooden batons that lay discarded nearby. 'With great pleasure. To undress? You should be so lucky.'

Bale grinned and raised himself up, giving Gamelin a playful kick in the ribs. 'Do not leave me to take these two on alone when our honour is at stake!'

So Gamelin sprang up beside him, each of them weighing a baton experimentally in their fists, while Cass and Rowan instinctively positioned themselves back-to-back, weapons drawn and ready.

'I have never fought a woman before,' Bale frowned, taking a tentative step forward and pausing, his baton poised indecisively. 'I don't wish to hurt you or exploit my superior strength—' But before he could continue, Rowan had darted forward and jabbed him, hard, with her baton, so that he doubled up, clutching his crotch and swearing, tears starting in his eyes.

'First,' Rowan said, surveying him dispassionately as he wheezed and grunted, 'you have fought women before, you just didn't know it.' She spun her baton into the air and caught it deftly in her fist. 'Second, based on the outcome of said fight, you *really* don't need to worry about protecting us from your "superior strength"' – her disdainful tone made it quite clear exactly what she thought of that notion. 'And third, didn't anyone ever teach you to watch your flank?' As he looked around, gaping in surprise, Cass moved swiftly forward from the position she had quietly taken up behind him and rapped him smartly in the side with her baton, sending him crashing to the ground.

'Mercy!' He gasped, hands in the air, and Cass stepped forward and put out her hand to help him up, feeling guilty for striking him when he was already compromised. But no sooner had he clasped her palm than he tugged, hard, pulling her off balance and sending her sprawling while he leaped to his feet again and readjusted his grip on the baton.

'So we're playing dirty are we?' Rowan grinned. 'Good.' And she hauled Cass to her feet without ever taking her eyes off the knights who were now circling them, eyes narrowed, taking wary sidesteps as they sized up their opponents.

Cass took up a defensive position again with her back to Rowan and firmly pushed down the tightness that seemed to grip her chest distractingly each time Gamelin circled past her and caught her eye.

Unsurprisingly Rowan was the first to strike, darting forward to engage Sir Bale, their batons coming together with a resounding knock, quickly followed by a smart 'rat-a-tat-tat' as they each rained blows upon the other, aiming to wind but always blocked by the swift defensive manoeuvres of the opposite's weapon. They were remarkably well-matched, Cass observed, admiring the swiftness of their footwork and the deft speed with which they readjusted their weapons.

She gasped as a sudden jab to her ribs brought her attention back to Sir Gamelin, who had taken advantage of her momentary distraction to land a first, slightly tentative, blow, and now paused nervously, as if he half expected to be chastised for it.

'She will not break.' Rowan rolled her eyes, still parrying Bale's blows with one hand even as she gestured towards Cass with the other. 'Try harder, Gamelin, or you will find yourself on your backside very quickly indeed.'

Cass laughed and allowed herself to be swept up in Rowan's infectious mood, the awkwardness quickly dissipating as she spun round to take a backhanded swipe at Gamelin, who blocked it and made a wild strike towards her head, which she ducked easily.

'You'll have to be quicker than that,' she teased, dancing swiftly behind him, light on her feet as Sigrid had taught her, and landing a jab to his elbow that almost made him drop his baton. He turned with a mock growl, gripping it afresh, his hazel eyes flashing as he aimed for her in earnest, a series of forceful downward blows that forced her to use both hands to deflect them. The air seemed momentarily to crackle between them, as she arched backwards and he leaned into the space her body had just occupied, their faces mere inches apart. She gasped, almost losing her balance, and saw his hand move forward, as if instinctively, to grasp the small of her back, to catch her, to pull her towards him, and then Rowan was there, tripping him from behind so that he fell sideways and rounded on her instead. Cass regained her balance and immediately Sir Bale engaged her, so she took up where Rowan had left off, with quick, sharp blows and unexpected jabs that forced him to take several steps backwards, on the defensive.

For a moment she heard Sigrid's low growl, as clearly as if her former mistress were standing beside her on the practice field. 'Do not give them a chance to use their weight against you in hand-to-hand combat. Strike pre-emptively, force your advantage, exploit your speed and dexterity. Make sure you are always fighting on your terms.'

She darted forward again, jabbing her baton into the soft base of his stomach and hearing the breath driven out of him in a satisfying rush. But before she could press the advantage, she heard Rowan curse under her breath and half turned to see her on the floor, her baton knocked some distance away. Then a strong arm grabbed her round the waist from behind and she felt the cold hard pressure of a wooden baton held against her throat from behind.

'Do you yield?' There was gentle laughter in the voice, and the baton was held carefully so that it did not constrict her airway or bruise her neck.

His chest was hard and warm against her back, his hand cupping her ribcage gently though his forearm was firm across her waist. For a single moment she allowed her mind to go somewhere else, to imagine a different scenario, to feel him holding her like this without a baton in his hand. Her eyes closed, and then Rowan's voice brought her back to herself, as she grudgingly muttered: 'We yield. This time.' Then he released her, and she suddenly felt the loss of his warmth, though the evening was not cold.

'They will be wondering where we are at the manor,' said Gamelin a little gruffly, avoiding her eyes, and he and Bale strode off, leaving Cass and Rowan to pick up the rest of the batons and follow them back inside for supper.

Chapter 10

They breakfasted in the hall the next morning with the dozen or so women who lived too far from the manor to return home to their villages each night. Cass was eating a piece of Bannock bread slathered in butter and honey, mulling over the best way to approach archery training when many of the women had never held a bow in their lives and there were not enough weapons at the manor for them all to practise with.

She knew Iona was working day and night in the forge. Every time Cass crossed the courtyard, the armourer's sprightly form was visible against the flickering heat except when she plunged hot metal into the water butt and disappeared behind great clouds of steam. Their reserve of swords was growing fast, but it would be some time before she had managed to make enough weapons for all the new recruits, let alone started work on casting new arrowheads. Meanwhile, Blyth had been scouring the countryside, visiting local villages to buy or borrow as many spare horses as possible, but they still couldn't yet mount everybody at the same time. Cass tried not to think about how badly it would hamper their efforts to defend themselves if invaders arrived before they had even managed to source basic weapons for everybody.

Just the beginning. Just the beginning. Just the beginning.

The words of the bloodied man haunted Cass, both when she was sleeping and awake. She watched the others sitting at the long tables hunched over their food. Rowan was muttering something about footwork. The younger squires were whispering together, their faces pinched with worry. Angharad was gazing into the distance, her porridge cold and untouched in front of her.

Their greatest fear until now had been that outsiders would discover their secret; unmask them as women daring to live lives deemed suitable only for men. Yet now the worst had happened, and Cass was discovering that there were worries and fears even greater. Suddenly the threat they faced was not only to the sisterhood and the manor but the whole community. If more raiders arrived before they had managed to train a fighting force to hold them off, then . . . She could barely allow herself to contemplate the devastation.

They would not spare them. Not women who dared to arm themselves and resist. She, Angharad and the others would be responsible for the slaughter. Had they undertaken too much? Was it madness to think they could ever train these women to resist an invasion from hardened fighting men?

Her gloomy train of thought was interrupted by a commotion at the great iron-bound doors of the hall that led out to the courtyard. There came a cacophony of yelling and of hooves ringing on the flagstones and Cass could hear Blyth's voice raised in uncharacteristic anger as a great pounding began at the door. Angharad rose to her feet and nodded to the two squires nearest the door, who only just had time to unbolt it before it flew open, clearly pushed hard from the outside.

A short puce-faced man with a rolling gait induced by a pronounced limp strode into the hall, looking around wildly. Angharad took a step forward but he completely ignored her, making a beeline towards one of the other tables instead, where a woman of about forty had been conversing animatedly with her neighbour. She turned pale as the man approached, a crust falling from her fingers onto the plate.

'Agnes,' he thundered, and she seemed to shrink in the

face of his furious scowl. 'Get up from that bench and get home immediately.'

She gulped and stumbled to her feet, but the woman next to her placed a hand on her arm and they all rose, all along the bench, as one, facing him.

'What is this?' he spluttered, his eyes bulging as the women faced him silently. 'This is between you and me, Agnes. You, me and our home, where you belong.'

Still the woman did not speak, though she cowered at his fury.

'You are needed at home, Agnes,' he spat, flecks of spittle flying across the table. 'Not here, taking part in this preposterous farce of dressing up and neglecting your true role.'

Rowan stepped forward, drawing a breath, but Angharad raised a hand to intercept, her eyes never leaving Agnes's face.

'And what might that be, John?' Agnes asked in a trembling voice, with the air of one screwing up every ounce of courage. 'It's not our home that needs me, it is you – you who cannot get along without me to cook and clean and tend to your every whim.'

He spluttered at her, but she continued, clenching the hand of the woman next to her so hard that their knuckles turned white, her face set in determination now she had begun.

'You are just as capable of looking after yourself and our home as I am, John. Just because you are lame and cannot join the fighting, does not mean you cannot be useful at home. Letting me be here, to do this, that is how you can best help our community now.'

'What do you mean, letting you do *this*?!' he exploded, gesturing wildly around the room. 'Live with a gaggle of other women like some kind of witches' coven and play-act with swords? What'll you do at the first sight of real danger, Agnes? You will turn tail and come running home, sobbing your fears to me! Well, I'll not be there Agnes, do you hear me? Not if you continue to follow this disgraceful course. There will be nobody at home waiting for you.' He drew himself up to his full height and nodded towards the door. 'Not unless you come home with me this instant.'

There was a long silence in the hall while everybody seemed to hold their breath, watching Agnes as doubt and defiance did battle across her face.

'Very well then, John,' she said quietly, and she sat down and picked up the crust again.

He huffed out an incredulous laugh, looking around as if to appeal to somebody to support him. But all he met were stony gazes, and he turned on his heel and limped out of the hall, followed by a short silence and then the clattering of hooves again.

Almost to herself, Agnes half laughed, half sobbed: 'I do quite like the idea of a coven, though. At least there'd be someone else to share the housework.'

There was another moment of absolute silence and then the hall erupted into the sound of cheering and fists banging on the table and poor Agnes almost choked on her crust as hands reached out from every direction to clap her on the back.

It was a grimly determined band who marched out of the hall to the meadow that morning.

Angharad had decided to split them into two separate groups, with half focusing on archery and the other half on sword fighting, so that they could make the best use of the weapons they had available. In order to decide who should be in which group, each would shoot a quiver of arrows at a target and then have a brief sparring match with Rowan, Gamelin or Cass while Angharad observed, dividing them up according to their strengths.

Alys was standing at the edge of the meadow with parchment and quill, as Angharad had asked her to make a list of the women allocated to each group.

'It's not so much a case of finding which task they're strongest at as which they're least terrible at, isn't it?' Susan whispered out of the corner of her mouth to Elizabeth, who tried to suppress a giggle.

Cass shushed them sharply, even though privately she had been thinking exactly the same thing.

'You were not exactly master sword wielders when you first arrived either,' Angharad snapped at them, and Elizabeth immediately ceased sniggering. 'But with patience and time your skills blossomed.'

She spoke with a tone of firm finality, and both turned back, shame-faced, to the arrows they were supposed to be collecting. But once they were out of earshot, Cass heard Angharad mutter to Rowan, 'Patience, I can muster. How much time we have, however, is the real question.'

As she spoke, one of the women swung wildly for Gamelin with her baton, missed completely and somehow managed to spin herself round and collapse in a heap, limbs and baton all tangled up together. As they all paused to watch her attempting to right herself, Cass saw Elaine, who was instructing the archers, take advantage of the momentary pause to rest her hands on her knees, her forehead creased with concentration as she took slow, deep breaths.

'What ails her?' Cass asked Alys quietly.

'The child is in the wrong position,' Alys answered in a grave tone, her worried eyes on Elaine. 'She should have been delivered by now, but the position of the babe is preventing her labour from progressing as it should. She should be resting in bed, not striding around a field shooting arrows.' She shook her head, lips pursed. 'It is her first child, and she does not seem to realize the dangers . . .'

'She will come when she is good and ready, Alys,' Elaine snapped a few minutes later, losing her patience as Alys attempted to feel her forehead for the fifth time that morning, checking for a fever that might indicate any sign of infection. 'And she and I will get through it together when she does. ARM UP!' This last exhortation was yelled at a young woman with wispy blonde hair who promptly unleashed her arrow directly into the soil at the base of the target.

Elaine sighed and trudged over towards it, but Alys beat her there and stooped to pull the arrow out of the ground herself. 'There is stubbornness, and then there's stupidity,' she said firmly, handing the arrow back to the girl but speaking to Elaine. 'Nobody is suggesting you aren't strong, Elaine, how could they . . .?' She trailed off at the stony look on Elaine's face. 'But you are going to need some help to get through this. You don't have to rely only on yourself any more. We are here to support you, if you'll only let us!'

Elaine began to grumble, but Cass saw her wince and put a hand to her side and she fell silent. After that, Elaine remained a constant authoritative presence in the meadow, shouting out encouragement and instructions to the archers, but she made less fuss when Alys came to check on her, and even swallowed the herbal medicine the older woman brought her with no complaint.

Slowly, the women were making progress. It was rare for an arrow to miss altogether now, although they still made a haphazard pattern across the target, and almost every one of the new recruits now could reliably block and parry a few basic sword strokes. Even Rowan had to grudgingly admit that Sir Mordaunt's knights were doing a good job of helping to train them, spending long hours out in the meadow carrying out repetitive training manoeuvres over and over with no complaint.

Those who had already known how to ride were progressing to horseback archery like Cass, and one or two had begun to shine under Rowan's close combat tuition. Edith, who had proven herself to be a quiet hard worker, was flourishing, her sword skills developing so quickly that Rowan had procured her a weapon of her own from Iona and decided to take her as her squire. And in the evenings the girl sat with Elaine, making herself useful by rubbing salve into her swollen feet or helping her to embroider linens in preparation for the baby's arrival, the dark head and the blonde one bent together in front of the fire.

It was on one of these quiet evenings that Cass, Alys, Rowan and Angharad sat discussing the grim reality of their situation. 'We need more news,' Alys huffed in frustration, glaring at the hall door as if it were deliberately keeping their scouts from arriving with fresh reports.

'They are covering great distances, and travelling at night to remain concealed is not easy,' Angharad reminded her, though she too glanced wistfully towards the entrance.

'We will not be ready,' Rowan said, keeping her voice low so that the squires could not hear. 'If they attack again soon, we will barely be ready to defend our own manor, let alone the rest of the community.'

'We have to,' Angharad insisted, sounding strained. 'We cannot let all the sacrifices that have been made be for nothing.' Her eyes were glassy, and Cass knew who she was thinking of.

Rowan shook her head. 'There is not enough time. We cannot train them fast enough. And any enemy who sees them, sees we are just women, sees our numbers . . .' She trailed off, not needing to finish the sentence. They all knew the rest. They would be demolished.

'Then we will not let them see us,' Alys said slowly, looking into the flames as if she were seeing them for the first time. 'Or at least, we will show them only what we want to.'

They all stared at her. 'Fire,' Alys muttered. 'We can use the fire,' she repeated, slowly. 'We will use the smoke.' She looked up at them, her excitement growing. 'Don't you see? Shadowy figures suddenly appearing out of nowhere between the trees. A mass of fighters looming from the mist like ghosts. We do not let them see us to realize most of our forces are a ragtag band of village women with newly acquired weapons and ill-fitting armour. We play on their superstitions and conceal our reality.'

Angharad called over some of the scouts. 'Visit the nearby villages and manor houses. Tell them to make piles of timber ready around their lands. If there is an attack, light the fires. They will serve as both a signal to summon aid and a veil to conceal our numbers. Go.'

'It will not work for ever,' she warned Alys, grimly.

'It does not need to. It just needs to buy us some time.'

Chapter 11

It was about a week later when Cass woke one morning knowing that something was wrong. She could not have explained how she knew it, but she opened her eyes with dread already heavy on her chest, so heavy that she could hardly draw breath. She climbed out of bed and reached underneath for the sword that had lain quiet for so long. As her fingers closed round the handle that should have been cold and hard it seemed warm to the touch, as if she had only moments ago put it down. And that familiar buzz of exhilaration, almost as if her whole body vibrated with energy, overcame her once again. But it was not strong enough to quell the fear that pressed in on all sides, suffocating, and she hastily buckled on a sword belt over her nightgown and forced the sword into the scabbard as she moved to the window and looked out over the courtyard below.

Nothing stirred. It was very early and the sky was luminous with childlike smears of pale pink, orange and yellow. The horses were quiet in the stable, and Cass knew they would be the first to raise the alarm if there were intruders near the outer walls. The air was warm, balmy and still, as if the world were holding its breath. It should have been the most peaceful of summer mornings. And yet still the terror would not loosen its grip on her throat.

The dread was heavy and sickening, turning her lungs to lead and seeping into her limbs so that it was as much as she could do to move to the door, unlatch it and push at the heavy wood with both hands, opening it inch by torturous inch. She had a woolly, lethargic sensation that something very bad was happening very close by, but Cass was underwater, her eyesight blurred and hearing muffled, forced to be aware of it while also knowing there was absolutely nothing she could do about it. It was a feeling she had never had before, and it terrified her.

The manor was silent as she padded out into the corridor and along a winding staircase, the narrow window slits in the thick stone walls allowing the pinkish dawn light to filter inside so there was a warm dreamlike quality to the place.

She came to a place where the corridor split in two and, as if she already knew which way to walk, her feet turned left and continued without hesitating, almost as if she was in a dream, sleepwalking a path she had walked many times before but could not remember.

It was not until she turned the next corner that she heard it. A long, harrowing animal wail. Cass froze, not breathing, and then it came again. A guttural cry with a serrated edge that tore at the air. She ran towards the door at the end of the corridor and burst through it, finding her sword in her hand without any memory of having drawn it.

But her sword would be no help in here.

Elaine was on the bed, her head hanging down between her shoulders, her back heaving with great raw gasps as she wrestled to regain her breath. Alys was next to her at the head of the bed, her hand clasped tight in Elaine's, and as Cass walked in Alys looked up at her over Elaine's wretched shuddering form and gave a terrified shake of the head.

That fear in Alys's eyes, and the helpless desperate look on her face was almost more terrifying to Cass than the sight of Elaine on the bed. Never had she known Alys to be anything other than gruffly confident; her lined face was always calm, her capable hands reaching immediately for a useful herb or a jar of ointment. It had not truly occurred to her until now that there might exist an ailment which

Alys could not fix. Yet there she was, not administering medicine or bustling about with reassuring busyness, but simply clutching the younger woman's hand as if her life depended on it.

'What can I do?' Cass whispered.

'Be here,' Alys whispered back, and Cass moved to the side of the bed and took Elaine's other hand in hers. She looked up, and those bright blue eyes that Cass was used to seeing so confident and certain were wide with fear. Her dark blonde hair was in its usual heavy plait, but tendrils had escaped and stuck to the sweat around the edges of her heart-shaped face.

'Stay?' she gasped out, and Cass nodded, because it was the only thing she could do.

The next few hours were worse than any battle or melee Cass had ever seen. There was nothing worse than her utter helplessness in the face of the forces that held Elaine pinioned ruthlessly to the bed while her body writhed of its own accord and her pale face contorted in agony. No death scream of a knight on the field had ever pierced Cass's heart like the low animal moans Elaine seemed not to realize she was making, and the knowledge that there was absolutely nothing she could do to ease them.

'The child has not turned,' Alys whispered, when Elaine had gone limp with exhaustion and she had carefully placed her hands on the great bulge of her belly, deftly feeling and prodding. 'She labours but cannot progress. And there's no way of knowing what the effect will be on the child if she does not deliver it soon.'

'She will live,' Elaine said through gritted teeth without opening her eyes, her face grey now and beads of sweat standing out along her neck and collarbone. 'Because she is strong, like her mother.'

Then she heaved again as if some great hand had twisted her insides and she let out a scream of such pure agony that Cass bit the inside of her cheek and tasted bitter metal.

She would never quite be able to remember afterwards what had come first, that awful scream, or the sensation that her sword was tingling somehow at her side, or the clash of weapons that drifted faintly through the window. All she knew in that moment was that her world had shrunk to that room, and that bed, and the three of them locked there together in an unholy struggle against death as it fought to grip Elaine in its greedy claws.

'Elaine,' Alys said quietly, though Elaine turned her head away, sobbing softly into her hair. 'Elaine, I must try to turn the baby. It is the only chance we have to deliver it. But it is going to hurt.' Her mouth was a grim thin line.

Elaine looked completely defeated. Limp and bedraggled, she was a shadow of the shining, crowned creature who had galloped into the great hall a few months ago, triumphantly arriving at the sanctuary she had chosen to keep her baby safe. She shook her head and tears leaked out of the corners of her eyes. 'No. I cannot. No more.'

'We have no choice,' Alys answered, and her voice took on a little more of her usual brusque motherly tone. 'I have seen you withstand grazes from arrowheads and blows from cudgels in the practice field. And you will withstand this too, because you are strong and you are brave and your child needs you, Elaine.'

Elaine mutely turned her head away, and Alys looked imploringly at Cass.

Nervously she knelt beside the bed so that her eyes were level with Elaine's. She laced their fingers together, never breaking eye contact. 'I am here with you. You once told me that being able to feel was my greatest strength. So we will feel this together. And you will both live through it, I promise.'

And Elaine gave the tiniest nod and tightened her grip on Cass's hand as she squeezed her eyes shut, and it was only once they were closed that Cass allowed herself to be flooded by the sheer panic that she had just promised something she could not guarantee, and the reassuring smile dropped from her face.

Cass did not know whether the shouts and the commotion

that rang in her ears were coming from outside or whether they were part of the chaos in her mind as Elaine neared the peak of her fight.

Alys placed her hands firmly on Elaine's stomach, and at the same time Cass heard metal grating on metal with an ear-shattering shriek.

Elaine drew in a shaking breath and there came a clattering of hooves and a long whinny.

Alys pressed down hard, both hands kneading at Elaine's stomach like dough, and Cass winced as Elaine screamed and there was a great crash of splintering wood.

Cass looked down at the bleeding rows of half-moons in the heels of her hands and realized that her nails had pierced her skin. Nothing could be worse than this helplessness.

Then there was one last great ringing of swords and Elaine shrieked higher and louder than ever, and her voice quieted and another took its place, a high-pitched furious wail that trebled and quavered in the sudden stillness.

Elaine lay deathly still, her face drained of all colour. There was blood on the sheets, too much blood surely, as Alys thrust the little raw red thing into Cass's arms and rushed back to bend over its mother, her hands working furiously once again. But there was no response this time, no protestation, no wailing, and Cass looked down at the tiny mite wrapped in a sheet in her arms. Its huge black newborn eyes blinked back up at her, as wide and deep as the night sky, and for a long moment in Cass's arms the child was quite calm and silent, staring up at her as if she was a trusted friend. She could not tear her eyes away from its piercing gaze as the tiny hand, fragile and translucent, the fingernails paper thin and purple, closed round her little finger.

Then the silence was shattered as the door burst open and Susan was there, dressed in armour, gasping for breath, blood running down one side of her face and plastering her hair to her neck.

'Saxons,' Susan breathed, between great shuddering gasps. She had eyes only for Cass, hardly stopping to take in the scene in front of her. 'Close – to – the manor . . .' She bent double, her hands on her knees, and blinked some of the blood out of her eyes. 'The fighting comes ever nearer – and the new recruits – not ready . . .'

Cass did not need to hear any more. She thrust the baby at Susan, who took it in her arms with a look of complete shock and sank weakly to the floor, cross-legged.

She was already halfway to the door before Susan's next words stopped her in her tracks. 'Angharad sent me for you – and your sword. The ruby sword.'

Cass stopped and turned slowly, feeling as if her hammering heart might break from her chest. She looked down at Susan, whose wide eyes gazed up at her from the floor, the child wriggling in her arms. And she could see the shadows that were Elaine and Alys behind her, but muted somehow, so that the only thing in focus was Susan's face, pinched and terrified, with those round eyes gazing imploringly into hers.

'The men from the manor told us about the sword,' Susan said quietly, staring at Cass still, as if in a mixture of fascination and fear. 'About the prophecy. Alys was there, she told us you needed time first to come to terms with it, alone.' Her chest heaved. 'Angharad needs you. There isn't any time left.'

Chapter 12

Cass knew which sword Angharad meant. And Susan's bloodied face danced in front of her eyes as she reached for it trancelike. It seemed to surge with energy at her side and she felt the force of it seeping infectiously into her own bones. She knew there was terrible danger, knew she might be racing to her death. Leaving Elaine felt like tearing herself in two, and yet her blood leaped within her, crackling with something between excitement and white-knuckle fear. The dread she had been filled with when she woke had dissipated. After those awful endless moments in Elaine's chamber – whether they had been minutes or hours she could not say – it was a sheer exhilarating relief to be able to take control again, to do something. Pushing aside her agonizing worry for Elaine, she focused on a threat she could throw her whole body into resisting. Here was a weapon that belonged in her hand, was part of her hand, part of her, no matter how hard she had tried to fight it.

She skidded briefly to a halt in her chamber, just long enough to yank her leather breastplate roughly over her head, not bothering to lace or buckle it, and she grabbed her helmet as she raced for the door once more.

Cass did not need any guidance to find the fighting. The sounds she had half-imagined in her dreamlike state as Elaine had given birth were all too real once she left the protection of the manor walls. Smoke billowed through the trees, acrid and thick in her throat, blotting out the bright sun so that the warm summer day suddenly seemed dark and threatening. The heat was oppressive and she felt sweat trickling down her neck. Pebble snorted and showed the whites of her eyes and Cass patted her, trying to calm her. Drawing nearer the little horse became so terrified Cass took pity on her, swinging her leg easily over to jump down and gently turning her loose, knowing she would return to the safety of the manor and Blyth.

Cass continued on foot. All around her, beneath the roiling clouds of smoke, the beauty of the woods shone out. Bright pink and purple foxgloves waved from the edges of the path and moss sprang lushly and green beneath her feet. Beneath the stench of the smoke she smelled the sickly sweet scent of a frothy wave of meadowsweet that bubbled up out of a damp ditch and her stomach clenched and threatened to heave at the contradictory smells, though she had eaten no breakfast. And all the while as she walked through the eerily still woods, she could hear the sounds of battle ahead of her. There were cries that sounded strange and animalistic, and shrill screams that made her heart pound painfully in her chest as she broke into a stumbling run, imagining Edith or Tess or Nell impaled and bleeding, the idea almost unbearable.

As she grew closer, she could hear low rough grunting and the crack of metal on leather. As the blurry mass of struggling figures became slightly clearer, though still hazy in the smoke, she heard Sigrid's voice in her ear and knew that her former mentor would have hung back warily, scouted out the situation and made the most of the element of surprise. But Cass had no room in her mind for caution or tactics, and the terrible images of her friends in her mind's eye would not allow her to hesitate for a moment. And beneath all that the sword in her hand seemed to be pulling her irresistibly towards the fray, so that she could not have stopped even if she had wanted to.

Cass burst into the clearing where the fighting raged,

seeing several great piles of dry leaves and logs aflame. Before she could stop to wonder why, Edith emerged from the smoke, defending herself valiantly behind one of the manor's white shields. The brute who pursued her was almost twice her size and she cowered beneath the onslaught of blows he rained down on her with a heavy wicked-looking axe, its wooden handle thicker than Cass's forearm, its blade cruelly curved.

Cass had never fought against a weapon like this before, and yet she did not hesitate. The knowledge of what to do seemed to pour into her like half-remembered music, and she brought up her sword as if it were the steps of a dance she had learned as a child and never quite forgotten. Her blade seemed keen and eager: it sliced at the man's wrist, eliciting a roar of pain as he dropped his weapon which bit heavily into the earth at her feet. She stepped over it, past Edith who whimpered with relief, and felt her sword drive itself deep into the man's belly at the exact spot where the chainmail hauberk split to accommodate his girth.

Then the sword slid out, slick and wet, and she surged forward without waiting for his body to hit the ground, towards Angharad, who was fighting two men simultaneously and seemed to have the upper hand with them both, and Rowan, who was battling at her side with gritted teeth, intense concentration on her face, her sword gripped in two hands and her shield discarded nearby.

Sir Gamelin and several of the other knights of Mordaunt's court were on the opposite side of the clearing, each battling grimly with one of the huge and thickset opponents.

She saw Nell and two other young squires scrambling desperately at the lower branches of a tree, trying to climb to safety as two tall broad-shouldered figures strode purposefully towards them. She raced forward again immediately, as if she knew that nothing could hurt her, taking one of the men by surprise from behind. She ran her sword through the back of his neck and out the front of his throat, then capitalized on the momentary shock of his fellow to spring forward and catch him a glancing blow on the side of his helmet. He recovered his wits quickly, brandishing a sword perhaps a foot longer than Cass's own, and as she circled him warily, waiting for his first move, she shouted at Nell to run and to take the others with her.

'Deep into the forest,' she bellowed, never taking her eyes off the man who towered over her, 'and do not come out until I call for you.' And she heard the pattering of their light feet as they fled, and prayed they had the sense not to run back to the manor, lest they lead the attackers there after them.

It was unlikely, Cass thought, that these Saxons were aware of the manor's existence; if they were, they would surely have attacked it at first light or before dawn, while all within were sleeping. No, it was more likely a raid into this area of countryside that had brought them by coincidence so close to the sisterhood, and that some villager or squire had raised the alarm and drawn the others to help.

She calculated all this even as her eyes locked on the pale blue of the stranger's gaze, peering into her helmet from beneath his own raised visor, his face wary and suspicious, as if trying to gauge what manner of opponent she was. They must have been bemused, Cass thought, to be set upon at first by a group of girls and then by reinforcements who wore armour and fought with weapons but had the bearing and stature of women. And a wild, hysterical laugh almost escaped her as that heady sense of exhilaration flooded her once more and the sword flew of its own accord to parry a blow she did not think she had seen coming and then dealt one in return – a slicing, perfectly placed attack that drew a thin superficial line of blood where the man's helmet met his armour.

And even as they continued to circle each other, each waiting for the other to make the next move, she knew one more certain fact: that the only way to protect the manor from exposure after an attack this close was to win. To win such a resounding victory that there were no survivors left to carry back the tale.

He came at her again with a yell of fury and a great hacking blow that missed her helmet by an inch as she dived sideways, leaping up from beneath him to catch his chin with a buffeting blow that knocked him sideways and seemed to daze him for a moment. Cass smiled inside her helmet – she knew it was only because he was so unused to fighting someone of such slight stature and so unmatched to his own size that she had been able to take him by surprise.

The sun rose higher above the trees and filtered through the smoke, bathing them in a stifling yellow haze. Time seemed to pass without Cass realizing, because she was sure she had only been fighting the man for seconds and yet it must have been longer, because the man Angharad had been fighting then she was gasping on the floor, and now she was fighting someone else, on the far side of the clearing. Then Cass saw her again, quite near at hand, tending to one of the women who had a wound in her side. She was aware of all this in her peripheral vision while the white heat of the fight consumed her sword.

The ground was hard and dry and her feet were hot and aching in her leather boots, so it could not only have been moments they had faced one another. Her arms had become heavy and tired, and the muggy air harder to force into her lungs, when she saw Elizabeth fall to her knees just yards away, exhausted and spent, and a man with an axe loom over her from behind.

And suddenly it was as if all the tiredness and heaviness was gone, and she felt the golden light that had seemed to glow inside her before, when she had trained with Sigrid, and when she had held the sword in the meadow. It overwhelmed her, rushing through her body, desperate to find an exit and she knew she could not hold it, that it must find its release.

The light was blinding and hot. That rush of power was replaced with stillness, even though Cass knew distantly that she was moving faster than she had ever moved in her life. And she felt the power explode out of her, and was lost in its brightness and the sheer, ecstatic, thrilling, terrible shock of it.

Then there was quiet, except for the crackling of the fire, and the sobbing of one of the girls, and the ragged, heaving breaths that seemed to be coming from her own lungs, and dimly she became aware that everybody was staring at her. And that there were no men left to fight.

Angharad swam into focus, standing quite still, her helmet beneath her arm, staring at Cass with a look that was both shrewd and shocked in her sharp green eyes. Rowan was gazing at her with open admiration, and then she heard a whimper, and looked behind her to see that a small knot of the newest fighters were clustered together, half-hidden behind a tree, and that they were not looking at Cass with gratitude or relief but with unmistakable fear.

Leaning on a tree, his chest heaving, his forehead creased with something Cass could not quite interpret, Sir Gamelin stared at her as though he had never seen her before.

And it was only then that she looked down and saw that there was so much blood on her sword hand that it dripped into a puddle on the hard dark earth.

Then came the sound of hooves, and before she could move or speak, Blyth was there, with Alys mounted behind on the same horse, leading Pebble, and Alys's arm was suddenly round Cass's waist and she turned her gently and led her away towards the manor. Cass made no protest, but went willingly, her sword still dangling in her hand.

'How do you live with it?' she whispered to Alys, as they began to walk and she remembered the words she had seen daubed on Alys's front door. WITCH. 'The exhaustion of being seen as something you are not? How do you cope with everyone seeing you as a threat when you are trying so hard to help them?'

There was another half-stifled sob from behind them, and Cass turned without meaning to and roared, 'You are welcome. And I would do it again if I had to, to keep you alive.'

Alys placed a steadying hand on her arm and led her quietly away. 'Well, that's one way to cope with it,' she said drily.

Chapter 13

Alys led Cass through the trees and sat her gently down on a large mossy rock beside a stream. She took Cass's face in her hands, and the sharp smell of soap brought Cass back to herself for a moment.

'Are you hurt?' Alys asked, peering searchingly into her face and indicating the blood that Cass was only now realizing covered her neck, her armour and her hair as well as her hands and forearms.

'No. It is not mine.' Her voice was flat and sounded as if it was coming from far away.

'Stay here,' Alys said firmly, gently pressing her fingers into Cass's temples to help her to focus. 'Concentrate on the sound of the water, the roughness of the rock, the smell of the moss. You need to ground yourself. Everything else can come later.'

Cass blinked at her, but pressed her fingers obediently into the mossy cushion she was sitting on. It was springy and slightly damp, cool and soft against her fingertips. She felt the haze recede a little.

'Good,' Alys muttered. 'I must attend to the wounded. But I will come back.' And she strode away without another word, leaving Cass staring down wordlessly at the place where the moss had turned rusty red as the blood from her fingers had smeared it.

She sat for a while, her mind unable to grasp the enormity of what had just happened. Replaying it in her head did not seem to work somehow; the pictures jumped back and forth and there seemed to be gaps and areas where things shifted in and out of focus. How many of them had she fought? Killed? She looked down at her hands again as if she suddenly needed to check that they were her own. The sword lay at her feet and she did not pick it up. What was this power? Was it in her or in the sword? And how could she control it? How could she know it wouldn't take over again, perhaps at a different time and in a different place? Were Rowan and the others at the manor even safe around her?

It was too much to try to think about, so she remembered

what Alys had said and tried to focus on her surroundings instead, finding something to anchor herself to the here and now. The moss smelled earthy and its scent mingled with the smell of rotting leaves from the banks of the stream. The water burbled merrily along, chattering to itself incessantly. She began to notice the sensations of her body again, as if she were returning to it, and she pulled her hot aching feet out of her boots and moved down the bank to plunge them gingerly into the cool water.

She leaned down and placed her hands, palms up, beneath the surface of the brook, watching the water eddy and flow around them. She did not rub them together but allowed the water to draw the blood away in long lingering tendrils that seemed to point back to her, no matter how far they washed downstream. You did it. You killed them.

She did not know how long she stood there before Alys placed a gentle hand on her shoulder and led her out of the water. She only knew that her hands had gone numb, that they felt like somebody else's, and that it was a relief.

'No casualties,' Alys told her reassuringly, as she steered Cass towards her horse and helped her to mount. 'On our side,' she added, with a sideways glance at Cass, who looked straight ahead, Pebble's reins limp in her frozen hands.

'The smoke signal worked,' Alys continued conversationally, as the horses began to move through the trees. She kept her voice calm and even, as if Cass were a young gelding she was trying not to spook.

'It was Sir Albinor's estate. They lit the fires to warn us. The smoke seemed to have the effect we had hoped on the enemy. It saved many lives today. And so did you.'

Cass did not answer, and Alys fell silent. They went back the same way Cass had come, though she did not see the foxgloves or notice the scent of the meadowsweet beneath the tang of woodsmoke clinging to her hair and clothes.

'Alys,' she said very quietly, just before they reached the gates of the manor, 'I think I might be a monster.'

Alys did not reply but pulled Cass along faster, and a little stupid part of her brain wondered if she was being taken to Angharad's rooms to be banished from the sisterhood for her brutality, or led to her own chamber to pack her belongings, but instead they left the horses at the stable and Alys took her straight up to Elaine's bedroom.

Susan met them at the door, her head freshly bandaged, the baby pink and healthy in her arms. She started when she saw Cass, whose white face and wild eyes made her look almost possessed, and Alys rounded on her at once.

She tutted. 'Do not drop it, Susan. That child went through enough to come into this world without you dropping it on its head within hours of its arrival. Now take it down to the kitchen so its mother can get some rest.'

They entered the chamber, where Elaine lay in fresh bedclothes, a little pink already back in her cheeks, her dark blonde hair in loose waves across the pillow. Her lips were parted so that Cass could see the gap in her teeth and a slight smile seemed to play across them as she slept.

Cass's heart leaped with relief to see her, and Alys nodded approvingly.

'A monster would not feel that way to see her friend lives,' she said gently but firmly. 'And that child lived today because of you. They both did. You are no more a monster than I am, Cassandra.'

Cass was quiet for a long time, watching the soft rise and fall of Elaine's chest. Hearing her full name took her back to her childhood, to her mother scolding her for coming home with torn and muddied skirts after making dens in the orchard, to winter nights snuggled close to her sister Mary by the fire, eating the last of the dried apples. When she thought about that child, she felt like she didn't know her any more, and that the person who had replaced her was a stranger. She saw moments from the last months flash in front of her: the crash and splinter of the lance as she had unseated her best friend Lily at a jousting tournament, the giddy whirl and swish of bright silk dresses as women danced in the firelight, the earth hard beneath her belly as she watched Mordaunt's manor prepare for an attack, the flash of her sword as it had pierced a Saxon neck.

'Who am I then?' Cass asked eventually, and Alys looked back at her evenly and sighed. 'I cannot tell you that, Cass. But I suspect it is time that you learned the truth. You need to go back to where you started.'

Cass frowned. She had not returned home since she had made a split-second decision to climb onto a horse behind Sigrid on the morning of her sister's wedding, leaving her home and family behind without even saying goodbye. She had managed to speak to Mary once, last year, and to tell her a little of what had happened, but the idea of facing her family again was more daunting than entering the lists to joust. She did not know if she could go back. What if she didn't like what she found? What if they were furious with her and could not forgive her for leaving? What if they embraced her with open arms and would not let her go again?

When Cass was a child, her mother had told them stories about people who were led below the ground by faerie folk and returned hours later only to find that time had passed so differently in the human realm that all their loved ones were dead and gone. She looked down at Elaine and remembered with a surge of guilt that Mary had been with child when they had last met. Elaine had so narrowly survived the battle. What if Mary had not?

That slight knowing smile played across Elaine's face again, as if her dreams were satisfying. And Cass thought how strange it was that the truth could look so very different. Here she was in repose, after facing death and defeating it to deliver her child without its father, a far cry from the picture she had imagined when she had first heard the story of Elaine: of the lovely frail maiden whose heart had stopped with grief.

Vaguely she put her hand to her face and found to her surprise that it was wet.

Alys was watching her, waiting patiently. 'If you do not go back,' she said softly, 'then you cannot move forward.'

So Cass found herself carefully pulling her silver locket from beneath her mattress and making her way to the stables the next morning to saddle Pebble, a leather bag with provisions for the journey strapped across her chest and her bow and arrow slung at her side.

It was just after dawn, and Blyth, who rarely slept inside the manor, was slumbering on a pile of hay in the corner as Pebble snickered quietly with excitement at seeing Cass, and she shushed her and led her out into the courtyard to saddle her where she would not disturb the other horses or wake the stable hand.

Angharad found her there in the greyish early light, her

cloak drawn over her nightgown, padding barefoot out of the manor. Her bright red hair was like a second cloak round her shoulders and she held her sword unsheathed, making Cass wonder wildly for a moment if she had come to prevent her from leaving.

'I saw you from my window,' she said, patting Pebble on the nose as Cass fastened the final buckle. 'Sleep doesn't come so easily these days.' She gave a wan smile. And she didn't have to say that Vivian's loss, and everything that had happened since, stalked her sleeping hours, waking her early with relief to be free of her dreams. Because Cass already knew. Even now her own nights were filled with a confusing jumble of Lily's screams and the clash of swords and Vivian falling, as if in slow motion. And every so often she would see again the woman with the glowing golden eyes and the strange spiral pendant who had bowed to her in the forest when she was a little girl, as if she were not looking at a grubby child collecting wood but a queen.

'Alys has told me that you ride for your family home,' Angharad continued. Cass nodded warily, and Angharad seemed to see the nervousness in her face because she put an arm out and pulled her into a swift, hard hug. 'It was a very lucky day for the sisterhood when you followed Sigrid here,' she said, releasing Cass and drawing back with a proud look in her eyes. Cass felt a painful lump come into her throat.

'And what you did yesterday proved that you are destined to be more than just a harbinger of good fortune, not just for us or for the people of Northumbria. You are special, Cass. More special than I knew, though Alys had tried to tell me.' Angharad glanced again at her sword, and Cass suddenly realized what she meant to do and felt a great pit of uncertainty open in her stomach.

'Kneel,' Angharad whispered, and Cass stood before her, hesitating and untethered.

'I cannot,' she shook her head eventually. 'I cannot become a knight without knowing who I am or why it is my destiny.'

She looked up at Angharad, expecting to see anger or disappointment in her face, but the older woman simply nodded, and Cass mounted Pebble, fumbling with the reins in her need to get away. Somehow the talk of raiders and invasion had always felt unreal to her: a distant threat for a distant time. And yet here it was, ever encroaching, like a persistent fly buzzing round her head, irritatingly distracting when she was grappling with what felt like much bigger questions about herself and her destiny.

How could she let Angharad make her a knight? When she still felt unsure whether she controlled her sword or it controlled her. When she was only just learning to master the art of shooting arrows from the back of a moving horse and certainly had none of the years of strategic experience of Sigrid or Angharad. When – a tiny voice inside her whispered – she couldn't even sleep at night without waking drenched in sweat, crying out in pain after seeing her best friend killed over and over again in her nightmares.

Angharad looked up at her then, as Cass sat in the saddle, gazing down on the fine gold circlet that rested on the fiery head. 'I will do whatever is necessary to keep the women here safe,' she said, looking deep into Cass's eyes. 'As you did, yesterday. Those women lived because of you, Cass. And the swords and shields we claimed from the fallen men will keep them alive longer still. You did not just take lives yesterday; you also saved them. Remember that.'

And as Cass turned Pebble's head towards the gates, Angharad called after her: 'We will wait for your return. And when you have found the answers you seek, we will fight the next battle side by side.'

Chapter 14

Entering the village felt like waking up from a dream. The hedgerows were still frothing with cow parsley, the fields asway with the fat heads of golden barley. The old half-blind sheepdog thumped his tail on the dusty track in lazy greeting, as if she had only been out to run an errand, as Cass trotted past him towards the farmhouse.

She reined Pebble in when they reached the orchard, as serene and shady as it had been that fateful day when she had vaulted the fence and lain under the apple trees, escaping the din of the house and the preparations for her sister's wedding. The only difference was that the branches had been overladen that day, dripping with spoiling fruit nobody had found the time to pick with the wedding approaching, and today the apples were smaller and greener, not yet ripened for the late-summer harvest. She looped the reins over a fence post and walked slowly through the long grass towards the house, plucking one of the unripe apples as she went and feeling its cool smooth skin reassuringly hard in her fist.

The back door was open, and Cass hesitated for a heartbeat. The sun was warm on the back of her head and it caught the thatched roof like burnished gold. For a moment it was as if she had never gone away. She could walk straight into the kitchen, wipe her hands on her apron and start peeling the potatoes for dinner. Her father would ruffle her hair as he came in from the fields and went to wash, and her mother would be bustling around, picking up after the little ones and tutting at them for leaving their things on the floor for her to trip over. There might be the smell of freshly baked bread or of fish if it was market day and they'd exchanged some vegetables grown in the patch outside for some of the river catch.

But she wasn't wearing an apron, and a sword swung at her side. The girl who had once lived here felt as distant to her as the shining knights of her childhood tales once had. She looked down at the simple doublet and hose she had donned for the journey and tugged self-consciously at her sword belt. She had dressed automatically, not stopping to think about the shock it would be to her family to see her dressed like this. But it was too late to change that now.

She pushed the door open with a creak. It startled her. That door hadn't creaked before. The room was empty. The plates and cups were stacked neatly on the table like they always had been. Sunlight filtered down from the window, painting the swept-earth floor a yellow ochre. It smelled just as it always had. The comforting richness of the wooden beams and the slight must from the straw-filled mattresses. A savoury aroma from the hanging dried onions and bunches of herbs.

It seemed so quiet. She could almost see herself sitting cross-legged on the floor, popping peas out of their pods and throwing one into the pot for every two that went into her mouth, sucking them gleefully while Mary frowned at her, carefully podding her own pile and emptying them fastidiously into the pot without poaching a single one.

The smile was still on her face when she heard the shrieks of laughter and in the next moment they burst through the door, little Grace, who had been only two when Cass had left her, and Jack, a few years older. His messy brown curls were slightly longer, perhaps, but they fell about the same sun-browned face and gangly limbs. They froze in the doorway, laughter dying on their lips, and stared at Cass.

The door opened again and her mother's form blocked out the light behind them.

There was a long silence.

'You grew,' she said at last, and Cass nodded.

Her mother ushered the children inside and set a basket of lettuces down on the table. Her eyes never left Cass, travelling from her sturdy leather boots to the newly formed hardness of her stomach and thighs, the muscles only lately grown along her upper arms. They lingered, widened briefly, on the sword with the red stone at its hilt, and came to rest on the silver locket at her throat.

The little girl was staring at Cass, her mouth slightly open, a smear of mud on one cheek.

'Oh, Miss Grace,' Cass said in a gentle, singsong voice, kneeling down to the child's height, 'you are quite the young lady now.' She reached out a hand and the girl jumped backwards and buried her head in their mother's skirts and Cass stood up, cheeks burning as if she had been slapped.

'Well, what did you expect?' Her mother's voice was low with carefully contained anger. 'That we would all remain here frozen in time until you chose to wander back to us? Did you think she would remember you? She was a baby the day you walked out without a backwards glance or a word of goodbye. It has been nearly a year.' She was trembling slightly, her knuckles white on the back of a chair.

Cass felt sharp tears stinging the backs of her eyes, threatening to fall, and shook her head mutely. She was not a knight, not even a squire, but a little girl again, being scolded for coming in late with leaves in her hair and mud on her shoes.

Then her mother sighed and dropped her hand from the back of the chair as if all the fight had gone out of her. 'Come here then,' and she pulled Cass into a hug that smelled of summer strawberries and fresh grass and a cool hand on her hot forehead and endlessly chasing around the garden on long summer afternoons and a wet cloth on scratched knees, and she breathed it in and sobbed into her mother's neck like a child.

Later they sat on the grass outside the back door with a cup of ale, backs leaning against the wall, while the children played around them.

'Your father won't know whether to kiss you or shake you.' Her mother tutted with a shake of her head. She was an angular woman, with dark hair pulled close against her head into a practical low bun. Her nose was sharp, her eyes heavily lidded, but there was a kindness to the set of her mouth that had always belied her brusque no-nonsense attitude. Still, Cass had never felt as entwined with her mother as she had with Mary. She glanced sideways at the crow's feet and frown lines that had deepened in the year since she had left, at the weathered, calloused hands clutching the earthenware cup. Her mother had not had the time or the luxury to spend the hours lying in the sun on their backs finding pictures in the clouds or running through the fields chasing mice that she and Mary had enjoyed. She had toiled long hard hours that bled into long hard days while their father worked the fields and helped the other local smallholders with their crops as they helped him when harvest time came. With four children to look after and a household to run it was no surprise that her mother had been a slightly distant figure, like her father, and that Cass and Mary had so often been left to their own devices.

Cass loved her parents and knew that they loved her, but it had been Mary she had cried herself to sleep missing on more than one of those first strange nights at the manor. And it was Mary her thoughts turned to first now she was home.

'The baby?'

'Aye.' Her mother nodded with a sideways glance at Cass. 'A boy. Hale and hearty and driving his mother half to distraction with lack of sleep, though she's otherwise well enough.'

Cass smiled. It was odd to hear the word 'mother' used to describe her sister. She felt a pang she struggled to identify, and then realized it was a kind of sweet pain – gladness for Mary and jealousy that she was no longer the most important person in her sister's life.

'She told us she saw you that day.'

'I asked her to,' Cass said quickly. 'It was not my choice that I could not send word back at first. And I wanted her to let you know I was safe and well. I did not want you to worry.'

'And you thought that would stop us? Hearing that you were safe? As if it did not spark a thousand other questions instead? Like where you were and who with and why you had gone and what kept you away, if you were not lying in a ditch somewhere, wounded or worse, as we had first assumed?'

Cass felt guilt clench her stomach hard, like a hand that would not let go, though she squirmed, shifting and crossing her legs, staring down into the dregs of her drink.

'She went through with the wedding that day, you know,' her mother continued, her voice tightening again in the way that Cass knew to mean that she was working hard to contain her anger. 'Walked towards her future husband with her mouth set and her face as white as the flowers in her hair and all her family watching her half-distracted with worry over what might have happened to you.'

Cass nodded miserably. Mary had always had such a

strong sense of duty. She would not have let Thomas wait
for her on her wedding day.

'Your father searched until winter set in,' her mother
continued, ripping open the place inside Cass where she had
buried her guilt, papered over with the half-lies she had told
herself, that her family would be better off without her to
worry about, that their minds would be put at rest when
Mary told them she was safe, that she would not have caused
them too much pain.

'Every day he rode out, trying to follow the tracks of the
horse that seemed to have taken you, begging other folk
to help if they could. He rode to every market town from
here to Caester Feld looking for you, stopping at taverns and
squares, asking if anyone had seen you.'

Cass's eyes blurred with tears. She had never thought,
not once, that her father would try so hard to find her. He
was a hard-working man, of few words, and the idea of
him undertaking such journeys and having conversations
with strangers on her behalf made her want to sob into her
mother's shoulder all over again.

The stone the children were using to play hopscotch
skittered suddenly to Cass's feet and she stretched to reach it
and throw it back, swallowing down the lump in her throat.
Little Grace gave her a quick half smile as she tossed her the
pebble, and the tightness in Cass's chest eased as she leaned

back again beside her mother, feeling the warmth from the wooden posts seep into her back, fortifying her.

'I am sorry,' Cass said simply and truthfully, and her mother's palm closed on hers and squeezed tight.

'You do not have to be sorry,' she said at last. 'I knew this day would come. I knew you would have to go from the moment he brought you to us. And perhaps if I had told you sooner it would have been easier. For all of us. Or prolonged the time you had with us. But he told us not to.' She sighed. 'Anyway, it is done now and there is no use keening over spilled milk.'

Cass felt as if she had received a hard blow to the head. Her pulse was racing, thready and skittering as if her heart kept missing beats. There was that strange itching in her fingertips again, as if the sword was warming at her mother's words and her hands ached to claim it as it came alive.

The sun was bright in her eyes and she raised a hand to shield them, looking at the woman she had always known to be straightforward and truthful. The woman she had thought was her mother. The woman now determinedly avoiding her eyes.

'Brought me to you? He?' She felt dazed, winded.

Her mother sighed heavily and pointed to the locket at Cass's throat. 'He left you that, the only link to your past. Mary was little, not yet quite two. She didn't remember a life without you. And we lived far enough from the nearest neighbours that it was an easy enough pretence to make. A new baby is always something to celebrate, and not many think to ask questions.'

Cass felt like she was wading through bog water, trying to find some solid ground or something to cling to as it threatened to suck her under. She shook her head and held up a hand to stop her mother, who did not seem to realize that she had started in the middle of the story and was maddeningly jumping backwards and forwards.

'He? Who was he?'

Her mother let out a long low breath and raised a hand to brush an errant curl from Cass's cheek, sadness and pride in her eyes as she studied her daughter's face.

'Merlin,' she said at last. 'Merlin brought you here.'

Chapter 15

Cass's first instinct was to laugh. Her mother, the woman who had never had time for frivolity or intrigue, was surely attempting to trick her, spinning a lie so huge, so preposterous, that Cass didn't know why she ever thought her daughter could possibly fall for it.

Cass could not think of a single explanation that made sense. She started to wonder if she was really here, or if perhaps she had been concussed at the battle in the woods and carried to Alys's hut. Perhaps she was dreaming, fantasizing strange, wild pathways that were not really hers to walk down. But still the rough wood was warm and firm at her back. Still the children jostled and bickered in the yard. Still her mother was watching her, waiting.

Cass's mind felt blank, as if it simply could not begin to absorb the enormity of this. She did not know what to ask or where to begin.

'Merlin?' she repeated at last. 'Adviser to King Arthur? The one they call a wizard?' Even as she said it the absurdity crashed over her and she laughed, a long quavering laugh that trailed off when her mother did not join her.

'Yes. You were just a tiny baby wrapped in a bundle of rags. It was a hot, clear summer's night, and the stars were brighter than I'd ever seen them.'

'No.' Cass was shaking her head. 'No.' But there had been a break in her mother's voice, a fracture so rarely seen in her sensible composure that Cass stared at her, wondering if she was imagining it. 'I was born on an early-summer morning at first light,' she said slowly. 'You told me so yourself when Grace was born, and Mary and I asked you about our own births. I remember.'

Her mother looked at her with tears in her eyes. 'That was what I told you to quiet your questions, but it was not true. What else could I have told you?'

'The truth!' Cass shouted, and the children paused for a moment in their play and eyed her uneasily, until their mother gave them a thin smile and they resumed their game.

'Please,' her mother said, her voice strained, 'let me try to explain.'

And though she had a thousand questions and objections, Cass clamped her lips tight shut and listened to her mother's story.

'It was late on a summer's evening. Your father and I had just gone to bed when a great thundering knock came at the door. We were terrified. I was nursing Mary and I remember cowering in the bed with her while your father took up a stout wooden stick and went to the door. A man and a woman were standing there with a tiny child. They begged for rest and for a drink, and we let them in. The infant was a scrawny little thing, with a scrunched-up face, crying as if its heart were breaking in two, but even in spite of all that I could see by the light of the candles that its eyes – your eyes – were the most beautiful mixture of blue and green.

'And once they had drunk, and eaten what little we had to share, the woman sat quietly by the hearth, soothing the child on her shoulder, while the man began to tell his tale.'

'What did he look like? How did you know it was Merlin?' Cass burst out, unable to stay silent.

Her mother shushed her. 'I am coming to that if you'll hold your tongue,' she said, sounding for a moment more like the brusque woman Cass remembered.

'He was tall and powerfully built, with long tangled dark hair streaked with grey. His beard and moustache were thick and wiry, but his eyes.' She shivered slightly. 'He had heavy, prominent eyebrows, and the most intense stare I have ever encountered before or since. His eyes were cold and blue and they seemed to see straight through you. Though he was telling his tale, though he was asking a great charity, still it was as if, all the while, his eyes were staring into us, examining our minds to see if we were worthy of you.' She seemed to rouse from the memory, with a little shake, and raised a hand as if to dismiss what she had just said. 'Fanciful nonsense, I am sure. But it was so strange and unexpected, late at night, and that was how it felt at the time.'

Cass had to stop herself from jumping in, urging her mother to tell the tale more quickly.

'He told us the child needed care, and that they could not provide for it,' she remembered, a soft look in her eyes as she gazed out into the middle distance, remembering. 'And that they had travelled a long way looking for a home that seemed fit, with parents who had a child a similar age who might be a companion for it. They had stopped in the village that afternoon, they said, and had spoken to a few other families, but had not found the right one.'

Her mother stopped and twisted the hem of her apron in her fingers for a moment. 'We had not been able to have a second child,' she said, her voice so low that Cass had to strain to hear it, and she knew what it was costing her mother to share such private details.

Cass watched her, startled to see wetness gathering at the corners of her eyes, but her mother wiped them impatiently with the back of her hand and continued.

'We agreed almost as soon as they asked it. Your father was a little more wary, more sensible, perhaps, but I wanted you so badly . . .'

'Afterwards I realized that some of it was strange, that the story did not quite fit together. Their clothes were rich for one thing, embroidered with gold thread and fastened with swirling metal brooches.'

Something stirred deep within Cass at these words, but she brushed it away, impatient to hear more.

'And when your father spoke to the villagers next market day nobody could recall having seen or spoken to two strangers that day, nor any time that week. It seemed so odd, in fact, that we took fright, I suppose, and decided not to tell anybody what had happened. I stayed home with you for months, while you wailed as if you were in perpetual pain and nothing I could do seemed to soothe you, and we put it about that I was in confinement, and didn't let anyone see you until later on, so that nobody knew you were not our own.'

Cass was breathing fast, her blood thrumming in her ears.

'It was Mary who soothed you in the end. She would put her little fat hand out to you with its dimpled knuckles and when you ignored her she would lie down next to you so that your whole body was cocooned inside hers and you would sigh as if some terrible thing that caused you great distress had been extinguished at last and you would settle down and fall fast asleep.'

'We always slept like that,' Cass murmured half to herself, and her throat ached.

Her mother nodded and reached out a hand to touch the tip of her finger to the locket round Cass's neck. That locket had started the whole wild adventure that had taken her to the sisterhood last year, when a bandit had stolen it from her outstretched hand and Sigrid had chased him down and returned it to her.

'This was the only object they left you with,' she said, and Cass remembered how significant it had seemed when her mother had slipped the chain round her neck on the morning of her sister's wedding. She remembered the words her mother had said, how they had seemed a little strange to her at the time. *It was never really mine, Cass. It is yours.*

'Ma,' Cass said gently, unable to hold her tongue any longer, 'was it the locket that made you think the man was Merlin? Because many couples who could not afford to keep a child might leave them with their only valuable possession – to assuage the guilt of giving them up.' She was trying hard not to cry.

But her mother shook her head. 'You are not listening, Cassandra; there is more to the story—'

And as Cass seemed ready to interrupt her again she snatched the locket from her neck with a sigh of exasperation and opened it, revealing the smooth empty inside Cass had seen a hundred times when she had played with it as a child.

'Look.' She turned it upside down and held it up to the golden rays of the late-afternoon sun and Cass took it in her fingertips and looked closer, squinting.

At the very bottom of the locket, etched inside the little lip that allowed it to close securely, there was a tiny engraving. It was so small that at first it looked like a scuff or a scratch – Cass had never noticed it before. But when she looked closely, there was a tiny design there.

'Is that a—'

'It is a dragon. The head of a dragon. The symbol of King Uther Pendragon, your father.'

Chapter 16

This time Cass really did laugh out loud. 'Ma, you cannot be—'

But her mother interrupted her again. 'I know it sounds ridiculous. I know. But let me finish the tale and then you can decide for yourself. Do what you like with the story, it is yours, but at least I will have done my part and given you the truth.'

Her voice was full of doubt and guilt and Cass took her calloused hand and held it in her lap, letting her head fall sideways briefly onto her mother's shoulder. 'Very well, I will listen.'

'After we agreed to keep you, your father and I went to prepare a safe sleeping place and to dig out some of Mary's old clothes from the wooden chest where I had kept them. When I returned, the couple were bent together, deep in a heated argument and did not hear me approach. Usually I would never have eavesdropped on a private conversation, you know that, but I was suddenly terrified that they had changed their minds, or that one of them had doubts about leaving the child with us. So I lingered, listening, in the hope that if I understood the argument I might be able to convince them to let us keep you after all.'

The sun dipped behind a cloud and Cass shivered, wrapping her arms round herself, goosebumps standing out along her forearms.

'But they were arguing about something else. The woman, who had hardly said a word until that moment, was remonstrating with the man, urging him to "tell the full truth".

'"She deserves to know," she kept repeating. I thought perhaps there was something wrong with you, that you were sick, or, worse, stolen, and that she felt I deserved to know if I was going to take you in, but she was not talking about telling *me*. She was talking about you. Saying that *you* deserved to grow up knowing who you were.'

Cass held tight to her mother's hand as if it was the only thing left to anchor her to the earth, to reality.

'She called him "Merlin",' her mother continued, the

words tumbling forth in a rush now, as if it was a relief to finally let them out after all these years. 'I did not mishear, Cass; she said it more than once.'

'But Merlin cannot be so uncommon a name that—'

'*Listen*,' her mother hissed, and she fell silent again.

'They left soon after that, and once she handed you to me, you started to scream incessantly, a terrible quavering wail that broke my heart. Your father tried to soothe you but nothing would console you, so I took you outside so that you would not wake Mary, and saw that there was a handkerchief on the ground next to the door. As I stooped to pick it up, the woman ran back to get it and the man waited a little way down the track, staring back at her. And while I held you and tried to calm you, she took it from me and spoke very quickly, all while looking down at the handkerchief and petting you so that from a distance it would not look as if we were speaking about anything of importance. She glanced up at me and her eyes shone like some warm metal, like copper or gold. She whispered to me that you were no ordinary child, but the daughter of King Uther Pendragon, that he had fathered twins and Merlin had taken them to be placed with separate carers for their own safety.

'As long as men coveted the throne, any child of Uther's would always be at risk. She told me I must never tell a soul, that Merlin had not wanted you ever to know who you were in order to protect you, and that you would be in grave danger if we ever revealed your true parentage. And then he gave an impatient shout and she pressed something into my hand and was gone. After she left I looked down and saw it was this locket. It wasn't until the next day that your father examined it in daylight and found the king's symbol there. We didn't know what to think. Your father said it was probably all nonsense, that the woman was delusional or had convinced herself of this wild story as a way of coping with the trauma of giving up her own child. He thought it would be easier if she made herself believe the babe was someone else's. But there was a lot about that night that troubled me. I went over it for years while I sat up nursing you late into the night, while I watched you grow and take your first wobbly steps, while you and Mary grew to love each other as closely as any two sisters related by blood.'

She sighed and shrugged. 'I cannot tell you for certain what the truth is, Cass. But she did not cry or hesitate to give you up as a mother would have done. It made sense to me that you were not her child, I knew it instinctively, as only another mother could. And what reason would she have to lie? She never returned, never asked anything of us. We never saw either of them again.'

Cass's head was spinning as if it would never stop. She

thought she might be sick, and she breathed slowly and steadily through her nose to try to calm herself. It was so hard to know where to begin, which part of the story to marvel at and turn over in her head as she tried desperately to make sense of it all.

'You're sure about her eyes?' she asked at last, and her mother nodded, baffled that this was the detail that most interested her. But she did not, could not, know that Cass had met a woman with eyes that seemed to glow with gold, that she had been the first person in her life who had seemed to see something in her that nobody else could. She did not know that the woman had worn a pendant with an infinite spiral or that Cass had seen the same symbol carved into a tree in the forest near the manor when she had ridden out with Rowan and Lily, hunting the elusive black stag. It was this detail, perhaps more than any other, more even than the tiny etching of the dragon, that made Cass wonder if her mother's story might actually be true.

Her hands fell limply to her sides and her fingers brushed the cool metal hilt of her sword. Cass stared down at it as if seeing it for the first time. She had pulled the sword from a stone. As improbable as it had seemed, it had slid out willingly into her hands when she had needed it most, and though she had convinced herself it must have been loosened by some coincidence, Alys had insisted that it meant something, that there was some prophecy about a great leader drawing out a sword in Northumbria. And hadn't Arthur, too, proved his kingship with the pulling of a sword from a stone? Though Alys had sniffed and told her that had been a stunt orchestrated by Merlin to cement Arthur's authority in the people's eyes.

It was too much to take in. She closed her eyes for a moment, leaned her head back against the wall and let the warmth of the sun caress her face. Twins. But that would mean . . .

'Arthur. You are saying that King Arthur is my twin?'

'Yes,' her mother said flatly, as if Cass had asked if there were apples left or if she needed to light the fire for supper.

There was a very long silence.

'I am sorry,' her mother whispered at last. 'I should have told you sooner perhaps. But there was always a good reason not to. You were too young; you would not understand. You were so close to Mary and learning she was not your real sister might have divided you. You were coming of age and had enough to think about without filling your head with nonsense about kings and strangers in the night. You were safe and happy and I had been warned that the truth would endanger you.' She paused. 'But really it wasn't any of that which stopped me from telling you the truth. It was a lot simpler. I loved you. You were my daughter, and I did not want you to know any different. I was a coward, Cass, and I feared losing you. I always feared that one day they would come back to claim you. When King Uther died I was terrified that they would come. But nobody did.

'When Arthur was crowned king, I secretly rejoiced, believing that you would never need to know your birthright now that your brother had taken the throne. I thought you were finally safe. And then, just a few short months later, we lost you. And when you disappeared, though I supported your father in his efforts to find you, secretly I thought part of me had always known.'

'You never told him?' Cass was falling – falling down a hole and spinning so fast that she could not think straight.

Her mother's voice faltered. 'I could not. Merlin was so persuasive, so forceful about the importance of complete secrecy—' She ran her hand across her lined face. 'It is difficult to explain. I was afraid. Afraid that if anyone found out, yes, even your father, I might lose you.' She paused, and the next words came from very deep in her throat. 'And part of me was so scared that if he knew who you were, that you were not only another man's child, but the daughter of a king, that it would put you somehow out of his reach. That he could never fully love you as his own. And I so badly wanted you to be our own, Cass.'

A half-broken chuckle left her. 'But the more you grew,

the more obvious it became to me that you were different –
that we would not contain you for ever. Keeping silent was
my way of trying to stave off that day as long as I could.'

She stopped and exhaled slowly, her whole body visibly
relaxing. 'Now you know everything. But there is one more
thing I want you to know. I love you, Cass. And I will always
be your mother in my heart.'

She leaned over towards Cass but her daughter recoiled,
looking at her as if she were seeing her for the first time.

'How could you keep this from me?' she gasped out
through white lips, and she stumbled away from her
mother's outstretched arms, away from the farmhouse
and the children beginning to clamour for food, through
the long grass skimming her calves, over the fence into the
orchard, escaping again, as she had on the morning of her
sister's wedding day. And it was under the same apple trees
that Cass sat now, her eyes pricking with tears, her fingers
running over and over the scar on her wrist, as she wrestled
with everything she had thought she was but deep down
knew she was not. She felt a burning mix of confusion,
betrayal and pity for the mother who had loved her so
fiercely she had kept her hidden, even from herself.

She stayed in the orchard until the sun began to sink
towards the horizon and then she made her way slowly back
to the doorway to watch her mother's back hunched over

the kitchen table. When Cass put her hand on her mother's shoulder, the work-smoothed palm came up readily, gratefully, to grasp it. And they did not need to speak again.

Cass stayed at the farm for four days, immersing herself in the food and the smells of her childhood, spending companionable hours with her mother doing chores and housework and all the while slowly, slowly trying to absorb all that she had learned.

There was time one evening to walk quietly around the farm with her father, asking him about the crops and the harvest, saying almost nothing about the locket or the truth of Cass's arrival, though he knew his daughter had been given the truth at last. And Cass knew that her mother had told him the full story, the truth of his adopted daughter's identity, and that he too had forgiven her for her silence because he too knew that it had been done for love.

As if by unspoken agreement, they talked of the things they always had done. There were no emotional declarations, no difficult conversations. Perhaps because talk of kings and courts was so far from the fields and the earth that made up his world. He treated her as his daughter, because that was who she was to him. And she was grateful for the anchor to tether her to the old reality that threatened each day to slip away from under her feet.

Her mother did not push her to talk more about it, nor did

she ask questions about Cass's life with the sisterhood. But when she woke on the second morning to find a serviceable woollen dress neatly folded at the end of her mattress, she put it on without complaint. It felt peaceful and soothing to retreat back into her old life, even while she knew it could not last.

One morning, before her mother had risen, she heard her father get up and followed him to the door, quietly telling him about the increased threat of Saxon bands and other raiders. Though they had seen no unrest yet, she urged him to have a plan in place to get their family and Mary's to safety if he should need to.

One whole, glorious day she passed with Mary and her chubby, babbling child, marvelling at its little cheeks and nose, her sister in miniature. They strolled through the orchard arm in arm, and Mary, who had always reacted to the smallest injury with the loudest wails, somehow managed to remain calm and pensive in the face of the enormity of Cass's revelations.

'We always knew you were different,' she said, shrugging, as if this changed very little, as if being the daughter of a king secretly fostered with a rural family were no different from having a few tomboy habits and preferring to run barefoot instead of wearing uncomfortable leather shoes.

'What will you do now?' she asked, as they sheltered

from the hot sun in the shade of the apple trees, and Cass's legs itched even now to expend their pent-up energy by climbing up to sit on one of the branches above her sensible placid sister.

'I will go back,' she said slowly. She had been thinking about it these last few days, while the slow rhythm of the farm cocooned her softly, and while it had occurred to her how easy it would be just to stay here, in her old life, as if she had never been away. The invaders would be somebody else's problem, Arthur could trouble himself with the security of Britain, and she could bury the strange, powerful sword beneath the roots of one of the apple trees and teach Pebble to draw a plough. There was no sure way they could fetch her back: Sigrid was the only one who had known where her family lived, and she was banished now, far from the sisterhood and its stronghold.

And yet it was when she thought of Sigrid that she knew she had to return. Sigrid had represented all she aspired to become. Everything a knight should be. Everything a woman could be. Knowing the injustice of Lord Mordaunt and his court, Sigrid had devoted herself unswervingly to finding him and securing justice. It would have been so easy for her to stop. But Sigrid could no more have done that than she could fly. It was simply who she was.

When she realized this about her own fate, a great

sense of calm came over Cass, replacing the panic and disorientation she had felt since learning the truth. Her fear at the decisions she would have to make disappeared. It was not about what to do or where to go or even how to cope with the enormity of what her mother had told her; she simply had to decide who she was. Everything else would follow. And she realized, sitting there quietly under the apple trees with Mary, that she had always known who she was. She had not needed her mother to tell her, not really. She had known it from childhood, from the moment she had run out of the house on the morning of Mary's wedding, from the second she had leaped onto the back of Sigrid's horse and left without a backwards glance. She now knew the answer to the uncomfortable uncertainty that had plagued her since she had first taken up the ruby sword, her worries about whether it controlled her or the other way round.

'Mary,' she murmured, as her sister half-dozed in the grass next to her, 'will you hold this sword?' And her sister took it without question, marvelling at the stone at the hilt, holding it awkwardly, wobbling in the air in front of her nose, but she showed no unease or sign that anything about it felt strange.

'How did it feel?' Cass asked, taking it back and feeling again that tingle of energy, somewhere between excitement and pain, that passed between her and the handle as she slipped it back into her belt.

'Heavy,' Mary said, settling herself into a more comfortable position and closing her eyes again. 'I don't know how you lift the thing.'

The sword was powerful, but Cass knew now that she was meant to wield it. It was her courage, her quest for adventure and her heart that lent the sword its power.

She knew who she was. Daughter of the king. Sister of Arthur. Wielder of the sword in the stone. And she was not afraid of it any more.

Chapter 17

She left for the manor on the fifth day.

Her father held her tight in his strong arms and she breathed in the warm smell of summer earth after rain as she rested her head on his shoulder, as she had done when she was small. She held her mother's hand tight, just for a moment, and, as she turned to leave, she heard her whisper: 'Everything you need is inside you, Cass. It always has been.'

The yellowhammers called their sweet song from the hedgerows as she left, like a melancholy farewell, and her mother went quickly back inside the house and shut the door. The children hung from the orchard fence and waved and shouted until she turned the corner at the end of the track and disappeared from view.

Cass's heart lifted as Pebble trotted along the woodland paths, breathing in the wild garlic and admiring the way the sun shafted down through the trees and dappled Pebble's gleaming neck. She felt a lightness and a certainty that had eluded her for weeks. She would return to the manor first, but it would not be her final destination. She knew exactly what she had to do.

There was something different about Cass's body as she rode, something that at first she thought was the sheer relief at the conflict that had hung over her these past weeks finally being lifted. Her thighs seemed to grip the saddle more firmly, her bow and sword felt lighter, but was it because her arms seemed stronger? The strange, fearful, exhilarating heat that sometimes surged through her when she went into battle suddenly seemed to be a part of her all the time. What had once been difficult to summon, a power that came and went seemingly as it pleased, was now permanent, like a steady background thrum. The light tingling in her fingertips, the sense of power crackling in her veins, it was always there now. Something had been awakened and was waiting, just beneath the surface, for her call.

She was thinking of stopping to allow the horse to drink and to eat the bread and cheese her mother had pressed on her for the journey when she heard angry shouting a little way ahead. Instantly alert, Cass slipped down and tied Pebble's reins to a branch, soothing her with a quick pat before slipping away, creeping forward from tree trunk to tree trunk, her hand on the hilt of her sword.

A young woman with short hair so blonde it was almost white and a delicate slightly upturned nose, was struggling against ropes that bound her to a tree on the opposite side of a small clearing. There was a scarlet split above her left cheekbone and blood dribbling from her lip. She glared up defiantly from beneath the hair that fell into her eyes.

'You will regret this,' she shouted defiantly at the three men who surrounded her, two burly and bearded, one smaller and skinnier, practically just a boy, with the first straggling growth of hair starting on his chin.

'It is you who will regret it, my pretty,' one of the burly men snarled threateningly at her, drawing out a dagger and pressing it to her neck so tightly that it left a mark.

The other man placed a hand on his forearm and he pulled it away. 'Let Nicholas deal with it,' he hissed, 'as we agreed. The girl is defenceless – perhaps it will make a man of him at last.'

The other man grunted as if he doubted this, but he nodded and shouldered his pack. Cass saw that they seemed to have recently dismantled a campsite: the charred and blackened remains of a fire had been scattered and three horses were saddled and waiting nearby.

'You'll remember this,' the second man sneered, with an unpleasantly blackened smile, 'the next time it occurs to you to go a-stealing, little girl.'

She spat at him like a cat, and he stepped backwards, looking distastefully at the spittle that had narrowly missed his boot.

'Rough her up enough to teach her a lesson,' he barked at the younger man, who was watching nervously. 'And then catch up with us.'

The two men mounted their horses and moved off, the sound of their hooves slowly diminishing as the youngster in the clearing remained stock still, staring at the bound girl.

Cass was about to leap out from behind the trunk and surprise him, confident she could overpower this weedy youth, when the young woman spoke again, and Cass was so surprised by her tone that she hesitated, still hidden behind the tree.

'Thank goodness.' She sighed in a plaintive musical tone, the defiance completely gone from her face and replaced with an open, innocent expression. 'I thought they would never leave us alone!'

The boy seemed bewildered. Cass could see the side of his face in profile as he hovered near the girl. He was sweating slightly, one hand gripped tight on the handle of his sword.

'Now,' the girl said briskly, as if this was a completely normal set of circumstances, one in which she found herself quite at home, 'I know you had no intention of hurting me and you cannot be held responsible for the actions of your father and his friend, that would be quite unfair. So if you untie me now, there won't be any hard feelings.'

The youth hesitated, clearly flummoxed by her confident demeanour, but he did not move to untie her.

'Listen,' she said, her voice suddenly emotional. 'I know what it's like to be pushed around by an overbearing father. I know how it feels to want to be your own person and feel like nobody understands.' The boy's eyes were riveted on her face and she held the eye contact, her big brown eyes soft with sympathy. 'In fact, that's how I ended up out here all alone in the first place,' she said with a sniff, and her eyes began to shine with tears. 'My sister and I tried so hard to please our father but somehow we could never seem to be the perfect young women he wanted us to be. One morning, he found fault with our cooking and threw my sister against the fireplace. There was a great gash on her forehead and her hand was badly burned.'

The boy's mouth was hanging open slightly.

'I ran,' the girl said, her voice catching. 'I left my poor sister behind, because I was terrified that if I didn't seize my chance and leave while he was distracted, I might never get another opportunity. One day I hope I will be able to go back and rescue her too. But in the meantime I had nowhere to go and nothing to eat. I never would have dreamed of taking anything that wasn't mine. I just needed a crust or two to get me through the day.' Her eyes were moist, and the boy stepped forward almost involuntarily, reaching out a hand to pat her gingerly on the shoulder.

'I know what it's like to have a rough father,' he muttered, as he fumbled with the ropes tying her hands behind her back.

There was a brief flash of triumph in the girl's eyes, then a bellow of rage and the two men stampeded back into the clearing, one catching the boy a glancing blow around his ears and the other seizing the girl round the waist just as she sprang up from the floor.

'This is what you think teaching her a lesson looks like, idiot boy? I'll show you a lesson!' And the poor boy cowered as blows rained down around him.

'And as for you –' the other man groaned as the girl took advantage of the distraction to sink her elbow into his stomach – 'you're going to learn some manners.' He pinned her arms easily behind her back with one meaty hand and lifted the other as if to strike her hard across the face. But Cass's bow was already in her hands, arrow drawn, and she felt the power shoot down her arm and into her fingers as she released it so that it flew into a tree trunk inches from the man's face and quivered there, her aim perfect. Before he could see her, she ducked behind the tree trunk.

The men spun round, scanning the surrounding trees, and Cass waited until they were looking in the wrong direction and quickly fired again, this time clipping the other man's shin with an arrow that whistled past and then buried itself in the ground. Concealed, she looked down at her leather-gloved hands in wonder. The second arrow, too, had whizzed straight to the exact spot she had intended, as if drawn there by invisible forces.

'Come,' he grunted furiously, shoving the youth unceremoniously onto his horse and leaping into his own saddle. 'She is not worth a fight,' he shouted to the other man, who looked reluctant to leave their quarry. 'Let the bandits have her and see if she keeps such an uncivil tongue in her head after that.'

The other man seemed to relent, casting one last acid look back at the girl before he, too, mounted his horse, and the three of them galloped away, the boy snivelling and drooping in his saddle.

'Show yourselves,' the girl shouted, positioning herself with her back against a tree and quickly drawing a dagger from her boot. 'But you should know that I am not alone. The group I am riding with are nearby and will return any moment.'

'Oh, really?' Cass grinned, lowering her bow and stepping out from behind the tree once she was certain the men had gone. 'Funny, I didn't see anyone nearby.'

The girl did not relax her stance. Her eyes travelled quickly and suspiciously over Cass's tunic and hose, the bow and arrow in her hand, the sword at her waist. She did not lower the dagger. 'Who are you? Why would you help me?'

'My name is Cass,' she answered, taken aback at the girl's wariness. 'What's yours?'

'Astra,' the girl replied after a pause.

'Well, Astra,' Cass said, 'it seemed like you needed a little help.'

'I was doing perfectly fine on my own,' she snapped back, but she lowered her weapon.

'My horse is nearby –' Cass jerked her head in the direction she had come from – 'and could carry both of us. I can ride with you to your home to help your sister.'

The girl laughed and slipped the dagger back into her boot. 'I don't have a sister,' she replied lightly. 'Nor a home.'

Cass looked her over, from the straight icy pale cropped hair to the threadbare woollen dress and dirty shoes bound in places with mud-caked cloth. Astra's face hardened with defiance under the examination and she lifted her chin, as if daring Cass to pity her.

'Here.' Cass sat down, took the parcel of food her mother

had given her out of her tunic and tore off a large piece of bread. 'Let's eat. And I will tell you about a place where your bravery and quick thinking will earn you food and a bed for the night.'

And as they ate, Cass told her about the sisterhood and Angharad and what they had fought so hard to create. Astra sat and watched Cass speak, chewing her bread thoughtfully.

But as the afternoon wore on, she said seriously, 'I may not have a sister nor a father but I have seen people turn on women for their beliefs.' She paused, and Cass wondered if she would elaborate, but her gaze was very far away, as if she had forgotten Cass was there at all. And then she suddenly seemed to come back to herself and jumped up, brushing the crumbs from her lap. 'I will believe in this sisterhood when I see it,' she declared. 'And if it is as you say then I will fight for it too.'

'Then come with me and see for yourself,' replied Cass simply.

The manor was eerily quiet when they arrived late that evening. Blyth peered down from the gatehouse above the walls and let them in, gently stroking Pebble's nose in welcome. Blyth offered a hand to help Astra dismount, but she ignored it, sliding nimbly down by herself and landing with catlike grace.

Cass left Pebble with Blyth and led Astra inside, expecting to find the hall busy with squires eating their supper, perhaps some of Lord Mordaunt's knights with them. But the fire had burned low and nobody seemed to have lit the torches in the brackets, leaving it dark and draughty. Astra looked around apprehensively, as if she did not think much of the place Cass had brought her to.

'They must have gone to bed early,' Cass said uncertainly. At that moment there was a wild shriek and little Nell flew into the hall from a door at the far end and threw herself at Cass, embracing her fiercely.

'You are back!' she cried, delighted. 'Elizabeth said you would not return, but I knew you would.'

Cass gave the younger girl's shoulders an affectionate squeeze. 'Where is everyone?'

'Most of the squires have gone to bed early,' Nell replied. 'And the women from the village, too. They've been training hard every day. Angharad is in her chamber, going through the latest dispatches from the scouts. And the men are in Gamelin's rooms, gambling on knucklebones,' Nell said, shaping her rosy lips into a round pout, 'but Alys said I was too young to watch, so I was on my way to the kitchen to find a snack.' She looked up hopefully. 'Will you teach me to play knucklebones, Cass?'

'I will,' Astra said with a grin, then added a defensive

'What?!' when she saw Cass's look of disapproval. 'It's never too young for a girl to learn how to earn an honest living.'

'Honest?' Cass scoffed.

'Well, I've got some other enterprising ideas, but I don't think you'd approve of those either.' Astra smirked, taking Nell's hand. 'Now show me the way to this Gamelin's rooms.'

Cass gave Nell a nod, smiling in spite of herself, and let her lead Astra away.

'And find Astra somewhere to sleep afterwards, will you, Nell?' she shouted after them.

Elaine came into the hall as they left, shushing the baby in her arms. 'You're home!'

To Elaine's great surprise the child had been a boy, not the girl she had been convinced she was carrying, and she had named him Hugh. He was a cheerful little thing, with bright blue eyes like his mother's, always waving his fat fists and taking in everything around him. But now his eyelids were drooping like crescent moons in his soft, pillowy face.

'He settles when I walk,' Elaine explained, pacing up and down the hall.

'What news?' Cass asked, her voice low to avoid disturbing the baby.

For a moment Elaine searched Cass's face, as if trying to decide whether she was strong enough to hear the news she had to impart. 'There are more of them than we thought.

The Saxons. Our scouts report a war host massing at Deva. Even with the fyrds he has gathered, King Ceredig may not be able to beat them alone.'

'How many?' Cass asked grimly.

'Too many.' The baby stirred and Elaine bounced up and down gently on the balls of her feet. 'But that is not all. There is another band approaching from the north. They have formed an alliance with some of the Scots, who are disillusioned with Camelot's rule and ready to expand their territories. We are at risk from both sides. Our northern and south-western borders are vulnerable, and we will not be able to hold them alone.' She exhaled heavily, as if glad to have expunged the grim news, and absentmindedly kissed the soft wisps of hair that curled above Hugh's ears.

'What is Angharad's plan?'

Elaine shook her head, and for the first time Cass saw fear in her sky-blue eyes. 'There is none, Cass. There cannot be. It doesn't matter what we do or how many local women we train. This is a greater force than we could ever withstand.'

Chapter 18

Cass passed a fitful night. Every creak of timbers was an enemy footstep, every swish of the branches of trees outside the sound of a cloak brushing over dry leaves as an ambush approached.

From the moment she woke the next morning, Cass saw that Nell had been right about the training stepping up in earnest. She could hear the clatter of feet outside her chamber before she had even risen from her bed, and by the time she had dressed and descended to the hall it was busy with members of the sisterhood, the new recruits from the villages and Mordaunt's knights, all breakfasting together, most of them already armed.

There was bustle and noise in the manor as there always

had been. But there was also fear, which laced the steaming dishes of the porridge set on the breakfast table and spurred on the younger squires as they pulled on their helmets and rushed out to practise in the meadow. It curled along the corridors and snaked up the stairs, tainting everything.

'We have lost a few,' came a low voice from her left, and Cass turned to see Rowan sliding into the seat beside her. 'Some left after the news started to come in about the Saxons gathering their war host. They prefer to flee with their families than to wait here and fight a losing battle.'

'But most remain?'

'They do.' There was a note of pride in Rowan's voice. 'We have been trying to build up their defensive skills as quickly as we can without scaring any more of them away.'

Even in the short time she had been gone, Cass felt there was something different about the women: the way they moved and carried themselves, reaching for what they wanted instead of waiting politely to be served. And there was something different about the way they looked at her too. There was a moment when she moved towards a pitcher across the table and Susan flinched from her hand, as if she was dangerous. She had flushed afterwards and quickly turned away, but Cass knew that things were different now. After the last battle, she could not pretend that she was the same as them any more.

She didn't know how many of the sisterhood Angharad had told about where she had gone and why, but she guessed that she had confided in Rowan, who had fixed Cass with an intense searching look as she walked into the hall, and she knew that before long she would have to tell them what she had found out, and by telling other people she would make a choice to accept her destiny, a choice she would not be able to take back.

'You've done well,' Cass murmured, seeing that Rowan was waiting for some kind of response. 'But—'

'Not so loud, please,' Sir Gamelin pleaded, taking a seat on the opposite side of their table and wincing as he gingerly massaged his temples with his fingers.

'Late night?' Cass asked wryly, bringing her conversation with Rowan to an abrupt end, and he nodded ruefully.

'Some young white-haired witch arrived just as we were about to call it a night and persuaded us all to play on a little. Then somehow the stakes grew higher and higher and the beer became stronger . . .' His eyes slipping in and out of focus. 'Come to think of it, I wonder if she added something to the beer,' he muttered slowly.

'And she relieved you of your purses?' Cass asked, trying not to laugh.

'That and more,' he answered, pointing plaintively to a white band of skin on his otherwise sun-browned little finger. 'My uncle gave me that signet ring.'

He looked so mournful that Cass laughed aloud, but when his gold-flecked eyes caught hers, dancing with amusement, she quickly looked down at her breakfast. As soon as she had eaten, she must see Angharad. The resolve with which she had returned from her family's home had only grown stronger with the latest news. She could see just one way forward.

At that moment, Angharad entered the hall. Her face was even paler than usual, her usually bright eyes dull with lack of sleep. Cass rose and took a step towards her, but before she could speak, Elaine rushed into the hall, her eyes wild, her hair dripping wet and flying around her in long, sodden clumps. She was staring frantically from side to side as she approached, as if searching for something as she passed each of the long tables.

'Hugh!' she shouted, her voice hoarse with fear. 'Hugh!'

Behind Cass, Rowan leaped to her feet. 'He is gone,' Elaine babbled frantically, clutching at Cass's arm. 'I put him down in his basket for a short while as I bathed in the next room and when I returned the basket was empty. He could not have moved by himself; he cannot yet crawl.'

A ripple of fear spread out around the hall, as people became aware that something was not right, and whispers replaced the excited chatter.

'Spread out,' Angharad ordered, immediately alert again

despite her exhaustion of moments before. 'Search the manor. Susan, alert the guards at the gatehouse. Shut the gates. Nobody leaves. Cass, the postern gate.'

Cass nodded and took off at a run as the women scattered, racing towards different staircases and doors, calling the child's name. Elaine sank down onto a bench in the middle of it all seemingly paralysed by fear.

Cass raced out of the main doors and into the courtyard. Blyth came to the door of the stables, startled, and gave a quick shake of the head when Cass shouted to ask if the baby was there. She careered round the corner, along the area between the manor and the outer walls, making her way round the back towards the postern gate that opened out onto the meadow.

Ahead of her, almost at the gate, was a dark cloaked figure, something muffled in a blanket in its arms.

Edith turned, one hand on the handle, the other clutching the bundle that wriggled and squirmed.

'You have found him!' Cass gasped out, her veins flooding with relief. 'Elaine was half mad with fear. She will be so grateful.' She turned, her chest still heaving, and was halfway back to the courtyard before she realized there was no sound of footsteps following her. She looked back. Edith remained motionless, her hand still on the handle. The child had started to cry, plaintive thin little wails, yet she made no move to comfort him.

'Edith?' Cass stepped back towards her uncertainly.

'He is not hers,' the girl said in a strangled sort of voice, and her hood slipped back, revealing the strange fervent expression on her pale face. 'He belongs with his father. With Lancelot.'

Cass's heart jumped into her throat. Automatically her brain began to race. She had no weapon, and if she turned to fetch one, the girl could slip out of the gate and be gone before she could make it back. Any false move risked her making a run for it. The only thing that seemed to be stopping her was that opening the gate would require her to turn her back to Cass momentarily to open the bolts.

Cass held up her hands, palms up. She had to think. She had to keep Edith calm, keep her talking long enough for someone else to arrive.

'Why, Edith? You have become close to Elaine these past weeks, and I have seen you care for that child as if it were your own. Why would you take it from its mother?'

'Because I love him,' the girl replied simply with a defiant lift of her chin. 'I love him as she never could, bringing shame upon him with an illegitimate child and defying the careful tale he created to protect his reputation.' She gave a bitter smile. 'He tried to give her a chance, you know. He sent his fellow knights to search for her, and they would have provided for her and the child in comfort, somewhere quiet where they could live without fuss, but she chose to sequester herself here instead, the stubborn fool.'

She looked down at the baby as if she had only just realized she was holding it. 'But now my lord has come to know that he has a son and he wishes to raise the child in the knightly fashion, and I shall be rewarded for bringing it to him. He shall see that I love him truly, as she could not, and he will realize that I am his true equal. Not those simpering, fawning hangers-on at court who swoon over him wherever he goes. It will be me he chooses.' A look of radiant certainty spread across her face, as Cass took half a step closer, her hands still outstretched.

'Edith,' Cass said, keeping her voice as steady as she could, though her heart was pounding, 'Lancelot abandoned Elaine. He told everyone she had died of unrequited love after he left her to fend for herself, her reputation ruined. Is that the kind of man that deserves your love?'

But the girl stiffened, looking over Cass's shoulder, and tightened her grip on the child in his blanket.

'Edith?' Elaine was standing behind Cass, her face slack with fear. 'Give me my baby, Edith.'

The girl shook her head, clutching the baby fiercely to her chest. 'He will not forgive me if I do.'

'Edith?' It was Rowan now, crowding into the narrow

alleyway, disbelief and fury in her eyes. 'What are you doing? You have become one of us. I trained you.' She let out a mirthless laugh. 'You have fought for us so fiercely . . .'

Edith shrugged, her face suddenly sullen. 'I have no quarrel with you. And we are all united against the Saxons. I had arrived at the village only a few days before you appeared, desperate for new sword hands. I had heard rumours Elaine was in the area, then news of a sisterhood of women living together began to spread and I suspected you might have taken her in. I had only intended to stay there for as long as it took to find a way to infiltrate the manor, and then you arrived, throwing open your doors freely. It was the perfect chance.' As she spoke, her hand was fumbling behind her, as she attempted to draw back the stiff bolt.

'He is crying for me, Edith,' Elaine called, a note of pure desperation in her voice. 'He is crying for his mother. Give him to me.'

The girl's fingers scrabbled frantically against the door, and there was a loud grating of metal as the bolt shot across and the door creaked open behind her. Her eyes lit up with triumph and then Cass was roughly shoved aside, as Elaine barrelled towards her. Edith turned and began to run, but Elaine was upon her before she had even taken a few steps, grabbing a handful of her hair and yanking her head back hard so she shrieked in pain. She ripped the child from Edith's arms and cradled him to her, speaking to him gently, shushing him and patting his back as Rowan and Cass rushed past her to seize Edith.

As the child quieted and nuzzled into its mother's neck, Elaine turned, ablaze with fury, and drew a sword from her belt, advancing on the girl who now sagged wretchedly between her captors.

'No,' Cass and Rowan shouted together, closing in so that they physically shielded Edith from Elaine's wrath.

'It is not necessary, Elaine,' Cass gasped out, reaching out a hand to place on her heaving shoulders. 'It is over. It is over. He is safe.'

'He is not,' Elaine seethed, 'as long as she is free to run to Lancelot and tell him exactly where he can find his son.'

The girl's head snapped up and her eyes gleamed in the morning sun. 'But I have already sent him word,' she crooned tauntingly, gleefully. 'He will find you soon enough and claim what is rightfully his. And he will have me to thank for it.'

Then Elaine leaped forward again and both Cass and Rowan jumped towards her, Cass staying her sword arm while Rowan took the baby out of harm's way. And when the moment of chaos had subsided, Edith had disappeared across the meadow and into the woods.

*

188

Rowan and Cass made their way to Angharad's rooms later, after they had settled Hugh and Elaine in her chambers with Alys to comfort her and two knights guarding the door.

Rowan's face was set and grim, but Cass felt her heart fluttering in her chest and climbed the stairs almost as if she were in a dream. The time had come, she knew, to reveal herself to Angharad and to the sisterhood.

Angharad sighed wearily and ran a slim-fingered hand over her face as she poured out goblets of warm spiced wine. 'Tell me about the girl.'

'It seems she was working for Lancelot,' said Rowan, gazing gloomily into her goblet.

'You seem to be taking this very personally,' Cass observed.

'Well, wouldn't you?' Rowan burst out. 'The hours I spent training that girl! And for what?'

'It's still a testament to your tutorship that she fought so well,' Cass said bracingly.

'Yes,' Rowan replied drily. 'Such an achievement for me to have trained our enemy. I'll be so glad to remember it's thanks to my good teaching when she returns with Lancelot and starts spitting arrows at us.'

Cass shook her head. 'They are not our enemies.'

'They will be if he is so desperate to get his hands on that baby. And now we've sent him a newly skilled right-hand woman to lead him straight to us and help him fight us when he gets here.'

'This is not our only problem,' Angharad reminded them. 'The gathering war hosts are far too great for us to defeat alone. We stand to lose our lands and everything we have built here if we do nothing.'

'Why would King Arthur allow Northumbria to be left defenceless?' Cass asked, her thoughts turning to the man she could not yet think of as her brother, so distant and glorious the tales of him seemed. 'He must know that Ceredig calls the men to the south. Surely he would not want the Saxons to gain a stronghold here?'

'He must not know,' Angharad said slowly, sipping her wine. 'Perhaps he is only aware of the forces massing at Deva. Most of the scouts he relies on in the far north will be loyal to the Scottish kings before Arthur. He may not be aware of the risk of the Scots' alliance with the Saxons until it is too late, until they have already gained too much ground and strengthened their position by taking northern territories. Taking lands like ours.'

The moment had come. She knew it, and the heat inside her knew it too. It buzzed beneath her skin until she felt almost effervescent.

'Then we must tell him,' Cass said quietly, gripping her goblet tightly.

'Oh yes,' Rowan agreed sarcastically, 'that's a great idea. Excuse me, I need to see the king. Yes I am just a poor woman from a remote northern settlement but I have some strategic information I think he'll be really interested in . . . That wouldn't get you clapped in the Camelot dungeons at all.' She rolled her eyes and slumped back in her seat. 'He will not listen to us.'

'I think . . .' Cass took a deep breath. 'I think he might listen to me.'

She told them everything, a look of complete astonishment on Rowan's face. Angharad seemed a little less shocked, perhaps, Cass suspected, because Alys had hinted to her that something like this may be coming.

'You think King Arthur is your brother?' Rowan asked at last, slowly, as if she wanted to be quite sure that her ears hadn't deceived her before she told Cass that she had truly, completely lost her mind.

'Twin brother. I know. It sounds unbelievable. But that is what my mother said.' And she pulled out the locket and showed them the tiny engraving.

'It could be a dragon.' Rowan put her head on one side and held it up to the firelight. 'But if you turn it this way –' she twisted it counter-clockwise – 'it could also be a sort of constipated pigeon.'

Cass took it back, grinning. But Angharad was staring

191

thoughtfully into the flames, her elbows resting on her knees, her pointed chin cupped in her hands.

'You must go to Arthur, Cass,' she said eventually, and Rowan stopped laughing. 'Go to him and use the locket as a reason to speak with him, or with Merlin, or one of his advisers. And whether they believe you or not, you can use the audience as a chance to pass on two messages.

'Two?'

'Two.' She ticked them off on her fingers. 'Firstly, you must tell him about the Saxons, about Deva and the deal with the Scots.' She handed Cass a heavy leather bag. 'Here are some of the coins and the brooches we collected from the bodies. They will prove to him that you are not lying about the battles we have fought.'

'And secondly?'

'Secondly,' she said, her voice fierce and her eyes flashing, 'you tell him that Lancelot and his other knights must swear to stay away from that child if he wants any more information from us about where the Scottish and Saxon forces are gathering in the north.' Angharad nodded, her face set. 'And with any luck we save our home into the bargain.'

Chapter 19

Cass had one stop to make before she set off the next
morning.

'Knowing that this is who you are does not
actually change anything,' Alys told her, blowing on her
lavender and chamomile tea to cool it. 'It just gives you all
the facts to make an informed decision.'

'You said –' Cass spoke slowly, not looking up from her
steaming tea – 'that the prophecy about the person who
would pull that sword from the stone spoke of a light to
hold back the darkness . . . a leader who would unite all
Britain . . .' She trailed off, unsure what she was trying to
ask. 'That does not sound like a destiny you can simply
choose to ignore.'

'It is still your life to live as you wish.' Alys shrugged. 'There are plenty of people who go to great lengths to avoid their own calling or destiny or whatever you want to call it. But remember one thing, Cass. Arthur was brought to court from the home he was fostered in, when Merlin decided the time was right for him to take the throne. But you . . .' She smiled, and her face seemed to light up with pride. 'You found your way here yourself. Unbidden. You have forged your own path. Don't ever forget that.'

'And if I show up at Arthur's court and he decides to have me killed because he sees me as a threat to his throne?' Her voice came out as a croak.

'If you have learned one thing from your time here, it is surely that powerful men do not consider women to be a serious threat at all. I suspect it is much more likely he will laugh at you than try to hurt you.'

'Well, that is a great comfort,' Cass said with a small smile. Then: 'Do you truly believe in all of this, Alys?' she asked, searching the lined face for the comforting certainty she yearned for.

Alys gazed steadily at her for a long time before she answered. 'I believe in you. I believe that your coming here was prophesied before you arrived and that you are just as capable of shifting the destiny of this island as Arthur or any other boy that a group of men have decided to anoint as their king.' She reached out her calloused hand and took Cass's palm in hers, patting it gently. 'It will be a difficult journey. And I would not judge you if you chose to turn away from it. But I also know you are good, Cassandra, and that you have it in you to succeed.'

Cass left Alys's hut and made her way to the stables, her cheeks wet as she fastened her silver locket carefully round her neck, only to find that she was not the only one saddling a horse that morning, nor the only one dressed in full armour.

'Did you think Angharad would let you make the journey alone?' Astra asked, casually, as she slipped on a bridle.

'She asked you to accompany me?'

Astra raised an eyebrow at the surprise in Cass's voice and shrugged. 'She needs her best swordswomen here and cannot spare them. But it might have helped that she spotted a tear in my eye when I confessed how you saved me in the forest and I would be forever loyal to you.' She grinned and Cass shook her head. 'What? I wanted to see Camelot, all right? And the borrowed armour doesn't look half bad on me either.'

She wasn't wrong. The leather breastplate shone between muscular biceps and Astra's sharp, striking features were only enhanced by the framing of the helmet. Yet beneath the cocky grin, there was something that reminded Cass of the vulnerability Astra had revealed on their journey back to the manor. And she suspected that she wasn't the only one who had become adept at burying pain deep to avoid feeling it too sharply.

More than anything, Astra reminded her of a stray cat, spitting and hissing when cornered but discerning about where it placed its loyalty and friendship. And without fully being able to explain it, Cass felt that she could trust her with her life.

As they busied themselves with the straps and buckles of their harnesses and saddles, Sir Gamelin rushed in.

'Cass—' He stopped short, suddenly realizing that there was not only one woman in the stables but two. He reddened, stuttered and started again.

'I heard you were leaving for Camelot and thought I might escort you –' he caught Astra's eye and quickly amended – 'ride with you . . . at least part of the way.'

'We are not in need of an escort,' Astra answered brusquely. 'You'd probably slow us down,' she added, grinning, as she pocketed a dagger.

'Perhaps it would not hurt for him to ride a little way with us,' Cass found herself murmuring and saw the surprise in Astra's eyes, but the other girl nodded without further comment. When they set off through the newly reinforced gates, Astra touched her heels to her horse's sides and rode a distance ahead of them, leaving their horses to walk side by side.

They rode in what felt at first like companionable silence, but the more time elapsed the more awkward the silence seemed to become until Cass felt that she could not bear it any longer.

'What is your horse's name?' she asked, blurting out the first question that came into her head.

'I do not think I can tell you,' he answered, a smile dancing around his eyes as he leaned forward to pat the neck of his handsome piebald stallion.

'Why not?' she demanded, surprised.

'It is an embarrassing name,' he replied unexpectedly. 'I did not choose it, but I fear you would judge me for it all the same.'

'You do realize this is only making me more curious to find out?'

'That is regrettable. But still.'

They rode on in silence a few minutes more.

'Why didn't you change his name if you disliked it so much?'

'It was too late. He wouldn't answer to anything else.'

She snorted, unsure whether or not he was teasing her.

'If you tell me, I promise not to let it colour my impression of you. My entire harsh judgement shall be reserved for the

197

previous owner of the horse and his questionable choices.'

'Nevertheless, it would have an effect on your perception of me every time you saw me riding him.'

Her heart rate picked up a little. 'And why should that matter?'

'Because your good opinion matters to me.' Goosebumps rose along her forearms and she forced herself to keep her eyes on the path ahead.

'And what if your refusal to reveal the name affects my opinion of you,' she teased, mock seriously.

'That would seem highly unfair considering the circumstances in which we last found ourselves alone in these woods together,' he countered, and she flushed in earnest this time, remembering the close crush of their bodies as he had sparred with her to try to force her to reveal her name.

'Very well.' Then, after a pause: 'But on that occasion you fought me for it.'

'Yes.' His hazel eyes twinkled again and her stomach fluttered in spite of herself. 'Fought and lost, although you did fight dirty if I remember correctly, so I am not sure it counts as a true defeat.'

'You visited your family?' he asked quietly a few moments later, his eyes scanning the horizon, leaving the question hanging in the air for her to answer however she wished.

'Yes.' She hesitated but in his reassuring presence the words seemed to tumble out of her and she found that it was a relief. Not to tell him of her identity, and the secrets her mother had revealed, but to find that she could talk to him about the other things. The more difficult, aching things that were harder to put into words, and which she might only before have shared with Lily when they were alone in their chamber at night.

With a slight thickness in her voice, she spoke of her family, the fact that they were not her family, not really, and the maddening, unfair, loving choice her mother had made to protect her by keeping her in the dark all these years.

'Family do not always know what is best for you, even when they have the very best intentions,' Sir Gamelin muttered, and Cass wondered if he was thinking about his uncle and about Lady Anne.

'King Arthur's twin. It cannot be so, can it?' He looked at her, his gold-flecked eyes serious, weighing her up.

She shrugged. 'I honestly don't know. It seems utterly fantastical, but there is the locket. And the sword. And my mother has never lied in my living memory . . . I cannot think of any reason why she would do so now.'

He gave a low whistle, shaking his head slightly. 'I knew there was something special about you, but this . . .'

She felt warmth spreading across her chest as if she had just swallowed a great draught of Alys's hot ginger tea and cast about for something to say to change the subject. There was something strange, tantalizing but also terrifying, about discussing the possibility of her destiny with him.

'Did you always want to become a knight?' Cass asked, wondering what it must have been like to choose this life, instead of having it thrust completely unexpectedly upon her.

He shook his head, with a little laugh that was half wry and half sad. 'I loved animals, as a child. I'd have been very happy taking over the farm. Getting to see the sunrise while you milk the cows. Spending your days out in the fields with the sheep, birthing the new lambs each spring. That's my idea of the perfect life. But my father had other ideas. There are two younger brothers at home to manage the farm, and my responsibility as the eldest son was to secure wealth and glory for my family.' He pulled a self-deprecating grimace.

'Better than being handed over to the man your parents have decided you will marry and bearing him children for the rest of your days,' Cass countered.

'I think a domestic life would have quite suited me,' he mused thoughtfully. 'No fighting and injuries . . . Quiet and peaceful . . .'

'Listen, I was in the room the other day when Elaine's child came and let me tell you there was nothing quiet or peaceful about it whatsoever.'

Out of the corner of her eye, Cass was close enough to see the fine stubble that covered his jawline, the way his smile crinkled the edges of his eyes. There was so little distance between them. 'Lady Anne seems nice,' Cass managed to say.

'Yes,' he answered in a low voice. 'She is a kind and gentle person, it seems. But I cannot—'

'We should increase our speed.' It was Astra, who had turned her horse and ridden back to them, her patience apparently having run out. 'We need to cover more ground before nightfall.'

Cass wondered if he might object, but Gamelin merely nodded. 'Then I will leave you here and return to the manor, where I can be of most use.'

Their eyes met for a brief moment.

'Be safe.'

'And you.'

They rode for three days, sleeping little, eating from fields and orchards along the way once their provisions ran out. At first constant anxiety plagued Cass, from worries about how they might be received to fear over what would happen at the manor in their absence. But as the hours went by and the terrain slipped past, she found a kind of peace in the tall, hedgerows and wide-open fields, the cloud-feathered blue skies and the dusty thud of Pebble's hooves on the hard dirt roads. They wore full armour, mostly keeping their helmets on, and when other travellers passed they gave the knights a wide berth, touching nervous hands to caps or ignoring them altogether.

Cass was grateful for their disguises, for the quiet. It gave her time to think about everything her mother had told her and how the story of her life had changed inside her head, as if all her memories were now swimming underneath a film of oil that distorted them and could never be wiped away.

She thought about the sword that hung at her belt and the mysterious power she wielded in battle, wondering about Arthur's famous sword, Excalibur, and whether it felt the same to him when he held it. Would she recognize herself in Arthur, feel some instant kinship? She thought of Sigrid, who had described her twin brother as part of herself, and given up everything to avenge his death.

Would Arthur even believe that she was really his twin?

The rhythm of Pebble's hooves became so hypnotic and soothing, walking in time with her own thoughts, that it was almost a shock when Cass looked up on the afternoon of the third day and saw Camelot rising up from the horizon. It was breath-taking. More splendid than any of the tales of her childhood could possibly have conveyed. Cream-coloured stone walls surrounded the city with guard posts at regular intervals. Across a drawbridge, through an ornate stonework archway, she could see a densely packed cluster of buildings and a maze of streets leading into the heart of the city. People hurried in and out, traders with trays of wares balanced on their shoulders, shouting impatiently to clear the way. Parents yelling at dawdling children who gazed up at it all, the expressions on their faces as awestruck as Cass felt. Chickens and stray cats ran underfoot and dung steamed in piles along the straw-strewn cobbles. And out of it all there rose a magnificent elevation, with small dwellings clinging to the sides of the rising hill and winding streets meandering up and up until they reached the crowning glory: a great castle at least ten times the size of the manor, with rounded turrets at the corners and higher towers rising within, their roofs seeming gilded in the late-afternoon sun, lending a warm rich glow to the whole magical scene.

They dismounted and led their horses across the drawbridge, unchallenged by the liveried guards in their white tunics emblazoned with Arthur's fierce red dragon. The noise and the smell rushed up to meet Cass as she was jostled along from all sides, swept into the current of the thoroughfare. They trudged onwards, passing blacksmiths' forges that rang with the sound of hammered metal and bristled with flying sparks.

There were women sitting at the sides of the streets with baskets of fish and eggs, some surrounded by clusters of haggling customers, others eying Cass greedily as she passed, her visor still covering her face. Every now and then a warning shout would ring out from a window and a bucketful of water or worse would sluice down into the gutter, prompting those down below to jump smartly out of the way.

Suddenly there was yelling and the ring of hooves on stone as three enormous stallions with gleaming coats clattered through the streets, scattering people in their path. Three knights sat astride them, their weapons sheathed in jewelled scabbards and their armour thick with chainmail and metal embellishments.

'The Orkney brothers are home for the tournament,' Cass heard a woman say excitedly, as they flattened themselves against the wall of a mud hut to get out of the path of the horses.

'Gawain! Gawain! I'm a knight like you!' a little child shouted in a shrill voice. And to Cass's surprise one of the riders slowed his horse and removed his helmet, releasing a sweaty mass of dark blonde curls and a wide grin in a suntanned face.

'Then I will need to practise harder if I am to come up against you in the next tournament,' he shouted in a rich, pleasant accent Cass had never heard before, with a wave that delighted the child, before riding on after the others up the hill towards the majestic castle.

They continued climbing upwards, and the hubbub lessened, until Cass could hear the sound of Pebble's hooves ringing on the cobbles again. The way became steeper as they passed empty dwellings, their inhabitants out at work or at play, and came at last to the enormous fortified gates of the castle itself, with thick metal slabs bolted into the wood and a great stone tower rising on either side.

A small wooden shutter set into the door opened at eye level and a man in armour peered out at Cass, who lifted her visor and adopted the low masculine voice she had not used in weeks.

'I have business at the castle.'

'Papers?' the man demanded, his tone flat and disinterested.

'Uh.' Cass swallowed. 'I do not carry any, but I must enter; I have an urgent message.'

'A message for whom?' The voice had become sharper, more suspicious, and the man was craning his neck now, trying to get a better look at Cass's face. 'Take off your helmet,' he barked before she could answer, and she hesitated, unsure whether revealing herself would do more harm or good at this juncture. But the decision was made for her. A small postern door in the tower opened and three guards rushed out, each holding a long spear. Two of them dragged Cass out of the saddle and pinned her to the wall while the third reached up and roughly yanked her helmet from her head.

There was a moment of shocked silence as her curls tumbled out, followed by raucous laughter.

'Playing dress up, are you, dearie?' one of the men asked, as if speaking to a small child, his wide smile missing several teeth.

Cass tried to draw herself up to her full height, no easy task while her feet dangled a short way above the cobbles, and with as much dignity as she could muster, demanded to be released. 'I come on behalf of those responsible for the death of Sir Mordaunt of Gefrin in Northumbria, with urgent news for the king regarding the Saxons and the Scots.'

They laughed louder.

'Hark how she talks.' One of them elbowed the other in the ribs, his eyes watering. '*Urgent news for the king regarding the Saxons,*' he repeated in a high squeaky voice, and they all fell about laughing again.

'Let me *go!*' Cass shouted, and to her surprise she was released and fell into a crumpled heap on the floor. She looked up, surprised, and saw Astra standing over her with the sharp blade of a dagger pressed to the throat of one of the guards.

Another guard chuckled nervously, his palms outstretched. 'Now, now, we didn't mean any harm by our little jokes.'

He took a slow step backwards towards the gate, and then suddenly Cass felt a white-hot pain fizz and explode in the side of her face. She gasped and looked down to see the arrow that had grazed her cheek, feeling the hot drip of blood at the base of her chin.

'Astra!' she shouted, and they both looked up to see that the ramparts bristled with archers, their bows pointed directly down.

'Did you think Camelot would not be robustly defended?' one of the men snarled as Astra released him, and before she could replace the dagger in her belt he had grabbed her by the shoulders and hurled her backwards so that she landed on her back in a large puddle.

'And stay out!' the other guard yelled, as Cass ran to help Astra to her feet. The slam of the door reverberated off the solid walls, and they found themselves alone once more.

'What now?' Cass muttered, trying to sound less deflated than she felt.

'We find ourselves lodging and food,' Astra answered, wiping mud off her chin with her sleeve. 'And we look for another way in.'

Chapter 20

'I had not thought we would need to pay for lodging,' Cass murmured, opening her leather purse and picking through the few coins within. Her cheeks burned and she felt like a silly child. What had she expected? For Arthur to throw open his doors and welcome her as his beloved long-lost sister? He did not even know that she existed, nor did it look as though she was likely to get close enough to enlighten him.

'I can help with that,' Astra said evenly, seeming unperturbed by Cass's near empty purse and the prospect of having nowhere to sleep that night. 'We just need to find the nearest market.'

'Astra, I do not think that stealing here is the best—'

'I am *offended*,' Astra huffed in mock indignation as she began to stride back down the road the way they had come. 'Shocked that you would call my morality into question. Why, I have never stolen in my life, not once, unless you count borrowing without asking, and even then I only did it with every intention of paying the goods back. One day. Perhaps not immediately but at some point.'

They retraced their footsteps to the main thoroughfare, where wooden huts and stone buildings leaned haphazardly against one another, creating a bustling warren of activity and powerful smells and noise. After a few false turns they found themselves in an open square of sorts, crowded with traders, women carrying baskets and sacks piled high with vegetables and bread and all manner of other wares. Cass loitered warily at one side of the square, watching, mystified, to see what Astra would do.

Within minutes the girl had borrowed three empty crates from a grocer, covered the middle one with a piece of cloth cadged from somewhere else, and set herself up a little way apart from the other stalls, sitting at her table for all the world as if she traded here every market day.

Cass watched in fascination as a woman carrying a heavy basket paused to ask Astra something, then nodded and sat down in front of her, leaning forward intently to listen as she spoke. Astra held out her hand and took the woman's wrist, turning her hand palm up and carefully tracing patterns on it with her finger, seeming to murmur away to her all the while. After a few minutes the woman stood up, looking pleased, a tinge of pink in her cheeks, and handed Astra a couple of coins before hurrying away.

All afternoon she sat there, Cass observing from a mystified distance, as men and women, young and old, stopped by her stall and invariably took a seat, listening, rapt, to whatever Astra was telling them. Sometimes she would study their palms, sometimes feel their scalp or simply close her eyes and press one finger to their temple, and all of them seemed completely enthralled, sometimes gasping in awe or shaking their heads in wonder.

One woman dissolved into tears and seized Astra tight, pressing a kiss into her shock of white-blonde hair before she walked away. Each seemed quite happy to part with their coins afterwards, and by the time she beckoned Cass over at the end of the afternoon her purse was fat and clinking.

Cass shook her head, not knowing whether to be admiring or judgemental. 'What did you do?'

Astra smiled mysteriously up at her, her eyes glinting. 'Give me your hand and I will show you.'

So Cass leaned forward, intrigued in spite of herself, and placed her hand in Astra's cool fingers.

'First,' she said, stroking Cass's hand gently, her voice

dropping to a low whisper, 'create an atmosphere of tension and mystery.' She stopped suddenly, her hands freezing, her eyes widening as she stared at something in Cass's palm, peering closer at a line there, causing Cass to lean closer in spite of herself, craning her own neck to see what had caught Astra's attention.

'Next –' Astra looked up at her, her cheeks slightly flushed, her eyes bright with excitement – 'a great revelation.' She took both Cass's hands in hers, squeezing them tight, and in a reverent breathy voice, she asked: 'There is something very special in your future, something quite extraordinary.'

Cass felt her heart beginning to beat faster, as images of spiralling necklaces, ruby swords and thundering hooves filled her mind unbidden.

'It is something you both desire and fear,' Astra continued, gazing intensely into Cass's eyes as if she could see through them into her very soul. 'Something you have longed for and dreaded, something that consumes your waking and dreaming thoughts.'

She shrugged, and dropped Cass's hand with a little laugh, and it was as if a light had been switched off and Cass found herself back in the bustling noisy marketplace.

'There's almost nobody who wouldn't read something into that and convince themselves it was a portent of a great love affair or a business venture they'd been considering or a marriage proposal.' She laughed, with an airy wave of her hand. 'Then it's just a case of letting their questions guide you to tell them exactly what it is they want to hear, and they'll go away happy and pay up without complaint every time.'

Cass smiled at her uncertainly, still not completely sure whether to be impressed or disgusted by this impish girl with her wiles and tricks. 'Where did you learn to do it?'

'My mother,' she said shortly, and for a moment Cass thought that was the end of the conversation.

'She followed the old ways, the old religion. It was in her blood, and mine, too, she always used to say. And much good it did her.' Cass stood up suddenly and started to tidy up, folding the cloth and clattering the crates together. 'We were run out of every town we ever tried to settle in, and eventually people's fear of her claimed her life,' she said without elaborating.

'She always believed in something bigger than herself, something she was a conduit for, some spiritual service she was performing. And look where it left her. After she died, I decided I'd never live in thrall to the stories and the superstitions. I'd make my own luck and my own purpose. And if I could lift a little money here and there from other people who were gullible enough still to believe, then so much the better.' She returned the crates with a friendly nod and came back to Cass, that defiant look in her eyes again. 'Considering how much the so-called magic took from me, I think I have a right to take something back, don't you?'

Cass opened her mouth to say that Alys would feel differently about the old stories, about their power, but then she shut it again. She could not bring herself to imagine what exactly might have happened to Astra's mother. But Cass knew more than she had ever wanted to about the pain of losing people you loved. And she understood a little of the soft, tender, hidden agony that Astra's hard, spiky exterior kept safe.

They spent the night in a barn that Astra's questionable earnings had paid for the use of. With no fire or candles, they went to bed with the sun after a meagre supper, each with a pile of straw for a mattress. Astra's slow, even breathing soon indicated she was asleep, but Cass's growling stomach, the throbbing scratch across her cheek and her racing thoughts kept her lying awake long after it was too dark to see the cobwebbed corners of the ceiling above her.

Her brother (so strange even to think that word) was so close to her. Closer than they had ever been since their birth, if her mother's story was true. And yet somehow, even in the brief time she had known about his existence, he had never felt further away. She shifted, and as she struggled to find a comfortable position on the prickly hay, her fingers

213

brushed the cool, hard metal of the sword she had pulled from the stone. Was she here because it had called her to Camelot? Because she had yearned to meet the twin she had known nothing of all her life? Because she felt a duty to protect Angharad and the others?

In the end, perhaps it didn't really matter. Unless Arthur acted soon, and with as many fighters as he could muster, there would be nothing left to protect anyway.

Chapter 21

Cass found herself on the other side of the castle gates sooner than she had expected.

When she awoke the next morning, she found herself alone in the barn, with no sign of Astra. Before she had finished splashing her face in the water butt outside, the girl had reappeared, with a loaf of bread and a wide grin on her face.

'There is a need for serving girls at the castle tonight,' she announced with an impish smile, throwing the loaf to Cass.

'And that affects us because . . .'

Astra adopted a mournful expression. 'Because Jane, the chambermaid I met at the market this morning, felt so sorry about my father's ill treatment of me and how badly I miss my poor dear sister that she agreed to sneak us in.'

Cass shook her head as Astra's smile reappeared. 'And if they're happy with us, we can stay on permanently. Or as long as it takes for us to get you into Arthur's chambers.' She shrugged, looking pleased with herself.

'Serving girls?'

'Yes. Apparently there's a tournament in a few days' time and all Arthur's knights are gathering to take part. They need more serving girls than usual for the feasts.' She threw Cass a bundle of clothes. 'So you'll need these.'

'We haven't got time to waste running round the kitchens pretending to be maids,' Cass said, holding up the beige cotton skirts and apron and grey shawl.

'There is time,' Astra said thoughtfully. 'Not much, but a little. The Saxons will not make their move until their forces are gathered to the fullest. The scouts told us many are still arriving and making their way inland to Deva. And the Scottish alliance is still forming. Better to infiltrate Camelot slowly and successfully than to have our heads cut off trying to storm the gates when the guards completely outnumber us.'

Cass felt conflicted. Part of her wanted to attempt to gain access to Arthur directly once again, but their previous reception didn't give her much confidence they'd be successful. She was running out of time, and she owed it to Angharad and the others to do anything that would get her inside those walls. Astra's plan was certain to do that at least. So she reluctantly started to change into the clothes Astra had given her.

They had barely arranged for their horses to be stabled and paid for their care than they were due to meet Jane, who chivvied them through a side door, along a narrow passageway and into a cavernous kitchen where maids and pages were scurrying about, scrubbing vegetables, chopping and kneading and pouring, all under the watchful eye of a tall sallow-faced woman with iron-grey hair.

'Who are these two?' she snapped immediately, as they entered the room, and Jane quickly bobbed a curtsy and explained they were two new serving girls hired for the tournament. The older woman frowned. 'We don't need two more for serving,' she said irritably, and Cass felt Astra tense next to her. 'One of them can stay.'

She looked them over appraisingly and jerked her thumb unceremoniously at Astra. 'You. Turn the spit.'

Astra moved wordlessly towards an enormous fireplace at the back of the room and began to turn a huge metal spit with two hands, rotating a whole pig's carcass which crackled and smoked as globules of fat dripped down to sizzle in the flames below.

Then the woman turned to Cass, her expression sour. 'You, out.'

Cass's breath caught in her throat. Her sword was carefully concealed down the side of her leg, the hilt strapped tightly to her waist beneath the borrowed clothes. As if it responded to this insult, she felt a bolt of electricity pass from her spine down the back of her legs and it pulled her up onto the balls of her feet, ready to fight if she had to. But before she could speak or move, there was a commotion at the door to the kitchen and a young woman burst in, wailing, her face blotchy and her eyes swollen from crying. She was clutching her forearm close to her chest, cradling it with the opposite hand.

'I don't care what the pay is, I will not work for her a moment longer,' she sobbed bitterly, before disappearing the way Cass and Astra had come in.

The tall grey-haired woman sighed heavily and briefly pinched the bridge of her hawklike nose between her thumb and forefinger. 'It's your lucky day,' she said to Cass with a thin-lipped smile. 'We don't need you in the kitchens, but Jane will show you to your position. Congratulations. You've just become the queen's newest chamber maid.'

There was only time for a brief panicked glance at Astra before Jane grabbed Cass by the hand and pulled her out of the room.

Jane set off at such a pace that Cass had to almost trot to keep up with her. She led her through a maze of stone corridors, the walls crowded with hangings and tapestries, with ornamental vases and statues placed at regular intervals and plush woven rugs on the floor, muffling their footsteps. Clusters of torches blazed in multiple brackets, setting off the jewel tones of the tapestries, which boasted scenes of lush forests, exotic fruits and majestic hunts.

At last, when Cass had lost count of how many turns they had taken and how many winding staircases they had climbed, the woman stopped and knocked at a door, waiting for a soft 'come in' before entering.

The room was beautiful, bedecked with wrought-metal furnishings and intricately etched wooden screens, with a crackling fire beneath a wooden mantlepiece covered in carvings of stags and hares. A long bench beside the fire was laden with furs and on a low polished wooden table there was a delicate bowl with a fluted edge piled high with apples, plums and strawberries. A beautifully carved wooden comb and a selection of shining metal arm rings lay on a tray on the windowsill, and a wooden bathtub stood in the corner, with soft cloths draped over its edge. She was in the queen's anteroom.

Jane looked Cass over, chewing her lip, as if she wanted to tell her something but wasn't sure how, then she gave a little sigh, moved to a door on the opposite side of the room and tapped on it gently.

'My lady?' She waited, then tapped again slightly louder. 'Lady Guinevere?'

The door opened and a girl stood there, her shining black hair braided into an elaborate crown on top of her head, pearls and golden hair grips twisted into it here and there so that her whole head seemed to shimmer. She had large grey eyes and pink cheeks, her lips darkened with rouge, her face round and unlined. In fact, she appeared so young that for a moment Cass looked automatically behind the girl for the queen, assuming that this must be another courtier. But then she spoke and her imperious tone immediately made it clear that this was Guinevere.

'Make me a bath,' she said, and her tone was so petulant, so childlike, that it sounded like she was aping the manner of a queen. Cass thought back to the time when her village had been abuzz with the news of the king's wedding and coronation. She knew that Guinevere was about the same age as her, yet she was powerfully reminded of little Grace back home sticking her bottom lip out and preparing to throw a tantrum.

Beside her she felt Jane stiffen as Guinevere passed close to them and picked up a stick from the fire, its other end smouldering. Next to the hearth, several large buckets of water stood waiting, and there was a big metal kettle hanging above the fire.

'The other girl was slovenly,' Guinevere crooned, and her voice took on a singsong quality as if she was reciting a nursery rhyme. 'Too slow, too slow, too slow.'

She waved the glowing red end of the stick from side to side in the air in front of Cass's face. 'I had to teach her a lesson. I didn't know skin would make a smell like that when it burned.'

The voice was so innocent, so lilting, that it took a moment for Cass to take in what she was saying. Then she looked at the burning wood and remembered the girl clutching her arm to her chest and felt her stomach turn over.

'This one will be quicker, my lady,' Jane whispered, her voice trembling, already backing towards the door, nodding frantically at Cass and gesturing towards the kettle.

Cass started, and then, seeing no immediate alternative, began to heave the water from the first bucket into the kettle above the fire.

Chapter 22

By the time Cass had helped Guinevere to bathe and dress it had become clear that the girl was not going to ask her anything about herself, even her name. She considered revealing her identity but remembered the previous chambermaid's wailing exit from the building and thought better of it. There was no telling how Guinevere might react. Cass was reeling, struggling to reconcile this volatile imperious girl with the beloved queen she had heard stories of. But as the day wore on, she started to suspect that she was not naturally cruel but rather very lonely and very bored.

'Play with me,' she whinged, as Cass tried to gather up the mess of luxurious silk and lace dresses she had discarded on the floor while selecting her outfit. She thrust a set of knucklebones in a gilded wooden box into Cass's hands, so she sighed and set down the gowns.

'I used to play with my sister,' Guinevere said quietly, and Cass wondered if she felt as lonely and lost without her sibling as she had when she had first left Mary behind for life at the manor.

'Now when she visits, if she wins, I just make her curtsey to me,' Guinevere giggled, selecting a small honey cake from a nearby platter and popping it into her mouth.

'Do you play with Arthur?' Cass asked, her curiosity about her twin getting the better of her. 'With the king, I mean,' she stammered, as Guinevere raised her eyebrows.

'The king is always busy,' Guinevere said in a slightly wistful tone. A shadow crossed her face for a moment. 'And Merlin does not like me to distract him with trivial things like games.'

'Merlin?' Cass asked eagerly. 'What is he like?'

'You ask a lot of questions,' Guinevere said sharply, and she seemed to look at Cass as if she were really seeing her for the first time.

'It is just all so new and fascinating to me,' Cass said quickly, lowering her eyes and scooping the little carved stone pieces out of the knucklebones box, passing them to Guinevere.

Cass did not see Astra again until she dutifully followed

Guinevere into the great hall that evening.

The hall alone could easily have contained the whole of Angharad's manor, with its soaring vaulted ceiling supported by wooden beams and a blaze of candles illuminating the silver and pewter goblets and platters that crowded the tables. There were stable boys and pages, maidservants and chambermaids clustered round the tables nearest the door, close enough to be in earshot if their masters or mistresses needed them, but far enough away that their combined body odours would not offend more noble nostrils.

Here Guinevere nodded curtly to indicate that Cass should leave her, so she slid onto the end of a bench, jostled by a page boy with dirty nails whose tunic was too big for him.

Cass greedily drank in the rest of the hall. The next few rows of trestles were occupied by squires and a group Cass guessed by their travelling cloaks were messengers or scouts. As Guinevere progressed further up the length of the room, she passed merchants and lords and ladies, their attire grander and somewhat cleaner, their cloaks fastened with metal brooches and arms encircled with bracelets and bands.

There was a rowdy table filled with knights in armour, their squires standing behind them as they sat at the benches, and Cass saw their travel-stained clothes and deduced that they had recently arrived to take part in the tournament.

Finally, the places at the last of the long tables were claimed by nobles and minor royalty; lesser kings, Cass guessed, or perhaps relatives of the king and his knights. There were ladies wearing gold circlets and jewels, and men with richly embellished tunics and neatly waxed beards, their goblets filled with wine unlike the pewter cups of ale she had noted at the closer tables.

But it was the very far end of the hall that drew Cass's gaze.

A tremendously thick wooden table, spanning the full breadth of the hall, its edges encircled with hammered metal, its shape perfectly round, almost as if some giant had taken a huge axe to a tree trunk and chopped off an enormous cross-section. Spaced evenly round its circumference were ornately carved wooden chairs edged with accents of gold, some carved with the names of their occupants.

Cass searched the table eagerly for Arthur, but she was disappointed. There were two chairs that were grander and more ornate than the others, side by side at the far side of the table so that they faced squarely across the expanse of the hall. But both were empty. Guinevere slipped into one of these seats with a sigh, as if the walk down the hall had tired her.

A little further round the table from the queen sat three men, quite clearly related as they all had the same wide good-natured faces scattered liberally with freckles and the same messy dirty yellow curls. Their builds varied, from the eldest, who was sturdy, with broad ox-like shoulders, to the middle brother, who was slight and thin-faced, and the youngest, who was the most handsome of the three, with a winning dimpled smile and a quick, easy laugh. Cass recognized the eldest as Gawain, who had delighted the child by stopping in the street. She watched him for a moment; he was clearly at ease in the splendour of the hall as he joked with his younger brothers, his arm slung casually over the back of his chair.

On the other side of the table, a few seats to Guinevere's right, was a short plump young man who swiped bad-temperedly at the pudding-bowl haircut that fell repeatedly into his eyes. Cass recognized him as Sir Kay; he was an ill-mannered knight who had argued with Lily when he had ridden north with some of his fellows last year. And a few spaces further to his right, she saw Sir Safir and Sir Elyan, the other knights who had travelled with him, their heads bent together in deep conversation.

She had warmed to these two knights when she had met them before and knew them to be courteous and kind, unlike Sir Kay. And for a moment she found herself imagining Sir Gamelin sitting among them. She pictured him gravitating towards Sir Elyan, perhaps joining in his conversation with Sir Safir, his eyes twinkling as they shared a joke . . . She flushed, though nobody was paying any attention to her or could possibly know what she had been thinking about.

Next to them was a knight so handsome that Cass felt compelled to study him more closely, as she might have paused to stare at a perfectly formed snail shell or a particularly beautiful rock by the side of a woodland stream. His rich brown hair flowed back in gentle waves from a high forehead, with a slightly protruding ridge above his pale green eyes lending prominence to straight, defined eyebrows. His nose was sharp, his cheekbones high and his chin darkened with a few days' growth of stubble. He wore no tunic only a cream cotton shirt, unlaced and open at the neck, and his strong forearms were lightly tanned. But even as Cass stared at him, a little dazed, he leaned over to swipe a leg of meat carelessly from the tray of a passing kitchen page without thanks or comment, hardly seeming to notice that he knocked the platter, sending gravy sloshing down his tunic. And when Sir Elyan looked up and frowned, the knight laughed and ruffled the boy's hair, causing him to spill still more.

'Don't worry your fragile sensibilities, Elyan,' the knight sneered in a high thin voice that carried across the hall, jarring strangely with his appearance. 'He is not too stupid to wash his tunic, are you, boy?'

The kitchen page flushed and straightened his tray as he

muttered, 'No, Sir Lancelot,' and hurried away.

Cass's gaze darkened as she looked again at the man who was laughing and tearing into the meat, knowing it was him who had abandoned Elaine, who had spread the word that she had died of unrequited love for him, rather than admit that he'd deserted her when pregnant. He had persuaded other knights of the round table to pursue her to Northumbria and still manipulated women like Edith, treating them cruelly enough to force them into scheming and betraying, just to gain his favour. Cass's grip tightened on her knife, but he never looked her way.

Near the three sandy-haired brothers sat a tall serious-looking youth with straight light-brown hair parted neatly at the centre, a thin thoughtful face with a long slender nose and delicate tapered fingers that tapped restlessly at the table next to his goblet.

'Little point wasting your time gazing at Galahad; he lives like a monk,' said a frank, cheerful voice, and Cass turned to see that a large girl with red cheeks and a stained apron that marked her as a kitchen maid had sat down opposite her. Strands of light-brown hair escaped haphazardly from the grubby white scarf she had tied round her head.

She smiled, reaching across the table to give Cass's hand a firm shake. 'I'm Ada.'

'Cass,' she said with a smile, grateful for a friendly face.

'You're new?'

Cass nodded.

'Kitchens?'

'Chambermaid – to Lady Guinevere.'

The girl grimaced and gave a low whistle. 'Keep your head down and your mouth shut is my best advice there.'

Cass laughed.

'It'll be madness the next few days with people flocking here for the tournament,' Ada told her knowingly. 'The squires can be grabby –' she sniffed disdainfully – 'but they usually respond to a swift kick between the legs.'

Cass smiled, knowing that she had more than a kick at her disposal if she should need it.

'But it's the knights you really need to look out for,' Ada went on, her voice lower now as she glanced furtively towards the round table. 'Galahad's no trouble, and the Orkney brothers wouldn't hurt a fly. Sir Kay can be a bore when he's in drink, but he's easy enough to outrun.'

Cass listened, suddenly seeing the shining table of knights in a very new light than the burnished haze of glory she was used to.

'But it's Lancelot you really need to watch out for,' Ada whispered under the cover of a rowdy jeer that had broken out further along their table as somebody had spilled their drink on their neighbour and received an elbow to the

229

eye in response. 'If he summons you to his chamber for anything, no matter how mundane the tasks sounds –' Ada was leaning across the table now, her voice urgent – *'do not go alone.* Take another serving maid with you, or better still one of the pages.'

Cass swallowed, thinking of Edith. 'And the same goes for Merlin,' Ada hurried on, and Cass's attention snapped back to the girl's earnest face.

'Merlin?'

'Not for the same reasons –' Ada shook her head quickly – 'but Merlin likes to experiment with herbs and draughts and the girls who go into his chambers do not always come out again quite the same.'

Cass stared at her. At that moment the great bolt-studded doors flew open again and flames from the torches surrounding the walls guttered and flickered as air rushed into the room and trumpets sounded.

There was cheering and a great scraping of benches against the floor as the king entered and Cass found herself swept to her feet along with the rest, craning her neck for a glimpse of him as he passed. She found that her throat ached and her eyes were hot. And the closer he walked, the stronger the answering force in her own body seemed to be; it was an inexorable pull, as if some fierce energy beneath her skin were yearning, reaching towards him.

She knew the king by his fine gold crown, by his tunic, which bore the colours of his men inverted: a dragon of purest white on a blood-red field, and by his eyes, which were as curious a mixture of blue and green as Cass's own.

In the briefest moment he had passed her, without seeing or knowing that she was there, and Cass, strangely deflated, sank back into her seat as another figure stalked past in the king's wake.

Cass would have recognized him by the deferential glances and the whispers, even if her mother had not described his long silver-streaked hair and piercing eyes. As Arthur's presence had prompted cheering and energy, Merlin's seemed to dampen and silence it, so that the noise died away in his wake.

He was a tall man, with slightly hunched shoulders, an imposing figure who seemed to shrink those around him as he passed, his shadow rising high on the wall alongside him.

Cass could not take her eyes from Arthur as he settled into the chair next to Guinevere's, inclining his head courteously to speak to her. She watched the easy way he conversed with his knights, noted the dimple that appeared below his cheek when he smiled. She was still gazing at him when she felt a sharp elbow nudge her in the ribs and turned to see that Astra had taken the place of the boy next to her, her eyes sparkling with adventure and hair messy and streaked with grease.

'You smell like a smokehouse,' Cass told her, putting a hand to her nose and waving Astra's attempted embrace away.

'Well, you try turning a pig over a fire for most of a day and let me know how you smell afterwards,' she retorted cheerfully, reaching across Cass to take a leg of chicken from a platter. 'What have you managed to find out?' she asked quietly.

'Not much,' Cass admitted. 'Except that the queen is not exactly as I expected.'

'Very little here is,' Astra agreed, her eyes darting around. 'I have seen a page whipped by his knight for insolence until his shirt was shredded, and a beggar turned away from the kitchen door asking for crusts even as we were preparing the feast.'

There was another peal of trumpets, and all eyes turned expectantly towards the round table where Arthur was rising to his feet.

'But I did learn something useful,' Astra hissed hurriedly in Cass's ear. 'I overheard a page ordering somebody to restock the wine in the pavilion in the walled garden because the king likes to walk there most nights before he retires.' She gave Cass a meaningful look. 'If you want a chance to speak with him alone, that is where you should try to intercept him.'

'You are all most welcome to Camelot,' Arthur cried in a confident voice that carried, eliciting cheers and the enthusiastic banging of tankards on the tables. 'My beautiful wife, my knights and I are ready to provide you the most hospitable welcome.' More cheering, while Guinevere preened, acknowledging the compliment with a nod of her head. 'We are most grateful to all those gathered here who have joined us on the battlefield, routed our enemies alongside us and driven back the invaders who threaten to infiltrate our lands and raze our settlements,' Arthur went on, his voice lower now and angry. 'Together we will continue to stand against all comers to protect our people and our lands.'

Cass wasn't sure what it was that drew her attention away from the king while all eyes were on him, but she glanced at Merlin, sitting a little behind the king, and was surprised to see his lips moving, his hooded eyes flashing, fixated on Arthur. She was almost certain he was murmuring the exact words Arthur was speaking, as if he knew them off by heart.

'And after we have made you comfortable and feasted with you,' Arthur was finishing, his arms outstretched, 'my knights and I will demolish you on the tournament field!'

There was a great roar of laughter that rushed around the hall like a wave, and Cass saw a satisfied smirk spread slowly across Merlin's face as the people chanted Arthur's name.

For a moment it seemed as if the opportunity to speak to Arthur might come sooner than Cass had dared to hope. As the king and queen swept out of the great hall at the end of the meal, Guinevere caught sight of Cass and gave a subtle jerk of her head, beckoning her to follow.

'Wow. She really likes you,' Ada whispered, her eyes round. 'She only usually chooses one of her chambermaids to accompany her. A favourite. Be careful,' she added, as Cass scrambled to her feet and hurried to follow the queen.

But as Cass stumbled into the aisle between the long tables and moved to follow Guinevere, she felt a strange prickling sensation like cold water being poured down her spine, and in a sudden rush that gave her the impression of being overtaken by a huge bat Merlin was somehow in front of her, blocking her way.

'What a lovely necklace,' he said so that only Cass could hear, and his voice somehow contained the rumbling of thunder and the crashing of waves. 'Where did you get it?'

Cass felt that she could not move, could hardly breathe. She looked down and saw that her silver locket had escaped from her undershirt and hung over her shawl, shining in the light of the nearest candle.

She looked up into the icy-blue eyes and understood immediately what her mother had meant about feeling that the inside of her mind were being examined as she met Merlin's piercing gaze.

'It is just a trinket,' she stuttered, trying to keep her voice level and unconcerned. 'A gift from a friend. She bought it from a pedlar, I think.'

He stared at her, appraising her, his eyes calculating, and she knew that he did not believe her, but before he could say anything else, Guinevere stopped in the doorway and looked back, stamping one of her feet and hissing, 'Come on, girl.'

Arthur had already disappeared, but seeing that Merlin had stopped Cass, the queen pouted petulantly and strode over to them, her opulent dress swishing. 'You keep my husband forever occupied with your meetings and your teachings,' she hissed up at Merlin, who was at least two heads taller than her. 'Are you going to keep my maidservants from me as well?'

Merlin looked as if he were considering his answer carefully, his eyes still steadily boring into Cass's, but before he could speak again the queen seized Cass by the arm, her long fingernails digging painfully into the flesh, and began to usher her forcibly out of the hall.

Cass glanced up as she left, looking back at Merlin's

glowering suspicious face, and as she turned away something glinted at the front of his dark robes, catching her eye. She gasped in spite of herself as she saw the pendant that he wore on a long dirty silver chain.

A metal spiral with no beginning or end.

Chapter 23

The queen kept Cass so busy that evening that by the time she was able to slip away the sky was inky black and the walled garden, when Cass finally managed to find it, was deserted.

Breakfast the next morning was not the relaxed, easy affair it was at the manor. There were no squires lounging on benches alongside the knights, chatting to each other about the tasks of the day ahead. The knights were served by pages and serving girls who stood silently behind their chairs or scurried back and forth to the kitchen bearing dishes steaming with delicately spiced squab, with vegetables soft and sweet and charred and smoky at the edges from being cooked over the fire. Then a sticky plum pudding generously laced with some kind of alcohol, swimming in cream and thick sweet sauce. And unlike at home, where everyone shared the same food, here Cass watched the rich, scented dishes pass her from the servants' table at the bottom of the hall where dark dry bread and grey porridge were doled unenthusiastically onto trenchers.

It was not easy to escape from Guinevere, who found reason upon reason for Cass to remain in her chamber, first polishing her jewellery, then airing her clothes, next spending hours plaiting her hair into narrow intricate designs, then unplaiting it when she changed her mind.

The room was spectacular. The queen's bed was surrounded by carved wooden posts delicately entwined with curling vines and intricate flowers. It was topped with a silken canopy of deepest midnight blue, embroidered with tiny silver and gold stars marking different constellations of the night sky. A heavily embroidered bedspread boasted more gold, and dark red and green thread, and all about the room was arranged expensive furniture finer than any Cass had ever seen before. Chairs were inlaid with gold panels and draped with rich glossy furs.

All the time Cass thought about how to find a way to get to Arthur, and all the time Guinevere talked, pouring out stories of her childhood in the countryside, her sister and the puppy she had loved and had to leave behind. She told Cass about the day Arthur had arrived at their manor, how the famous story of the new young king spotting her picking flowers in the garden had unfolded a little differently than Cass had heard it.

'Arthur was there, of course, but he had his head buried in a book the whole time. He was new to his kingship and so worried – anxious about how to perform and what to say, how to move and speak. He would sit for hours at the fireside with my father, asking him questions about military campaigns and battle strategy.'

Guinevere traced the whorls of golden embroidery on the bedcover with the tips of her long slender fingers. 'It was Merlin really, who found me in the garden. He asked me how old I was and whether I liked learning. It seemed like a strange question at the time, but I have understood it more since. There is so much to learn to perform precisely as I am supposed to. The right kind of wave. The right way to dress. When to be seen and not to be seen. How to best support my husband by keeping quiet and keeping out of his way.' She broke off and clapped her delicate hands. 'A ride. Let us go on a ride!'

Guinevere's eyes seemed almost too wide, their pupils like deep wells in the grey irises, threatening to swallow everything in the luxurious overdecorated room into their depths. 'And I shall dress you up,' she said slowly, her voice

239

breathy with excitement as she gazed at Cass like an exciting new doll.

Cass opened her mouth to object, and for a moment something dark and dangerous swept across the pretty naïve face, something that threatened banishment if she did not comply.

'We must dress up if we are going to be seen outside the castle gates,' she said, her voice somehow dull and hard at the same time.

Cass shut her mouth again.

At the foot of the bed was a beautifully polished trunk of some dark shining wood, and Guinevere threw this open and began pulling out a bewildering array of dresses, including rustling silk and luxurious velvet trimmed with lace and jewel-toned ribbons. She picked through them as though this were quite routine, occasionally holding one up against Cass, muttering about colouring and fit. At last the queen selected a gown of teal velvet, with a front panel embroidered with delicate flowers and laced with fine gold ribbons.

'This should do nicely,' she said, and Cass found herself ushered into a separate dressing room, where Guinevere pulled and prodded and laced and buttoned and coaxed her feet into a pair of velvet slippers that were softer and finer than any shoes she had ever worn, though at least a size too small. And suddenly her hair was being tugged and combed with Guinevere paying not the slightest bit of notice as she first protested that she could tend to her own hair, and then tried to explain that the curls would not do as they were told and were best left to their own wild ways. Now something was being patted delicately onto her cheeks with soft fingertips and her lips stung and throbbed and there was a sharp scratch as something was slid into her hair, making her gasp, until at last the activity stilled and she was apparently ready.

'There!' Guinevere was flushed, her eyes shining with excitement as she clapped her soft hands together once again, bouncing on the balls of her feet and surveying Cass from head to toe in the glass propped against the dressing-room wall.

The woman who looked back was somebody Cass did not recognize. The gown hugged and accented her body in a way that emphasized her waist and the curve of her hips, while her collarbone stood out above the elegant square neckline, her pendant nestled safely beneath. Her hair fell in soft shining waves, some kind of oil giving it a gentle sheen, and the chestnut brown was lent a coppery shimmer by the accents of gold and pearl tucked cleverly among the curls. A fine gold chain fell in a semi-circle over her forehead and her eyes seemed to shine. Her lips were a bright, bitten scarlet that matched the thin slash of the cut across her cheekbone where the guard's arrow had passed close enough to scratch her.

Struggling into the saddle of the horse she was expected to ride with both feet flung to one side and her voluminous skirts somehow puffed out around her, Cass had to admit a grudging respect for Guinevere, who seemed to manage her palfrey deftly enough in spite of the burdensome clothing.

As they rode out of the gates of Camelot the guards bowed deferentially to the queen, and almost immediately excited whispers and murmurings began to vibrate through the crowded streets. By the time they had reached the lower gates to the city, the narrow alleyways were so thronged with people that they were forced to slow to a walk, picking their way through the crowds. But Guinevere, who Cass had feared might be frustrated by the delay, seemed almost to come alive under the admiring gaze and comments of the people, throwing out coins and silk handkerchiefs on every side and eagerly accepting the posies and nosegays children stretched up on shy tiptoes to pass to her.

Yet the moment they cleared the drawbridge, she struck her horse repeatedly, forcing it faster and faster until its tail streamed out behind her and Cass was obliged to urge her own borrowed mount into a gallop to catch up.

Guinevere stopped at last at the crest of a slight ridge where the fields rolled away like great swathes of fabric in front of her. Her usually pale cheeks were flushed, her chest heaving, and Cass felt that she had witnessed the queen come to life, almost in the same way that she felt when she gripped the handle of her sword. For a moment the girl turned to her with a look in her eyes that was half frantic, half pleading.

'Let's just go, right now,' she gasped out, still panting to catch her breath.

Cass was startled, taken aback by the suddenness of the demand. 'Go where?'

'Anywhere. Nowhere.' She raised and dropped her hands in a bitter gesture of indifference. 'Just you and me. We could ride away from all of this.'

'I—'

Guinevere cut Cass off, letting out a strange little laugh that seemed almost to strangle itself in her throat. 'I jest, of course.' She laughed prettily, her breath now under control, and looked back carelessly over her shoulder. 'They would never let me get far,' she whispered, her voice hoarse. And looking back behind them, Cass saw half a dozen guards whose horses bristled with spears, swords and bows, carefully following the queen from a respectful distance.

All the rest of that day Cass looked for a chance to slip away, to seek out Arthur, but Guinevere clung to her with an intensity that was almost frightening, The queen was full of contradictions and Cass did not quite know whether to pity her or to recoil from her in horror. But she slowly realized that beneath the cruelty and the brittle doll-like facade was a young woman not unlike herself in circumstance: uprooted suddenly from her family home, mourning the loss of a sister who was both playmate and confidante, trying to find her feet in a bewildering world of weaponry and politics and men.

Perhaps Guinevere sensed this, or perhaps she simply relished the opportunity to talk and talk to a maid who seemed to scare less easily than the previous girls. Cass felt it and opened up to her more in the brief moments Guinevere wasn't chattering away at her. She spoke to her about Mary and the farm that she had grown up on, not because it was a good strategy to create a bond with the queen, who could be a powerful ally, but because it simply felt natural to share some of that aching loss, and in sharing it to ease both of their pain a little.

Chapter 24

Arthur called a gathering of his most senior knights and advisers the following morning, and, Astra having overheard and passed the news on to Cass at breakfast, they contrived to sneak into the back of the hall at the allotted time. Astra had brought two huge pewter jugs full of water as an excuse for their presence but nobody challenged them, packed as the hall was with servants and pages, squires and nobles, all jostling for position and craning their necks to catch a glimpse of the goings-on at the round table. A witan in Arthur's court, Cass very quickly learned, was nothing like the informal meetings at the manor, where everyone, from squires to stable hands, was encouraged to participate.

'Plans are underway, my lord,' a tall man with a reedy
voice and beige robes was saying, as Cass pushed through
the crowd, holding the jug in front of her face as a kind of
shield. The closer she came to Arthur, the more her fingers
seemed to tremble with excitement, or was it some kind of
buzzing energy that seemed to pull her towards him?

'The statues will be larger than any other in Britain and
will depict Your Majesty and the queen side by side on
thrones of marble.'

'Good.' Arthur looked strained, Cass thought. Merlin
lurked behind him, ever present, like some kind of stooped
gargoyle, his hand clenched on the back of the king's chair.
Cass noticed how frequently Arthur's eyes flicked upwards
to his adviser's face, how he seemed to look to him for assent
and approval when he spoke.

Arthur brought his fingers up to his cheek and pulled
absently at his earlobe and she felt a shiver run down her
spine. Her own fingers often fiddled with her earlobe when
she was anxious or thinking things through.

'Tell me about the preparations for the tournament,'
Arthur demanded, and several advisers stepped forward to
report that the tournament field had been prepared and the
stands for spectators constructed, while another confirmed
that around fifty visiting knights had arrived to take part.

'And we are ready to face them,' Sir Gawain roared,

eliciting cheers that rang out around the room.

But Arthur still looked worried, Cass noticed, and he frowned at the noise.

'Let us hope that your bluster translates to a better performance than it did at the last tournament, Gawain,' Arthur burst out sharply, and Cass, who felt strangely as if she knew him, could see that the fear and frustration in his tone was not really directed at Gawain.

'I was injured, my lord,' Gawain said in a chastised voice, his neck ruddy and his hand automatically going to his wrist.

Sir Safir spoke up, his voice calm but firm. 'My lord, we must discuss the Saxon threat. The invaders in the west—'

'I have repelled the invaders,' Arthur shouted over him. 'The Irish sea wolves have scattered back homewards with their tails between their legs . . . those that were left, anyway.' He thumped his fist on the table and looked expectantly at those around him, who broke into dutiful applause.

Cass noticed that Merlin's fingers on the back of Arthur's throne were so clenched that they had now turned bone white.

'Quite so, my lord,' Sir Safir acknowledged. 'But the Saxons continue to gather. We must plan our campaign. We should not wait for them to assemble in greater numbers before we strike.' Beside him, Sir Elyan nodded his agreement.

Watching Arthur closely, Cass felt her own heart begin to beat faster. As his eyes skittered from side to side, it was as if his fear of being exposed as out of control, not strong enough, flooded into her own chest. She reeled in wonder that she was able to name those feelings without ever having spoken to her brother.

'The Saxon raiding bands have proved easy enough to rout before,' Lancelot said, lazily spinning the hilt of a dagger, the point of which was balanced on the tabletop in front of him.

Merlin leaned forward to whisper in Arthur's ear and the cacophony of worry that had been battling in her body suddenly seemed to quiet, like a calm sea after a squall. But though it should have been a relief, she felt only cold fear, as Merlin straightened with a slight smile playing about his lips above the grizzled beard. And Arthur, his eyes hardening, jaw clenched, spoke again, not directly to Safir but to the whole room.

'Of course we are fully aware of the threat from the Saxons,' Arthur declared, his tone firm and controlled. 'Our scouts monitor the situation and report to me personally every other day.'

'Naturally these reports are not made to every lower knight, but directly to the king,' Merlin chipped in, his malevolent gaze lingering on Sir Safir, whose frown deepened.

'And I am happy to be able to reveal,' Arthur continued, his voice carrying around the hall, 'that King Ceredig, our ally and a fearsome fighter, journeys already to meet our foes. With the support of several fyrds from around Britain, and, naturally, with my strategic instruction, he will confront the Saxons where they gather, near Deva, and will rid the land of them for good.'

Cass and Astra exchanged shocked looks. So Arthur already knew about Deva and the Saxons gathering there. Then what on earth was he doing feasting at Camelot and preparing a tournament instead of riding to meet them, with or without King Ceredig's support? Should she try to shout now, to add her voice to the melee? Would anyone listen to her? She glanced nervously behind her at the guards with spears and swords who stood at the entrance to the hall.

'My lord,' Sir Safir tried again, and Cass saw that Sir Elyan was whispering urgently in his ear. 'My scouts suggest the Saxons may number too many for King Ceredig and his forces to—'

'*Your* scouts?' Merlin's voice was not raised and yet it cut like a dagger through the air and Cass felt her whole body tense. The silence became thicker, as all the assembled members of the household seemed to hold their breaths.

'My lord,' Merlin purred, looking down at Arthur, 'is it considered necessary for your knights to have their own scouts reporting to them without the knowledge of the king?'

Arthur's eyes narrowed, and Cass felt as if panic were

gripping her by the throat. She couldn't breathe, her muscles beginning to tighten, her eyes watering. Beside her, Astra looked at her in concern as she gasped for breath. The murmur of voices from the round table faded into the background as her vision began to blur and her friend put an arm round her and half supported, half dragged her out of the hall.

Downstairs in the kitchen, seated on a stool and sipping a cool cup of ale, Cass frowned and tried to clear her head. Astra knelt beside her, worry written all over her face.

'If you are taken unwell, we should—'

'I am not unwell,' Cass interrupted, pressing her hands tightly round the cup to try to stop them from shaking. 'It is . . . something else.' She did not tell Astra that she suspected she was somehow channelling her twin's emotions, because she feared it would sound ridiculous, mad even. Yet she was convinced of it. Already, now she was more distant from Arthur, her heart rate had calmed and her vision returned to normal. But an anxiety remained that was all her own. If Arthur was so unsure of himself, so tightly controlled by Merlin, there was all the more reason for her to speak to him, and quickly. If he was not forced to heed the warnings of the threat the Saxons posed, the result could be disaster, not only for everyone in Camelot but for the rest of Britain too.

Chapter 25

The garden was fragrant with night and late-summer blooms. Jasmine and honeysuckle hung low and heavy, coating the air with syrup. A warm gentle breeze caressed Cass's face as she crouched like a shadow at the base of one of the high stone walls.

The moon was nearly full, and its glare lit the garden almost as if it were day. The stars were so bright that, for a moment, Cass allowed herself to imagine them straining down to catch a glimpse of this meeting of two leaders of Britain, prophesied to reveal themselves by the drawing of a sword from a stone. Then she shook herself and laughed at the idea that the stars should ever bend for her.

It had been some hours since she had left the servants'

sleeping quarters and her joints were aching and stiff, but still she waited, her eyes fixed on the wooden pavilion at the opposite end of the walled garden. White roses climbed its sides, their thorns hidden in the shadows, their buds threatening to burst into bloom.

There was a rustling in the bushes and Cass's whole body tensed, but it was just a mouse scurrying out of the leaves. Cass watched, motionless, as it sniffed the night air, its whiskers twitching. Then its ears swivelled in the direction of the pavilion, and it was gone as suddenly as it had appeared. Cass felt her heart begin to beat faster as she strained her eyes to look towards the opposite end of the garden. A tall figure, swathed in a cloak, had appeared, and was walking slowly across the grass towards her.

This was her chance. The opportunity to confront Arthur, to reveal her identity, to implore him to mobilize his forces and protect the north. And yet she hesitated. If she stood up now, everything would change. There would be no going back.

She waited, frozen, while the footsteps swished a slow path through the evening dew, nearer and nearer.

Suddenly Cass found herself upright, her legs having sprung of their own accord, and later she would swear to herself that she had never made the decision to move. And that was when the man pulled back the hood of his cloak and it did not reveal Arthur's shining crown, but the grizzled, tangled mane of his adviser Merlin.

'Are you lost, little girl?' he asked in a voice that was a threat not a question. And Cass realized it had been no accident that he was there instead of the king. He had been watching her. Waiting for her. Like a cat in the shadows, waiting to pounce.

'Why have you come here?' Merlin asked. 'What do you want?'

For a moment the story about being a simple serving maid danced on the tip of Cass's tongue, but she looked into the ice-cold blue eyes and knew that it would be a pointless lie. Merlin had known exactly who she was since he had set eyes on her. So she decided to risk everything and tell the truth.

'I have come to warn Arthur of a great threat. The Saxons gather in larger numbers than he realizes and—'

But he cut her off before she could warn him about the Scots.

'There is nothing here for you, girl. This is Arthur's kingdom, and Arthur's alone.'

Cass blinked.

'If it is gold you are after, my men will escort you home with coffers full of it, but you must swear never to return.'

'Gold? No, I—'

'Arthur will never know that you exist,' Merlin hissed, his

eyes flashing with anger. 'Nothing you can do will change that. He is the High King; his is the crown of all Britain.'

Cass felt hot frustration and shame bubbling inside her, burning her stomach. Did Merlin think that she wanted to steal Arthur's crown?

'I harbour no ambitions to the throne,' she cried angrily. 'But if you do not heed my warning, Arthur will lose everything . . .'

Merlin took a step towards her, and suddenly a long thin knife with a ferociously sharp blade had appeared in his hand. 'You have threatened the king,' he crooned very softly, and Cass felt the sun-baked stones of the wall press into her shoulder blades as she realized she could back away no further.

But just as Merlin raised the blade, something moved above her on top of the wall and a shadow dropped beside her, catlike, throwing a handful of dirt and gravel into Merlin's eyes and grabbing her hand.

'RUN!'

Cass did not wait to be told twice. Together they streaked across the garden and back into the castle, the sound of Merlin's thundering footsteps behind them.

'Where—' Cass gasped out, but Astra just pulled her on, practically wrenching her arm out of its socket in her haste. They ran up a spiral staircase, along a corridor lit by torches in brackets, their feet stumbling over luxurious rugs and passing alcoves with foreboding statues of solemn men. Behind her, Cass heard a crash and muffled swearing as Merlin knocked something over, but she did not stop or look back, even when her lungs screamed in protest.

'Followed – servant – taking – food – earlier – king's – chamber—' Astra gasped out, to explain how she knew where to go, and Cass silently thanked the stars that she had intervened in the forest that day and brought Astra back with her to the sisterhood.

But she was tiring – they were stumbling more, running slower – Cass wasn't sure how much longer she could continue, and as they dragged themselves exhaustingly up yet another spiral staircase, she saw the terrifying spectre of Merlin's shadow climbing the stone wall behind them.

At last they reached a long corridor and Astra gestured frantically towards a door at the end of it. Even as they began to advance, a group of six armed guards leapt up from where they had been seated and began to charge towards them, unsheathing their weapons as they went. Cass and Astra hesitated, but as they turned to look behind them Merlin emerged, grunting from the top of the stairs, furious and sweating, and they turned back to the shouting guards, who were brandishing their swords and screaming at them to surrender.

Slowly, Cass dropped to her knees and closed her eyes, unsure whether the fatal blow would come by sword from in front or knife from behind.

For a long agonizing moment there was silence. Then she heard the shuffling of feet and looked up into those blue-green eyes that were so like her own.

Chapter 26

Cass had thought the queen's rooms were grand, but Arthur's chambers made them look like a hovel. Handsome objects lined every surface, from daggers in jewel-encrusted sheaths to leather-bound manuscripts with painstakingly detailed maps inked on their open pages. Every inch of the stone floor was covered by great thick luxurious rugs of bearskin and other glossy furs. The furniture was made of a beautifully grained dark wood: cross-legged chairs with fruit and leaves carved all over their backs and arms, screens draped with silks and velvet, and an enormous table banded with polished silver. Torches blazed in the sconces and other doors led off, towards the High King's sleeping, dressing and bathing chambers, Cass presumed.

She and Astra stood awkwardly on the rug in front of the fire, Arthur, with Merlin beside him, barely looking at them.

'I was in the midst of ejecting these interlopers from the castle, my lord,' Merlin said smoothly, and Cass noticed how quickly he had managed to regain his composure. 'There is no need for you to become involved.'

'They were caught trying to get into my chambers,' Arthur replied, pacing worriedly. 'I am already involved.'

'That is unfortunate, Your Highness.' Merlin moved towards Astra and Cass as if he would take them by the arm and drag them towards the door.

'I dare you to try it,' Astra snarled, baring her small white teeth, and Arthur glanced up at her in surprise.

'We have news for the king,' Cass interjected, as quickly as she could, wishing Arthur would look at her, really look at her. But he seemed so distracted that he only glanced at her as she spoke.

'They are beggars,' Merlin said acidly and dismissively. 'Trying to spin tall tales, no doubt, to gain the sympathy of the king. I am sorry you have been disturbed, my lord, when you have such important matters to attend to.' He nodded towards the silver-circled table, which was covered in scrolls with broken wax seals, quills and pots of ink, and Cass felt her heart constrict again with that maddening, suffocating anxiety and panic. He did not know what to do, he could not do it, he could not be king . . .

Again she felt the terror threaten to envelop her, but she fought it, digging her fingernails into her palms and reminding herself that she was Cass: she was standing with her two feet on the soft rug, she was in danger of being dragged away by Merlin before she had the chance to tell Arthur about the Saxons, and this might be her only chance.

'The Saxons are massing at Deva—' she said loudly and clearly, and Merlin froze.

'We know this,' Arthur cut her off, and his tone was sharper now. His eyes narrowed. 'Is this some trick of Safir's? The threat is under control. And if you seek to undermine my authority as king . . .'

She felt the panic heaving, roiling in her stomach. 'I come to warn you that the Saxon forces do not only mass at Deva,' she rushed out, stumbling over the words in her haste. 'They have joined with the Scots further north and plan to expand their territory together.'

Arthur's face hardened; he stepped towards her with his hands outstretched, as if he would put them round her neck, and then he stopped dead and what little colour was left in his face drained from it completely. He was staring at the locket Cass wore round her neck.

'How do you know this?' he whispered, his voice hoarse,

and Cass found that she was overwhelmed with the uncertainty and the pain that was being stirred in him, in them, by the sight of the necklace, and could not answer.

'We are part of a sisterhood,' Astra spoke up, her voice clear and steady. 'A group of female knights.' She paused to accommodate the inevitable snort of outrage that came from Merlin's direction. 'We have defended our lands against bands of Saxon raiders, and learned from our scouts that the rest of their forces are allying themselves with the Scots in the north.'

Cass struggled to find her voice. 'Your Majesty, please grant me a private audience so that I might explain. There is more to tell—'

Arthur hesitated. He looked dazed, his eyes moving automatically to Merlin as if for guidance.

'Female knights, you say?' Merlin asked, and his lips curled.

'Yes. We have the war trophies to prove it – you will see they are Saxon things.'

'It will take a little more than that to prove we should take your story seriously,' Merlin said dismissively, and Cass's heart sank. 'The tournament starts tomorrow,' he said, and Cass saw that his eyes suddenly seemed to sparkle as if with inspiration. 'If you are who you say you are –' his eyes flicked over Cass again like some cold amphibian eyeing its prey – 'then take part. Compete, if you are truly trained in the ways of knighthood, and, if you are successful, the king will hear what you have to say.'

Cass felt anger and frustration surge inside her and clenched her fists as she leaned towards him. 'There is not time for that. We do not have time to play games and mistrust each other. Even now the Saxons and the Scots may be marching south. Every day people might be losing their homes or seeing their villages ransacked. The ride is many days from here; there is no time to waste.'

But Merlin smiled and his teeth were broken and discoloured. 'Fight,' he repeated dispassionately, 'if you wish to earn the right to be heard by the king.'

Chapter 27

Cass sweated inside her armour and adjusted her grip on the borrowed lance.

For weeks her focus had been on training for battle, honing her horseback archery skills and strengthening her sword arm. It had been so long since she had last ridden in a tournament that she feared she might have forgotten everything she had been taught.

The field was far grander than any she had ridden before. The knights' pavilions were bright and crisp, fringed with gold tassels and stocked with fruit and wine for the competitors, though Cass had not touched a drop. Grand wooden stands faced the lists, adorned with fluttering pennants, and everywhere the wings and claws of Arthur's bright red dragon crowded in.

Cass had been allowed to retrieve her horse and armour from their lodgings, Astra walking quickly alongside her, chewing on her bottom lip.

'I don't like it,' Astra had said worriedly. 'It smells like a trap.' She had insisted on posting herself in the corridor adjacent to Merlin's chambers, always carrying a cleaning cloth or a pitcher of water so that she could feign busyness if she were questioned, but really taking careful notice of who came and went from the rooms of the king's chief adviser.

As Cass had led Pebble to the tournament field, Astra had melted into step beside her as if from nowhere, her head studiously bowed as she whispered quickly to Cass out of the corner of her mouth.

'You need to watch your back,' Astra hissed. 'After you were granted permission to fetch Pebble, one of Arthur's menservants visited Merlin's chamber and there was a great commotion – it sounded as if Merlin was berating him and there was thudding and crashing as if he was throwing furniture around the room in his rage. I crept closer to the door and heard him screaming. Something about having your own armour and that meaning you must be trained—' She paused suddenly, taking a discreet step away from Cass as a couple of knights rode past them, so that it seemed as if they were both merely walking in the same direction.

When the knights had overtaken them, she continued quickly. 'Afterwards he sent immediately for Lancelot, who remained in his chamber for a long period, though I could not hear anything of what they said.'

There was no time to say any more, as they had reached the pavilions by then and Astra had peeled away to find a seat in the stands.

The sun's glare made Cass grimace as she surveyed the lush green grass and the lavishly painted red and gold lists. Pebble snorted and stamped impatiently, as keen as Cass to throw herself into action.

She drew a few curious glances, but most of the members of the round table who bustled past were so busy with their own armour and weapons that they did not even seem to notice her, jostling among a crowd of visiting lesser knights who had come to take their chance at the kind of glory only a Camelot tournament could promise.

The king sat in a cushioned chair at the very front and centre of the stands, Guinevere beside him in a pale pink silk dress. It struck Cass how much they looked like puppets with their stiff posture, perfect clothes and matching gold circlets shining in the sun. Behind them, always at Arthur's shoulder, towered Merlin, his shoulders slightly hunched in his long dark robes as his eyes ceaselessly roved the stands, the pavilions and the field.

As she crossed the field to the other end of the lists, Cass saw the queen's eyes flick towards her momentarily, then she snapped her head straight ahead again, as if Cass was somebody she did not recognize at all. And though this was not unexpected, Cass found to her surprise that the queen's anger at her deception stung a little.

Cass waited, as the steward announced the first bout. 'Sir Gawain rides against Sir Bedivere,' he bellowed, and the crowd roared its approval as the two knights burst into the arena and cantered around the field, acknowledging the cheers and shouts. Gawain winked jovially at the audience, his helmet under one arm, and they rewarded him with renewed screams and clapping, clearly relishing the fleeting contact with one of the best known of the round table knights. Bedivere was a handsome knight with dark brown skin and a bald head that gleamed in the sun. Each carried the same dragon-emblazoned shield, and their lances were capped with wooden balls to prevent serious injury.

As each withdrew to opposite ends of the lists and pulled on their helmets, couching their lances under their arms, the crowd grew silent and watchful, waiting for the exuberant call of the trumpets. It came, bursting out into the clear blue sky, and the knights pricked their spurs and thundered towards each other at terrifying speed, their enormous warhorses tearing huge clods out of the grass and scattering them in their wake.

They came together with a thunderclap of exploding wood as both lances splintered, but neither knight was unseated despite the force of the blows, and the crowd burst into applause and they rounded to face each other again, their squires hastily replacing the broken lances with fresh ones.

This time Gawain adjusted his aim slightly, catching Bedivere at the very edge of his shield and it tilted, throwing the tall knight off balance so that he crashed heavily to the ground, his horse continuing on without its rider. Bedivere rose, unhurt, and acknowledged the cheers of the crowd while the triumphant Gawain swept his helmet from his head and beamed around before resuming his place in the lists to wait for the next competitor.

Another challenger came, then another, and Gawain dispatched them all with the same immense force and accuracy, never losing his own seat despite the gargantuan blows of the other knights' lances. Cass watched closely, ignoring the other knights who caroused and drank, sprawling on the grass outside the pavilions as they awaited their turn to ride.

She studied every detail of Gawain's technique: the inflexibility of his shield arm, the way his lance jerked imperceptibly upwards at the very moment of impact, destabilizing his opponents. And just once or twice, with a movement so fleeting she almost thought she had imagined it, she saw him rest his shield on his knee and rotate his left wrist in its protective gauntlet as if it pained him. Then he whirled to compete again, as invincible as ever, his shield held proudly aloft. But Cass noticed that he kept the shield very still, letting the blows glance off rather than parrying them, and she remembered what he had said at the witan, about having been injured at the last tournament.

The bouts continued, each more impressive than the last. The slender Galahad was thrown so forcefully from his seat by the strength of Gawain's lance that he actually flew through the air across the field, landing with a cacophony of crashing metal and wood near the base of the spectators' stands. But he stood, aided by a squire, and staggered off the field apparently only winded, as Gawain watched on in obvious relief.

'Sir Gawain,' the steward shouted yet again, and then a hint of scepticism entered his tone as a manservant whispered in his ear, 'riding against Cassandra of the mysterious sisterhood of so-called female knights.'

For a moment there was total silence on the tournament field, then the knights' pavilion and the stands both exploded with noise. Cass sat numbly in the saddle, watching as if from a great distance, while angry knights remonstrated with the steward and others openly gaped and pointed at her, some laughing, others sneering and goading her.

She saw the steward turn towards Arthur, a question on his face, and the king nod back at him.

'Take your places,' the steward shouted, shaking off the knights who continued to protest and grumble loudly as they stomped back towards the pavilion.

Cass felt energy jolt through her, and Pebble must have felt it too, because she lurched forward, surprising Cass and almost unseating her. As Cass struggled to regain her position, she dropped her lance, and the crowd surged to its feet, laughter and jeers raining down around her. Something hit her on the helmet, splattering wetly through her open visor, and she panicked for a moment before she realized it was just a squashed and rotten tomato. The juice dripped unpleasantly down the side of her neck, the smell sickly and fermented.

Cass recentred herself in the saddle and squared her shoulders, trying to block out the ridicule and insults of the spectators, who were now shouting about her place being in the kitchen and not on the back of a horse. She gratefully accepted the lance a taciturn squire returned to her and urged Pebble forward to their starting position at the end of the lists.

Gawain, who had looked as shocked as the others but, she

noted with gratitude, had not jeered or protested, nodded courteously to her before putting on his helmet. Ignoring the heckling crowd, she couched the borrowed lance tightly beneath her armpit as Sigrid had taught her, allowing her elbow to take the weight instead of her wrist, straightening her back as she closed her visor, narrowing her field of vision to a thin strip. She focused on Gawain, letting everything else dissolve into silence, waiting for the cry of the trumpets.

It came at last, a rousing invitation that spurred her forward, Pebble relishing the opportunity to unleash herself, mane streaming as she raced enthusiastically down the lists.

Cass felt that she was moving in slow motion, every muscle in her body strained to bursting, every nerve jangling with the awareness of how high the stakes were. She desperately needed to succeed: to win the opportunity to speak with Arthur, to convince him of the urgency of the situation in Northumbria and implore him to send his forces to bring relief. And, finally, to meet the brother she had never known.

As if time had slowed almost to a crawl, she saw Gawain advance, his movements graceful and streamlined in perfect co-ordination with his rippling mount.

She could not hear the baying spectators, nor feel the sweaty chafing of her armour or the strain from the weight of the lance. Her whole focus narrowed to the oncoming knight and the point near the bottom of his shield where she calculated she must strike to take advantage of the weakness in his wrist and have any chance at all of winning. Just an inch too low and she would miss the bottom of his shield altogether, a couple of inches too high and she would catch him too close to the centre of his shield, allowing him to deflect the blow easily and to unseat her with his considerably superior strength.

She controlled her breath, keeping her arm steady, just as Sigrid had taught her all those months ago in the meadow when they had perfected the accuracy of her aim using gold rings that she pierced deftly before they slid down the length of her lance to land at her fingers. But there were no gold rings here, no stern, calm mentor to shout instructions and advice. There was just Cass and her lance and the shield bearing down on her so fast now that it was almost on top of her.

She held her breath, stilled her arm and swung her lance down, its tip smashing directly into the exact point of the shield that concealed Gawain's wrist. He twisted sideways, letting out a sharp gasp of pain, and his lance swung round, Cass ducking swiftly so that it sailed harmlessly over her head, as the weight of it unbalanced the rider and he slipped out of his saddle and crashed onto the grass.

Then everything suddenly returned to its normal speed and volume, and the waves of shrieks and boos emanating from the stands rang inside her helmet as the bright blur of the pavilions rushed towards her and the steward announced her as the victor in the joust. She glanced up at the stands and saw Arthur clapping politely and Merlin's lip curling away from his teeth behind the king.

Gawain stiffly clambered to his feet, looking a little dazed, and over by the pavilions Cass could see his brothers bursting with laughter at his defeat. But he merely nodded to Cass and walked off the field, rubbing his wrist.

It was not over yet. The other knights had dismounted, and drawn their swords, their mocking laughter now turning to low muttering, and Cass, watching the glowering darkness on Merlin's face, knew that she must also triumph in single combat to satisfy his conditions for earning an audience with the king.

Cass eyed the other knights warily. Their armour was newer and more expensive than hers, with more pieces of metal. Their swords were expertly made, and Cass knew as well as anyone in Britain the tales of their prodigious skill in combat. In both height and weight there was not one of the knights of the round table that did not dwarf her. Perhaps the only thing in her favour was that the format of the tournament was different from others she had taken part in, with each knight fighting just one other in single combat, rather than taking on many opponents one by one. Her stamina, she knew, was better suited to a quick and furious bout than a long protracted battle. Particularly because the only possible strategic advantage she could think to exploit was the element of surprise.

They'd seen her stumble in the saddle. They'd watched her drop her lance. They'd heard the laughter and the jeering of the crowd. And most of them probably thought her defeat of Gawain had been a fluke.

So let them, she thought grimly. As she walked forward to be matched with an opponent, she deliberately dragged her leg slightly, so that it might appear she was wounded, and let her shoulders sag and her head droop in apparent exhaustion. And although her ruby-hilted sword seemed to vibrate with eagerness to spring upright, she forced it to trail limply along the ground instead.

It was not particularly surprising that Sir Lancelot let out a derisive bark of laughter when the steward indicated he and Cass should step together into the sparring ring.

'I cannot fight this little girl,' he protested, his voice much louder than it needed to be, playing to the crowd. 'It would take less exertion than shooing a stray cat out of my chambers.'

The crowd lapped up the farce, laughing and slinging jibes as Cass stood still, feeling her cheeks burn but determined to maintain her stony expression.

'It will be a quick fight then, sir,' she replied. And she slipped her helmet on and drew her sword up in front of her at last.

Lancelot appealed directly to Arthur, his hands spread as if to express the absurdity of the situation. 'My lord, I am a champion of women, as well my fellow knights of the round table know. I cannot fight one.'

The crowd murmured its approval, yet from beneath her visor, Cass saw some of the other knights exchange quick looks, and she wondered for the first time how many other women like Elaine there might be, perhaps some who had not been lucky enough to find a sanctuary like the sisterhood.

She felt hot rage flowing through her, and she stepped forward and gave a sharp hard blow to Lancelot's shield. 'Enough! Let us begin!'

Arthur nodded and Lancelot whirled to face her, his sheer breadth and solidity as imposing as a stone wall.

'Step into the circle,' the steward demanded, indicating a roughly drawn furrow in the grass with a diameter just the length of a horse. 'The first combatant to step fully outside the line cedes the battle.'

Cass felt her stomach fizz. She had not practised this style of combat, though Rowan had told her about it. It was a popular way of fighting at tournaments, when knights wanted to pit their skills and dexterity against each other without inflicting serious harm. Of course, Arthur would not want to lose any of his men. But she saw how Lancelot's eyes flicked towards the dais, as he tested the blade of his sword with his thumb, and it was not the High King he was looking to but Merlin, whose eyes darkened as he nodded imperceptibly.

Chapter 28

Cass stepped inside the circle, firmly planting both her boots on the grass, but before she could think, before she could even fully raise her shield, Lancelot was upon her, a whirling tornado of metal and muscle.

It was all Cass could do to remain upright. Any thought of attack, or inflicting blows of her own, was completely obliterated by the need to stay alive. She brought the pommel of her sword up beneath her shield, using both hands to reinforce it against the onslaught of strokes raining down on it. The pressure was so great she was forced backwards, her feet shuffling closer and closer to the edge of the circle, unable to avoid stumbling gradually further and further back.

Lancelot's plan was clear – overwhelm her with his

strength and force her out of the circle at the very outset before the fight had even really begun.

She felt the heel of her right foot slip and knew it had reached the furrow in the grass. She saw Lancelot's eyes flash triumphantly inside his visor, sensing victory was near. The crowd were baying, chanting his name, eager to see their hero humiliate the imposter with a swift and crushing defeat.

For a single moment, he paused, readjusting the grip on his sword, and it was the second of respite Cass needed to think.

Before he could strike again, she ducked, somersaulting sideways round him, and back to the centre of the circle. And as he whirled round to face her, she spoke quietly so that nobody else would hear. 'A champion of women?'

He swung his sword again and she took the blow full on her shield as she rose back to her feet, the power of it sending her staggering backwards a step.

'I have a friend who might say otherwise.'

It worked. He swung his sword again, but the hit was slightly off target – it glanced off the edge of her shield, giving her the chance to raise her own sword for the first time.

'She has just had a baby, a beautiful little boy.'

She heard him panting inside his helmet.

Cass put every ounce of her energy into the first stroke of her sword, and as she swung it through the air, she shouted: 'HER NAME IS ELAINE.'

The blade crashed into Lancelot's shield and he stumbled backwards a few steps. Cass heard the gasps of the onlookers and thought she caught ripples of whispers in the stands. She pressed her advantage, bringing her sword up again before he had regained his footing, this time with a fast stinging jab beneath the shield. It caught him in the hip, forcing a sharp gasp out of him, though his chainmail prevented her from drawing blood.

Lancelot had recovered from the shock now, and her goading had only enraged him further – he bore down on her furiously, and for a brief moment Cass thought of Gamelin and his story about his sister and the bull that had chased them in their childhood. She saw Gamelin's crinkling smile and amber-flecked eyes, then Lancelot's sword smashed hers aside with a clang that rang out around the field and left her wrist singing with pain.

The blow had awoken her sword – Cass began to feel it glowing with energy in her hand and the pain in her wrist was enveloped in a gentle warmth that seemed to cushion it as her sword flew through the air faster than lightning, lighter than a feather, smashing Lancelot's weapon aside as if it were little more than a piece of straw.

Cass did not hear the gasps of the crowd now, nor was she aware that Lancelot swore inside his helmet in disbelief, that Merlin's eyes flashed or that the High King rose from his seat. She was lost in the power that consumed her, in the dance to music only she could hear. She parried every attack Lancelot attempted with ease, sweeping his sword aside and returning each stroke with two of her own – harder, faster and more cleverly aimed than his.

Little by little she forced him backwards, inching forward with every blow until she aimed a particularly vicious strike at his unprotected armpit from below and he gave a sharp cry of pain and stepped backwards, one foot entirely outside the circle.

Then the shrieks and cries of the crowd increased to such a pitch that Cass looked up and saw Arthur leaping from the stands, running towards them, drawing his own sword, the great Excalibur, though he wore no armour and carried no shield.

'I invoke my right as king,' he roared, and Lancelot stepped out of the circle without a word, allowing Arthur to take his place facing Cass.

Her whole body buzzed and thrummed with the golden thread of power that flowed between her and the sword, but as she faced Arthur he seemed to be glowing too, his sword shining with an other-worldly light. When the two weapons neared each other sparks seemed to fly and crackle between them.

It was like a dream. A never-ending whirl of thrusts and

parries, swipes and feints, blurred together so fast that it was all Cass could do to hold on, to remain in her body as the power surged through her veins. And then there was the strange dreamlike experience of seeing his eyes, so like her own, widen in wonder, the green and the blue swirling together. The pale face beneath the freckles like fighting a ghost in the mirror.

It seemed to go on for hours, days, seconds. They chased each other round the circle like flowing water, neither one ever putting a toe outside it. And throughout it all, despite the eeriness and the exhaustion, four words thrummed in Cass's ears like the beating of a drum. *He is my twin. He is my twin. He is my twin.* She knew it to be true now beyond doubt, knew it in her bones and her tingling fingers and her skin that shivered with power.

Then there came a shout from the steward that the time limit had expired, that the fight was officially declared a draw, and she stopped, dazed, and Arthur stared at her, gasping for breath, looking as shocked as she was, as if he, too, were rousing from a strange waking dream. And without waiting for Merlin, without acknowledging the spectators in the stands, without speaking to his knights or shaking Cass's hand as joint victors should have done, he simply said, 'Come,' and turned back towards the castle, leaving her to follow him.

Chapter 29

When they reached Arthur's chamber, he instructed the armed guards at the door to allow nobody to enter, then swept inside, with Cass in his wake.

Arthur crossed the room to two ornate chairs on either side of a fabulously high fireplace, each piled with soft sheepskin, and unstoppered a bottle of wine that sat on a small table between them. Sitting heavily, he poured a large goblet of wine and, wordlessly gesturing Cass towards the other chair, began to drink.

She walked slowly across the room, pulling off her helmet and gauntlets, and sat stiffly, feeling the sharp ache of her muscles subside and shaking her head as Arthur moved his hand towards the wine again.

'Tell me everything,' he said quietly, and Cass felt her chest crack open with relief.

It was difficult to know where to begin. She tried to start with the sisterhood, but he had so many questions that she had to jump backwards, to her childhood, and then forward again, to everything her mother had told her.

'Not my mother,' she corrected herself slowly. 'The woman who adopted me. When Merlin took me to her on my real father – *our* real father's – instructions.' He opened his mouth, but she reached into her clothing and brought out the locket with the dragon engraved in it and held it out to him without a word.

Arthur did not seem able to speak. But he did not need to. She could feel it all. The thrill of the shock. The panic this unexpected news had broken open inside him. The confusingly entangled urges to eject her from his chambers and to embrace her.

He half rose from his chair, sat down again abruptly, rose again, took a few steps towards the door, turned on his heel and walked back towards her, reached out a hand and then dropped it fitfully back to his side. After he had stared at her for a few long moments more, Arthur crossed the room to a beautifully carved wooden chest and drew out of it a velvet pouch. Coming back to Cass, he undid the drawstring and shook out into his palm a silver locket so like her own that she drew it out of her armour, as if to check it was still there.

'I thought I must have been mistaken, when I saw you wearing it,' he muttered.

They held them side by side, then Cass's open to display the engraving. He turned his own over to show her the same tiny dragon carved into it.

'My father . . .' He stopped and looked at her. '*Our* father . . .' He paused again, his eyes searching her face as if looking for signs of their kinship. 'He told me he had ordered Merlin to leave the locket with me so I would always be marked as the son of Uther Pendragon, the future king,' he said quietly. 'I never really knew him. Merlin told me later that my birth had to be concealed because of the circumstances . . .' He trailed off again, uncomfortably this time. 'I had to be kept hidden away. I was not brought to court until shortly before Uther died. And it was always Merlin I spent most time with, not the king.'

She felt her breathing slow and knew that he was calming, not much but enough for them to be able to talk. 'Our mother?'

'Tricked. By Merlin at our father's behest. He had become obsessed with her beauty and consumed with his desire to possess her.'

Cass flinched. She knew the story but she had tried not to think about it too much since learning of her true parentage.

Merlin had used dark magic to confuse their mother, Igraine, so the story went, making her believe that Uther was really her husband, Gorlois of Cornwall. Uther had entered her chamber and Arthur had been conceived that night. *And me too*, she thought with a jolt.

She had always hated the way the story was told; the words were all wrong. Desire, confusion, conception, instead of power, lies and rape.

'She died soon after I came to court.' Arthur paused, looking down into his wine. 'She did not want to know me, and I cannot blame her.'

He poured himself another goblet of wine. 'It was only really after Uther's death that Merlin announced who I was. Not everybody was willing to believe that Uther had an illegitimate son or that he was the rightful heir to the throne. But then there was the sword and the stone, and that seemed to convince them.'

Cass felt light-headed. It seemed unreal to be sitting here in the High King's private chambers, hearing him describe how he had come to the throne.

'I am sorry,' he said a little stiffly, 'for asking you to prove yourself. But it is difficult to know who I can trust. And uncertainty causes panic.' He took a long sip of his wine. 'Give them certainty, Merlin always said. Give them certainty and you will have control.'

'Control for you or for him?' Cass asked without thinking, and she saw immediately that she had gone too far. She felt it: a hot rush of fury that took her by surprise and seemed to burn inside her stomach.

'He has been good to me,' Arthur retorted sharply. 'Closer to a father than Uther by a long way. It was his guidance that helped me to repel the Irish sea wolves and the Picts, his guidance that led me to ally with the military leaders who had the experience and the knowledge I did not.'

His guidance that helped those shining victories to pile up at the feet of the newly crowned king? Cass wondered, remembering the excitement and celebration that had spread giddily through her village when news had reached them of the dazzling victories and heroic exploits of the new young king. The loyalty that Arthur inspired also gave him control. All at the hand of Merlin.

'I do not trust him,' she began vehemently, wondering how to put into words what she had seen on the tournament field, her suspicion that Lancelot had been acting on Merlin's orders when he had fought her so fiercely. But what proof did she have?

'You do not know him,' Arthur snapped angrily, speaking as the king now, not as a brother.

Cass looked at him, noticing how he swept his golden-brown curls impatiently out of his eyes just as she did, how his right eyebrow rose like hers when he was angry. She didn't want to argue with him. She wanted to drink him in, to ask him more, to find out what else they had in common, to talk to him for hours about their childhoods, about their real parents. To ask him if he could sense her in the same way she seemed to feel so connected to him. But the urgency of her mission weighed heavy on her. There would be time for all that later. Already it might be too late.

But as she opened her mouth to speak to him about the threat, about the alliance between the Saxons and the Scots, the door crashed open and Merlin filled the doorway, his face contorted with rage. Though he quickly rearranged his features into an expression of deference as he approached Arthur, Cass could see plainly that blue fire still burned in his eyes.

'My lord,' he began, and Cass could tell that he was thinking quickly as he played for time, picking up the wine bottle and then moving over towards a table, his back to them, as the splashing of wine pouring into goblets could be heard.

'Do not tell me not to believe it, Merlin,' Arthur said warningly, and he picked up the lockets and thrust them towards Merlin as he turned. 'She has the locket. The very same locket I was told was proof of my birthright.'

'And so it is,' Merlin snapped back. 'Proof that you are the once and future king, you alone. And has it not proved so? Have you not repelled your enemies and begun already to unite Britain as it has never stood united before? Do you really want to risk all that for the jealous ambitions of a cunning country girl who was never supposed to leave her farm?'

'Jealous? Ambitions?' Cass interjected angrily, leaping to her feet. 'I already told you, I have no desire to rule, sir, if that is your concern. I have only come to warn of gathering forces that threaten precisely the peace and unity you are so proud of.' Though she could not help herself from muttering, 'Not that it has been entirely Arthur's doing or yours to achieve it.'

This seemed to inflame Merlin's rage still further.

'Stupid girl,' he hissed, seeming to expand until he filled her field of vision. 'You understand nothing of kingship, nothing of peace and battle and glory. I chose *you*, Arthur,' he blazed, rounding on the king. 'She was the spare, an unexpected complication. I left her with a decent enough family, where she would grow up happy and ignorant. But now she comes back to threaten everything we have built together.'

'I have no fight with you,' Cass insisted, refusing to be cowed. 'We are on the same side. But we must ride north, and quickly, if Arthur's forces are to face the Saxon threat in time.'

'Impossible,' Merlin snapped, before Arthur could open his lips. 'Arthur rides west to join King Ceredig and to repel the invaders, as he has done so successfully before. And the legends will show it was his arrival that swung the battle in Britain's favour.'

Cass laughed incredulously. 'So you hold his forces back until the last moment in order to sweep in and claim the glory?' she scoffed scathingly. 'And you would pursue that glory at the cost of catastrophe in the north?'

Vaguely she was aware that Arthur was stirring beside her, raising his hands to his temples, a frown line appearing between his eyebrows.

'Catastrophe?' Merlin spat. 'We have only your word that there is any such threat. It would suit you very well, I am sure, to send Arthur off on a wild goose chase to offend our Scottish allies and leave you here to spin your lies in his absence.'

Cass laughed in furious disbelief. 'There are no lies!' She did not think she had ever been so angry. She felt hot blood pounding in her ears, and when she glanced sideways at Arthur and saw his fists tensed in an exact mirror of her own she knew that he felt it – felt her fury just as she had felt his fear and panic.

'Are you so consumed with power that you cannot comprehend any other motivation? My friends will die if we do not act. They and thousands of others in the north. And then your precious united Britain will fall to pieces as it is picked apart from different directions by the vultures you ignored even when you were warned of their coming!'

'Enough!' Arthur yelled, holding up both his hands to silence them. 'Let me think. I must think.'

Merlin, panting slightly, looked down at the young king. 'Of course, my lord.' He bowed his head. 'And in the meantime, we will drink to Britain if we are truly all on the same side.' And he thrust a goblet full of ruby-coloured liquid into Cass's reluctant hands.

'Why?' he sneered at her, with a suspicious look, as she tried to pass the goblet back to him. 'Why will you not drink a toast to Britain if you truly have no ulterior motive here?'

Cass noticed that Arthur's eyes flicked worriedly towards her at these words, so she raised the goblet to her lips and drank a deep draught of the wine within, before placing it down on the table. 'I mean to cause you no difficulty, Arthur,' she tried again, willing him to listen. 'I come only to warn you of a terrible threat before it is too late.'

'We could ride to Ceredig first,' Arthur said slowly, his eyes still on Cass. 'And from there travel north—'

'NO,' Cass shouted, frustration shooting out of her, completely forgetting that she was addressing a king. 'There is no time. Leave Ceredig and the others to the west – he has the Northumbrian fyrd at his disposal already and others have ridden to his aid. You must ride north immediately.'

Merlin took a quick threatening step in front of Cass, his body far too close to hers, and she smelled the grease and the tang of rotten food that came from his beard. 'You will know your place,' he hissed. 'You will know what happens to those who dare to challenge the High King.' And his eyes seemed to shimmer and to change, with a deep green emerging from the centre like a whirlpool, spinning so fast that Cass thought she might be sucked into them if she did not look away.

With a gargantuan effort she dragged her gaze elsewhere, and found herself panting, her hands clammy.

It happened very, very slowly. The room tilted slightly to the left. It was strange because Cass thought she was standing quite still, but then everything, from the richly cushioned chairs to the golden goblets started sliding almost imperceptibly to one side, so that things started crashing up against each other at the edge of her field of vision. Things were not where they were meant to be. Her stomach lurched.

Fear wrapped its tendrils round her and slowly began to tighten. She could not fill her lungs with air. This was surely the magic people whispered of when they spoke of Merlin. He smiled softly at her from a great distance away, as she gasped and fell backwards into the chair.

Somewhere, faintly, she thought she could hear laughter, or was it shouting? A woman's tone and the angry raised voices of the guards. But they all seemed far away, as her throat tightened and everything blurred, until darkness swallowed her whole.

Chapter 30

When Cass woke, her mouth was so dry it felt grainy, as if she had swallowed dirt. She gagged, and a cup was placed gently into her hands. She gulped at the warm liquid gratefully, though it had a strange bitter taste. Her head swam and her thoughts were muddled. She was lying in a bed and sunlight was streaming in through the window, but the room was hot and muggy and somehow hazy.

She turned her head to the side and winced as pain shot through her skull and her neck ached. There was a fire lit, with a small pot simmering on it, filled with water and herbs. Then a figure rose from the fireplace and bent over her and shock pierced her like an arrow as the burning golden eyes she had seen so many times in her dreams swam into focus.

She started and tried to push herself up out of the bed but her limbs felt as if they were weighted down with rocks and her head swirled and pounded at the effort. The whole room spun and lurched and she retched, spitting thin bile over the side of the bed and onto the floor.

The woman tutted. 'Hush,' she said, and Cass remembered her voice as clearly as if it had been yesterday that she had stood under the trees and asked Mary for money in return for telling her fortune.

'You must lay still,' the woman said, and the voice was like the wind and the streams and the creaking of the trees.

Cass did as she was told, not because she wanted to but because the sickening whirling of her vision would only calm when she lay back. Her heart battered her ribs as the memory of the previous night rushed back to her, and she looked up fearfully at the woman and saw the endless spiral pendant that dangled from her neck.

'You have the same magic?' she asked, her voice scratchy and hoarse. 'You and Merlin?'

The woman laughed, and the myriad lines and grooves on her weather-beaten face tightened and puckered, though her eyes shone as bright as ever. 'Not magic in the sense you are thinking of,' she replied gently, patting Cass's hand with cool, smooth fingers.

'It was no magic that floored you yesterday, unless you count powdered mushrooms as a kind of faerie potion,' she continued grimly, and Cass's gaze flicked in panic towards the cup of bitter liquid.

'An antidote,' the woman said soothingly, and she raised the cup to Cass's lips again. 'I got here just in time,' she added, as Cass closed her lips tightly, refusing to drink again. 'If I had not, or if you had drunk any more of the wine, the effects might have been irreversible.'

She sighed at Cass's stubborn expression and set the cup carefully back down. 'You are not the first to mistake its effects for magic, my dear, though others are not usually given so strong a dose. Merlin leans heavily on the use of such things to maintain his air of mystery and power.' Her voice was as bitter as the drink.

'B-but you are the same,' Cass stammered, her eyes falling on the necklace again.

'Not the same,' the woman corrected, and she ran her brown thumb over the swirls of the pendant. 'But connected. Our paths are intertwined, his and mine.' She fell silent for a moment, gazing at the fire as if lost in memory. 'My name is Nimue,' she said eventually. 'Merlin and I both draw our strength and trace our history from the old magic of the moss and the stones, the water and the air. We were present at your birth and we did what we thought was right at the time.' Her face grew troubled and she stroked Cass's hand absently.

'But I followed you, Cassandra Pendragon. I visited you over the years in different guises, though you never remembered or recognized me – and why should you? A shabby pedlar woman, a travelling mummer in the village at Yuletide—'

'You followed me to the manor,' Cass blurted, and the woman nodded. 'The spiral I saw marked on the tree that day in the forest . . .'

'Yes. But I had already begun to doubt Merlin's decision long before that. He had assumed that Arthur would become the heir, and chose to leave you with a kind family where you could lead a normal life.'

'Because I was just a girl,' Cass said quietly, and the older woman nodded.

'But as I watched you grow, I saw that Merlin had made the wrong choice. I came to believe that he had anointed the wrong twin.'

The swirling haze was inside Cass's head now, not just in the room, and she felt like she might be sick again. Was this why Merlin had been so suspicious of her and so angry? How long had they fought over her, over which twin should rightly claim the throne?

'You wish me to be queen?' Cass asked faintly, struggling

to keep her eyes open as her mind seemed to flicker and drift.

'I believe you to be the leader who is destined to guide Britain towards the light,' Nimue answered simply. 'What form that leadership may take, I do not claim to know.'

She offered Cass the cup again, and this time she took it and drank deeply and immediately the thick fog in her head seemed to clear a little.

'I think you have made a mistake,' Cass began, and the woman smiled.

'And that is a very good example of why you might be a better leader than the boy who never questioned his right to the throne.'

Cass opened her mouth again, but Nimue cut her off. 'There are more urgent matters to occupy us now. Arthur gathers his knights and sends messengers to the kings of East Anglia and Mercia. He calls on their fyrds to meet us on the ride north.'

'But Merlin . . .'

'Merlin is gone for now,' she said carefully, looking down into the tea. 'Banished by Arthur on pain of death. Though I have no doubt he will one day return.'

Cass felt a wave of relief, of surprise and gratitude towards the brother she had only just begun to know. 'And Ceredig?'

'He has the forces of Wessex and Northumbria as well as his own men. You were right – the threat from the Scottish alliance is more urgent. You must ride north.'

Cass nodded. 'But first I must persuade Arthur.'

Cass found Arthur in the walled garden, pacing back and forth.

'You cannot just expect to come here and start issuing commands,' he barked at her almost the moment she approached. 'I am king. These are my decisions to make.'

'I am not trying to make decisions for you. I am just trying to warn you!' She clenched her fists in frustration, but then she felt it. His fear. The terror of being left to stand alone as king without Merlin's firm guidance. The need to stay in control.

'The locket doesn't really prove anything, you know. Not to anyone beyond myself and Merlin. I am the one who drew the sword from the stone,' he snapped.

Cass shook her head. 'Thank you,' she said quietly. 'For listening to me about Merlin.'

'I did not do it because of you,' he retorted. 'I cannot have one of my closest advisers keeping secrets of such magnitude from me. And when I realized what he had done to your wine . . .' He paused and looked directly at Cass for the first time since she had entered the garden. 'I felt it,' he said almost fearfully, 'the strangeness and the dizzy fog, before you fell.'

She held his gaze, her eyes bright. 'I feel the connection too.'

'Well, it doesn't change anything,' he burst out, and Cass would have been hurt except that she could feel his terror. 'I am king. I will decide our course of action. I am quite capable of ruling without his help!'

'I am sure you are,' she answered, trying to keep the impatience out of her voice. And that was the moment she realized that she could use Arthur's insecurity, his keenness to keep the grip on the crown that Merlin had indoctrinated into him, in her favour.

'Arthur,' she began again, and this time her voice was softer. 'I did not come here to tell you what to do. How could I? I am just a girl who grew up on a farm, with little understanding of the complexity of politics and what it takes to unite and rule a great country.'

She chanced a glance at him. Surely this could not possibly work? And yet already she felt it in her own chest – a gradual unfurling of the tightly clenched anger and fear that were bound so closely together. 'I came to ask – to beg – for your help. Northumbria will not survive without you. Its people cry out your name. They look for you to ride to their rescue, for their king to save them.'

Cass stopped, worried she was overdoing it, but Arthur was already imagining the adoring crowds. She could feel his chest expanding with relief and imagined glory.

'I will consider it,' was all he said. But she went away with a small smile on her lips. And it did not surprise her when she was summoned to his chambers the next morning.

'I have decided we will ride to Northumbria. We will leave Ceredig to drive out the Saxons and defend Deva. The northern threat is more severe as it endangers my alliance with the Scottish kings. They will come to wish they had never betrayed me.'

Cass nodded, sensing that the less she said the better. If Arthur needed to believe this was all his idea, then so be it. Just as long as he came. But her gratitude that he would leverage his considerable forces to strengthen the northern border was not enough to prevent her from having one more difficult but necessary conversation.

It was not hard to convince Arthur of the realities of Lancelot's behaviour, of his treatment and abandonment of Elaine and his attempts to kidnap his baby son. What was more of a challenge, however, to Cass's dismay, was convincing him that this was a problem.

'The child is his, is it not?' he asked distractedly, already returning to the papers on his desk, already consulting maps and making plans.

'It is a tactical choice, not a moral one,' she said coolly, hating herself for taking this approach. 'Angharad and the others will never give you the information you need to find and fight the

Saxon–Scots alliance unless Elaine and her child are protected. And Lancelot is a loyal deputy to leave here in your place.'

Arthur's eyes flickered and Cass knew he was thinking of Sir Safir, who she had not seen anywhere in the castle since the witan. 'Then I will order him to stay in Camelot and protect Guinevere,' Arthur capitulated ill-temperedly. 'She is just a child playing at being queen, chosen by Merlin to charm the crowds. She cannot stay here alone anyway. I'll fabricate some pomp about him becoming the queen's most loyal chief knight-protector.'

He pushed a distracted hand through his curls, only serving to make them even wilder, and Cass hid a smile, because even when he infuriated and baffled her there were moments when it was like looking into a pond and seeing her own reflection.

Cass frowned. 'Is that wise, my lord, given his behaviour towards women?'

'Nonsense.' Arthur waved the question away. 'She is untouchable. And Lancelot may be many things but he is loyal.'

Cass was already moving towards the exit, sensing that Arthur's temper was subsiding into weariness, that he needed respite from all this turmoil.

And as she left she saw him sink down onto a stone bench and close his eyes.

Chapter 31

The ride north was very different to Cass and Astra's journey to Camelot. It was an awesome sight, the crowd of knights with their shining helmets and eye-catching white and red shields pouring through the streets and out of the city walls. Their warhorses gleamed and tossed their proud heads, and the standard bearers hoisted their flags high. Neatly covered wagons drawn by oxen and loaded with tents and supplies and even a field forge rolled smoothly behind them.

Everywhere they rode, people came out to cheer and wave and shout their support, with women throwing flowers at the hooves of the knights' horses and children running alongside them for as long as they could until they faded into the distance, still laughing breathlessly and waving with all their might. She saw how they seemed to adore Arthur, their cries reaching fever pitch as he passed without a helmet, the better to allow his crown to shine in the sun, and how their cheers straightened his back and flushed his cheeks.

This all seemed strange to Cass, who had seen battle and knew the grim reality they rode towards. These people had little idea, she thought, of the smell of blood and burning flesh, or the cost of knowing you had taken a life. For them, she supposed, it was a simple matter of defeating the faceless enemy and securing their safety. Allowing their lives to continue undisrupted. And for the first time Cass wondered about the ordinary people the Saxons had left behind. Had they cheered and waved handkerchiefs as those tall broad-shouldered men with guttural accents had ridden away from their towns and villages, laden with armour and weapons? Had they thought of the future attacks those men and their weapons would carry out as a distant, unreal necessity?

The days were gruelling, with great distances covered between dawn and dusk. There was no time to waste, and Cass was glad of the pace, urging Pebble onwards to keep up with the bigger horses. The further north they drew, the more acutely her fears crystallized, and the harder it became not to see the manor burn in her sleep.

But the nights were jovial and filled with laughter and

feasting beside campfires, and Cass soon became more familiar with the various knights of Arthur's fellowship.

Galahad, Cass noticed, was quiet and softly spoken, and kept himself apart from the other knights. He retired earlier than they did and Cass learned he had a reputation for being particularly abstemious, only drinking the weakest ale and eating a very plain diet.

Bedivere was kind and protective, always riding close to Arthur as if he saw it as his personal duty to protect the king from any danger.

The three brothers, Gawain, Agravain and Gareth, the first three of a five-strong clan to be sent to Arthur's court by their father, King Lot of Orkney, were a close-knit, jolly bunch, quick with jokes and raucous laughter, usually at one another's expense. It was their custom to sit together at dinner each night, and, alongside many of the other knights, to revisit their past conflicts and victories, occasionally accompanied by loud and ribald battle songs on nights when a keg of particularly strong ale had been opened.

As they made camp on the first evening, in the shelter of a thickly wooded hillside, the younger brothers seemed nervous, looking over their shoulders as they drove in the wooden tent pegs with their mallets, and when Sir Kay asked them what was amiss, they loudly told him they were keeping their eyes open for any sighting of the gigantic

Green Knight, who was said to live not far from here. Cass looked around nervously, before realizing that the other knights within earshot were all chuckling appreciatively and sending amused glances in the direction of Gawain, who was bent over a stubborn peg, his ears reddening visibly.

'If you should see a very large fellow in green, Cassandra,' Agravain, the slight brother told her earnestly, 'enormous, really, with thighs like tree trunks and hands the size of shields—'

'Then run as fast as you can in the other direction,' Gareth, the handsome youngest brother chipped in, grinning broadly. 'Only first give him Gawain's best regards. And whatever you do, don't *ever* be left alone in a room with his wife.'

'Still the same joke, brothers, all these months later?' Gawain called over his shoulder, as the others burst into peals of laughter. He straightened and turned at last, his face shining with exertion. 'I am telling you, it happened exactly as I described it to you. I can no more explain it than you can, but it was real.'

'Our apologies, brother,' Agravain replied sincerely, holding up his hands. 'It sounds very plausible, really it does.' Then his mouth twitched, and Galahad, who was sharpening his sword nearby, gave an explosive snort.

'I tell you I met him,' Gawain burst out, exasperated.

'And he had only consumed four flagons that morning,

Agravain,' Gareth added, reproachfully, 'so shame on you for casting aspersions on the accuracy of his account.'

And they all fell about laughing again, leaving Gawain to shake his head and disappear, muttering, into his tent.

Sir Kay was as rude and obnoxious as Cass remembered him, but the other knights were quick to put him in his place. He generally gave Cass and Astra a wide berth, presumably because he considered a female knight to be far beneath his notice or attention, a state of affairs that suited Cass very well. But Astra seemed unable to resist goading Kay, by riding up suddenly behind him and spooking his horse, or asking him long and complicated questions about weaponry as he became increasingly flustered and annoyed. Cass rolled her eyes at her friend, but in truth Astra's presence was a welcome tethering point in the midst of this new alliance.

'Without you,' Cass told her as they sat beside the campfire late that night, 'I am not sure I would ever have gained access to the castle, let alone to Arthur. Thank you.'

Astra squeezed her hand briefly, before rising to try to wheedle some of the less guarded knights into a game of dice, but she flashed Cass a broad grin over her shoulder as she went.

On the morning of the second day, Cass rose early, while most of the men were still asleep, and walked up the steep slope, away from the circle of tents that hugged the base of the hill. Picking her way across the uneven ground, looking for sticks to build up the fire, she came upon a stream that wound its way through the trees and eddied into a small pool among the elegant white trunks of a glade of birch trees.

Cass stopped and stared. Next to her on the leaf-strewn floor was a neatly folded white tunic embroidered with a blood-red dragon. And rising out of the pool, allowing the water to cascade down through her short hair and over her naked breasts, was Sir Galahad.

For a moment they stared at each other, both completely frozen.

'Oh, piss,' said Sir Galahad. She sighed and gave a resigned shrug before wading out of the pool and beginning to roughly dry herself with her tunic.

'Well?' She turned to Cass, and the corner of her mouth quirked upwards at the astounded look on the young woman's face.

Galahad picked up a length of cloth that had been folded beneath her tunic and began to wrap it tightly round her torso. 'Did you think you were the first women to realize the benefits of dressing as knights?'

Cass opened and closed her mouth. 'Um, yes,' she admitted bluntly.

'Well, you're not,' Galahad said somewhat unnecessarily, pulling on a white linen shirt before struggling into her damp tunic. She sat down on the mossy bank and started pulling on her boots.

'My name is Gaia,' she said, looking up at Cass, who was still staring down at her in disbelief. 'I have been a member of the round table for two years. And a much more satisfying and successful life it has been than anything I had to look forward to as a woman, believe me.'

'But . . . you have never—' Cass was unsure where to start.

'Never been exposed? No.' Gaia shook her head, a note of pride in her voice. 'Mind you, I really had to lean hard on that whole "purity" thing.' She grinned. 'It helps with maintaining privacy, you know. But every now and then, it helps to find somewhere remote where I can be myself for a while.'

Cass gave a delighted laugh. 'No wonder Sir Galahad rides on so many solo quests. So Arthur has no idea?'

Gaia shook her head. 'And I need it to stay that way.'

'I won't tell anyone. I promise.' And Cass headed back to the camp, leaving Gaia to enjoy her freedom in peace.

They arrived at the manor on the eve of the third day. It could not begin to compete with Camelot for size or grandeur, but (after the first flush of relief that it was still standing) Cass felt a glowing sense of pride at the elegance of the building with its stone and wood facade, glowing gently in the last of the day's golden light. The guards threw the gates open and dropped to their knees in shock to see the High King ride in with his knights.

Blyth quickly summoned some pages to help with the horses and spoke quietly to Cass. 'You'd best go straight round to the meadow. There's something you'll want to see. And the king also.'

So Cass led them to the postern gate and out to the meadow striped with the long shadows of early evening, the cornflowers and poppies thinning now as autumn approached, replaced by yellow toadflax and pale purple fleabane.

But it was not the wild flowers that drew the eye, but the neat lines of knights, their weapons new and bright, their armour polished, horses tightly controlled as they streaked across the field in sharply disciplined rows, spitting coordinated showers of arrows that thundered into the very centres of their targets with a startling crack.

There were women fighting, their swords flashing against the rose-tinted sky as they leapt and whirled, and Cass was reminded powerfully of the first time she had ever set foot in the meadow and the sheer admiration she had felt for Rowan and the other knights-in-training. Suddenly it was as if the whole field were flooded with Rowans, completely unrecognizable from the ragamuffin band she had left behind not two weeks ago. Their strokes were powerful and precise, their riding accomplished, their aim outstanding.

She felt pride explode, hot and bright, in her chest. This was not a motley band of left-behind women scrappily trying to defend themselves. This was an army, and one any fighting force would be wise to fear. They had used smoke to create a legend, to dream up the tale of a legion of fearsome women warriors with terrifying and prodigious skill. It had been intended to spread fear and confusion, to give them a psychological advantage over their enemies. But now, Cass saw clearly, there was no longer any need to rely on stories and smoke screens. The legend had become flesh.

As Cass led Arthur along the side of the meadow, followed by his knights, a gradual hush fell over the field, as one by one the women realized they were in the presence of the king. They lowered their weapons, some openly gaping at him, and Rowan sprinted over to envelop Cass in a hard sweaty hug.

Angharad approached, her chestnut-brown leather breastplate gleaming in the sun, her sword still in her hand, sweaty tendrils of red hair plastered to the sides of her forehead and neck.

'Your Majesty.' She bowed before Arthur. 'You are most welcome here.'

Arthur and his knights were staring at the women on the field, seemingly speechless.

Cass's chest swelled with pride again and as Arthur turned to her, she lifted her chin and said simply: 'See?'

Chapter 32

Arthur's knights camped in the meadow that night, though Angharad insisted on vacating her chambers for the king. The lesser knights ate round their campfires, but Arthur and his more senior confidantes were treated as guests of honour in the hall.

'He recognizes you as his sister, then?' Rowan asked Cass in a low voice, as they dined that evening. At the long head table, Angharad was resplendent in an ivy-green gown and golden coronet, entertaining her guests as graciously as if royalty visited every week.

'It seems so, though not without some obstacles.' And Cass quickly filled Rowan in on everything that had happened in Camelot. She had managed to speak briefly with both Angharad and Alys that afternoon, and now told Rowan the same story: how she and Astra had infiltrated the castle, the obstacles they had overcome to get to Arthur, and Merlin's attempts to stand in their way before they had finally succeeded in gaining Arthur's ear and his trust.

'Merlin's influence remains strong, though,' Cass murmured, frowning up to where Arthur sat, quiet and pale, looking smaller than usual without the hulking figure of the man who was usually standing at his back. She could see, rather than sense, his nerves: the tightness in his jaw and the way he clenched the stem of his goblet. Here, surrounded and embraced by the sisterhood, it was as if the immediacy of Cass's emotional connection to him had dimmed a little. It was still there, tugging, but further beneath the surface.

Cass glanced along the row of knights and stifled a giggle: the younger Orkney brothers were gazing, completely bemused, at the women who filled the hall, many of whom had swapped their leather armour for silk dresses before dinner. Bedivere and Gawain, along with some of the other senior knights of Arthur's retinue, were leaning in towards Angharad and the king, who sat beside her, carrying out a discussion in low urgent tones.

On a table at the far end of the hall she noticed with amusement that Astra was regaling the squires with a no-doubt exaggerated account of their exploits in Camelot, the younger girls staring up at her in awe. Cass smiled, thinking that Astra deserved all the glory that came her way after everything she had done to help her return successfully with Arthur and his knights.

The most senior and trusted members of both Arthur and Angharad's inner circles remained in the hall after dinner, poring over maps and discussing strategy until the fire burned low in the grate and Angharad urged them all to seize the few hours remaining to them to rest before they set off.

As they stood to leave, rubbing joints stiff with long hours of sitting, she paused and clapped her hands, and smiled as she announced that there was a piece of joyful news amongst the bad: Sir Gamelin and Lady Anne would be married in less than sixty days, on All Saints Day.

There were cheers and the clinking of pewter mugs, and under the confusion of the noise Cass's eyes found Gamelin's hazel gaze for a moment, before they both looked away.

After just a few fitful hours of rest they set off, their combined forces making a bigger and grander procession than any Cass had ever ridden in. She never would have believed that the straggling band of women that had gradually and reluctantly gathered to the manor could have transformed into a powerful fyrd she felt proud to ride at the head of.

Gamelin rode ahead of her now, alongside the other knights who had formerly served Sir Mordaunt, and she watched his armoured back and the way he ran his hand occasionally through his light brown hair, but he never turned and she was glad of it.

Lady Anne had stayed behind, along with the other women who could not or chose not to fight, along with a skeleton force of squires and a few junior knights who would guard the manor in their absence.

She hated herself for having watched so closely, as Gamelin had bidden his future bride farewell, and for the surge of relief she'd felt when he'd touched Lady Anne's outstretched hand only briefly, then turned and ridden away without looking back to see her waving. Cass shook herself and looked away from him to the others who rode up ahead in their bright red tunics.

Arthur and his knights had shown Angharad great courtesy and respect, and Cass had not been the only one surprised at how readily they seemed to accept the existence of the sisterhood.

'Perhaps they think we'll be useful as human shields, if not as fighters,' Rowan muttered suspiciously, unready to trust the new alliance until she had seen it tested in action. 'Or perhaps,' she added, turning to Cass, 'they have seen you in action and think us all supernaturally gifted swordswomen?' And Cass had wondered if this could be true, or whether Arthur's alignment with the sisterhood was more about accessing the valuable information their scouts had gathered about the Saxon and Scottish forces and where they were massed in the north.

She had wondered, briefly and uneasily, on their ride to Northumbria, if leading Arthur to the manor might be a terrible mistake. Might Merlin have tasked him with seeking out the sisterhood in order to enable him to destroy Cass and those who had trained her for good measure? But Merlin was gone, and there was little choice when the manor stood to fall anyway if she did not bring reinforcements to stand against the Saxons.

'They plan to take the border towns and villages first,' the lead scout had reported breathlessly the previous evening. She stood by the crackling fire, evidently quite startled to find herself addressing the High King, but then squaring her shoulders and continuing nonetheless. 'They gather at the mouth of the River Glein – but they have not yet massed their full forces. The Scots have joined them, several of the lesser kings, though not so many as we feared, and they are joined by some mercenaries also, but there are still spaces left in their camp, as though they expect more. They are unlikely to invade until all those who have promised their alliance arrive.'

'Then they are as weak now as they will ever be,' Arthur said grimly. 'And they will not be expecting a pre-emptive attack?' He raised a questioning eyebrow at the scout, who nodded her confirmation.

'We have been careful not to be seen. They expect to take Northumbria by surprise.'

Arthur seemed satisfied. 'With any luck, our victory will dissuade any others from being foolish enough to join the rebellion. We will march north tomorrow and take them unawares.'

'We?'

They all turned to see Sir Kay slouching in the shadows just beyond the ring of light thrown by the fire.

'We have humoured this charade long enough to obtain the information we need, my lord – surely you do not intend us to ride into battle with a bunch of hose-wearing women? And risk the enemy laughing us off the battlefield?'

Cass saw Angharad stiffen, but she remained silent and looked at Arthur for his answer.

Arthur paused for a long moment, and it occurred to Cass that perhaps he was not used to fielding challenges like this directly – it would probably be Merlin who would have replied in his stead. And, not for the first time, she felt a little sorry for the young king, who seemed very alone without his ever-present adviser at his back.

'Do you see any other fyrds here ready to ride north and take on the Saxons and the Scots, Kay?' Arthur asked sharply.

Gawain piped up from the other side of the campfire, where he was lying on his back with his hands laced behind his head. 'Sir Kay, you saw me fight this "hose-wearing woman" mere days ago. She was more than a match for me.'

He said it simply, truthfully, and Cass felt her chest swell as Angharad and Rowan cast her looks of admiration.

'And I am just a squire, Sir Kay,' Cass chimed in, with laughter in her voice. 'It is the sisterhood's knights you really need to watch out for.'

'No,' said Angharad, and she rose, looking at Cass. 'My lord –' she turned to Arthur – 'this young woman has shown prodigious skill in combat, saving the lives of many under this roof several times over. Had she not ridden to Camelot you would never have known of the size of this threat until it was too late. She deserves to be knighted if you would do the honours?'

Arthur hesitated, but before he could reply, Cass held out a hand to stop him.

'I am honoured, my lord,' she murmured. 'But I would receive my knighthood from the knight who created the means and opportunity for me to train, who helped me to see everything a knight could be, and who I follow into battle unquestioningly as my leader.' And she turned to look at Angharad, whose green eyes were very bright.

Cass felt her whole body seem to thrum with the enormity of it. There was an overwhelming sense of certainty, as if every second of her life had been leading up to this exact moment and she had simply been waiting, all this time, to step into the shoes of the person she was supposed to be. The knight she was destined to become.

Angharad told Cass to kneel, there before the fire, amongst all the gathered knights, and she touched her sword lightly between her shoulder blades – once, twice, a moment and a lifetime between the blows – and held out a hand to help her to her feet.

The other women roared their approval, many of Arthur's men joining in, and briefly Cass saw her brother's face turned towards hers, and for once there was no suspicion or defensiveness there, but something that looked a lot like open admiration.

But it was the women's voices that were the loudest, and just for a second Cass imagined Lily standing in their midst, whooping loudest of all, her face lit up with joy, Sigrid giving her a nod of pride, and Vivian and Leah clapping her on the back, and as she threw herself into the arms of the sisterhood, for once Cass did not try to hold the tears back but let them fall freely.

Chapter 33

They rode north at dawn. It was tense and silent, and felt very different from the laughter and joking of the preceding days. She rode with Rowan, Astra and Elaine, who had obstinately refused to listen to any of Angharad or Alys's arguments, threats or pleas and trotted smartly forward with her sword fastened at her side and her baby strapped to her back. Once Elaine knew that Hugh was safe from Lancelot and that the other knights did not know that she was the *same* Elaine, there was nothing to be said to keep her at the manor.

'Remain here? While you fight for our safety and our home?' she had said with an incredulous laugh. 'I would sooner go directly to the Saxons and surrender myself and my child.'

So Alys rode close behind her, full of dark mutterings about accidents and inappropriate environments and recklessness, with saddle bags bursting with milk and swaddling clothes and carved wooden dolls.

The other women were quiet and focused, and Cass knew they grappled with the enormity of the task before them. But there were no fears spoken aloud or questions asked. Only determined faces and white fingers gripping weapons a little too tight. All except for Astra, who seemed as confident and carefree as ever, whistling as she rode and fingering the hilt of one of the several daggers she wore at her belt.

After two days' ride they stopped in the late afternoon in an area of thick woodland, tethered the horses and sent scouts to crawl unseen to the place where the trees thinned. Beyond, they reported, a gentle grassy slope led down to the mouth of the estuary, where the Saxons and the Scots had made their camp along the bank of the river.

'We wait till nightfall,' Arthur said, and Angharad agreed.

It was the longest afternoon of Cass's life.

They could make no noise, light no fire and allow no horse to roam outside the cover of the trees. The guards they posted to the treeline swiftly and silently dispatched a lone Saxon soldier who wandered dangerously close, dragging his body out of sight and hiding it in the undergrowth. Cass waited with the others until she could bear the nervous energy and the sight of young Susan's earnest shining face no longer.

She walked away, back into the thick relief of the tightly packed trees. Their overlapping canopies blocked out the sun, leaving it cool and quiet. The only sound was the breeze in the leaves and the occasional soothing call of a wood pigeon.

Despite the soft, mossy shade, her skin felt fiery and uncomfortable beneath her armour, prickling with a power that longed to escape. Her fingers worked methodically over every buckle and fastening, checking and rechecking, though she already knew they were tight and secure. Her nerves were as taut as a drawn bowstring.

She had fought before, killed before, but never like this. Not even when they had stormed Sir Mordaunt's stronghold had there been such a long and torturous wait beforehand. The anticipation was almost unbearable. There was too much time to think about what was ahead.

She twisted the handle of her sword over in her hand, feeling the cool dispassionate metal of the blade, knowing now that it would surge with power when she needed it to. But still there was a small part of her heart that couldn't be certain that she wanted it to.

She paced back and forth, her boots making no noise on the soft ground, as the woods darkened gradually around her and the trunks of the trees faded and smudged into vague foreboding pillars.

She thought about the role she had played in recruiting and training the women from the villages, as well as the younger squires at the manor, and she saw their faces pass in front of her – Martha, Tess, Elizabeth, Susan, Nell and so many others. Her stomach twisted with nausea as she thought of them, just a short distance away, preparing to fight with every breath in their bodies to protect their home and the sisterhood. She knew full well that there could be no battle such as this one without casualties, that not all of them would travel home together. And the weight of it, the sheer responsibility, dragged Cass almost to the ground and she sat heavily with her back against a tree trunk.

She thought about Gamelin and the moment their eyes had met in the firelight at the mention of his wedding. And though there was no hope of anything changing, the thought of losing him filled her chest with pain.

And she might too lose Arthur, who had so often been withdrawn and distant on their journey, making it impossible for her to have the chance to really know him. The knights of the round table who had come to feel like friends in just a few short days.

Angharad. Rowan. Alys.

It was almost dark.

She realized she had been tearing grass from the ground

in fistfuls, and let it fall in a scattered mess as Gamelin stepped out of the trees.

'It is time.'

And suddenly, without Cass knowing which of them had stepped towards the other, their bodies were entwined and his lips found hers and they were kissing as if they might never let each other go. All the tension and the fear and the anticipation that had been bottled up unbearably inside Cass flowed out into that kiss, as his hands tangled in her hair and pulled her closer, his sword clattering against her armour, his other hand at her waist, pulling her towards him. The kiss deepened, igniting a hunger that filled her whole body with a burning need as she felt herself melting, becoming liquid in his arms.

Then a robin gave its rapid, urgent 'tic, tic, tic' alarm call as one of the horses shifted nearby, and as quickly as it began, they had broken apart again. Chests heaving, they turned wordlessly and walked back to the others together but his little finger brushed against hers and Cass's lips tingled.

She could taste him still as they mounted and rode to the edge of the wood.

The night air was fresh and exhilarating on Cass's hot face. Far below, she could just make out the lumpen shapes of the Saxon encampment. All was dark except for the twinkling lights of a few campfires.

'Watchmen,' Gawain breathed, pointing them out. 'We will deal with them.' And he beckoned to his two brothers as Arthur nodded his assent.

They left their horses and set off, running lightly over the grass until their silhouettes were swallowed in the dark.

They waited, helmets on, weapons ready. At the very last moment Elaine kissed the sleeping baby hard on the forehead and handed him to Alys, turning resolute tear-filled eyes to the dark shapes of the enemy camp and not watching as Alys disappeared into the wood with the child in her arms.

One by one the flickering lights were snuffed out like candles and Cass knew that Gawain, Agravain and Gareth had extinguished their targets. Then Arthur gave the signal and they spilled out of the trees and began to ride slowly down the hill towards the river, keeping their horses to a walk so that they might approach unheard.

Closer and closer, unbearably close, they came to the tents, and still they crept quietly forward, waiting for Arthur's signal. At last, just as Cass was ready to burst with the fear that they would be heard and lose the element of surprise, he bellowed a great war cry, which was immediately taken up along the lines as they spread out, galloping amongst the tents and raining spears and arrows and sword strokes down upon every bewildered half-asleep Saxon or Scot who stumbled out.

It was easy for the first few minutes. There was chaos and confusion, screams of horror and fear. Most of the figures on the ground were unarmed and without their helmets. Very quickly Pebble began to stumble a little and slowed down, picking her way forward, and Cass knew that it meant their way was blocked by bodies. But more men poured out of the tents, and the more the thunder of hooves and the clash of weapons rang out, the more alert the emerging fighters were, some having managed to pull on their armour, most now with weapons in hand.

Torches leapt into life and someone reignited a couple of the campfires, which lit the scene with an eerie red glow as the remaining Saxons rallied and began to fight back.

Cass saw Astra throw a dagger with each hand and then leap from her horse to reclaim them from the bodies they had felled. She heard Angharad's piercing battle cry as she thrust again and again with the point of her spear and saw Elaine at her side, releasing a volley of arrows that pierced the tent walls and drew yelps of shock and pain from within.

She felt rather than saw a spear whistle past her face, so close that it moved her hair, and she heard a sickening impact behind her and twisted in her saddle in time to see one of the village women fall from her horse like a stone, and Martha's face split into grief and shock beside her.

'Martha,' Cass shouted, as she sat there, unmoving,

staring horrified at the body on the floor. 'Martha!'

And Martha started, wild-eyed, nodded, and rode forward again, despite the tears streaming down her cheeks.

As she watched her go, Cass's heart ached for the woman who had already endured so much in her long life and raged that she had been dragged into this bloody war of men fighting for land and sovereignty. Then she felt the unmistakable surge of power and rose to meet it, lifting her sword and channelling the heat and the fury she felt into it.

One by one, men fell at the point of her sword as she ploughed great swathes through the rows of tents, leaving men gasping and bloody in her wake.

Ahead of her, she saw Susan get up, terrified, in front of the fire, as a Saxon warrior raised his heavy shield to batter her to the ground. Cass was not close enough, but even as she urged Pebble forward, she saw Sir Bale ahead of her and the tip of his sword took the Saxon through the back of the neck and left Susan shaking but unharmed, her face white against the flames.

Just as it seemed that they must surely overwhelm their opponents in the carnage and confusion, Cass heard a warning shout from one of Arthur's men and turned, along with the others, to see what looked at first like a wall of flame emerging from the treeline and sweeping towards them like a great fiery wave. As it came closer, Cass saw that it was not a single wave of fire, but a huge crowd of men, some of them on foot, some on horseback, holding aloft blazing torches and readying weapons as they bore down upon the Britons.

The beleaguered camp had clearly sent messengers to call for urgent reinforcements. And Cass's heart sank as she saw the scale of the Scottish forces quickly advancing in their direction.

It was Angharad and her fighters who met them first. Torches sputtered and went out, trampled beneath thundering hooves. The women fought fiercely and the advancing line of Scots faltered. Then Arthur and his knights threw themselves into the fray with abandon, hacking and hewing, hurling spears and loosing arrow after arrow.

Cass did not wait, she could not; she was pulled on by an invisible force that seemed insatiable, burning through her as hot and bright as the flames that flared around her, throwing the silhouettes of falling men into sharp relief. And in the moment that the foremost Scottish king saw Arthur's standard and recognized the blood-red dragon, he faltered and seemed to stumble in confusion.

Chapter 34

At daybreak victory was theirs.

Dawn brought with it a dreary drizzle that settled on their hair in a fine mesh of glittering drops and many of the women huddled together, shivering. There was relief but not outright celebration at their victory, for there were bodies to bury: the corpses of several of Angharad's squires and around a dozen of Arthur's, plus two lesser knights.

Until today there had always seemed a marked separation between the members of the two fellowships; Arthur's knights had kept their distance, even though most seemed to accept the female fighters. But the blood and heat of the battle seemed to have forged a new alliance, and they worked together as one now to dig and fill the graves.

Cass sought out Arthur in the grey dawn, but found him preoccupied, busy with politics and arrangements for meetings to discuss a truce and foundations for peace at the border.

He would stay on with his knights to hold meetings with the lesser kings of the Scots who had been spared. The Saxon forces had been almost entirely destroyed, though some had fled, heading south, likely to join the others in their stronghold at Deva. And while many Scots had died beside the river, a few would be allowed to return north with their tails between their legs, carrying the message of the High King's superior military might and a warning to others that further attempts to ally with the Saxons would end in catastrophe.

Cass did not fully understand this. She knew Arthur intended it as a gesture of generosity and grace: a way to show his beneficence as a king who would allow them to retain their sovereignty north of the border in spite of their treachery, in return for a powerful alliance and their future loyalty. But still it seemed strange and lopsided somehow that ordinary men had poured their blood out into the waters of the River Glein for a dream that kings and nobles would quickly negotiate their way out of before returning to their castles and their lives.

'You were right,' he told her quietly, and she was surprised at how much the words meant to her and the tears that pricked her eyes when he said it. 'Thank you.'

She smiled at him, and then they were hugging each other, and it was not the hug of a commander and one of his troops, but of a brother and sister clinging to each other for a long moment in the aftermath of a great ordeal and the relief of a threat averted. But even as they broke apart she could feel his worries creeping back in: the pressure to strike the right balance now between authority and magnanimous forgiveness; the other allies who might need to be pacified and reassured about the situation; the knights he must reward for their service in the battle. And she understood how the thoughts crowded and overwhelmed him and took herself away.

Rowan had protested that Angharad should be present at the negotiations: after all, it had been her forces who had played an equal part in the victory, and she, too, deserved some strategic reward. But Angharad insisted that she had no interest in the dealings of kings or wrangling over deeds and land and fealty. As long as their border remained untroubled, she said, she needed nothing else. Cass knew she was grateful, too, that the decision to make a surprise attack at night had been so successful in keeping the number of casualties they had suffered low. So they left Arthur to matters of state and made their way slowly homewards.

Cass kept her distance from Gamelin as they rode. She did not trust herself not to betray her feelings if their eyes should meet, not to blurt out something inappropriate if she allowed him within earshot. A few times he seemed to allow his horse to drift towards her, as if he would speak to her, but always she touched her spurs to Pebble's flanks and sped away to ride next to Rowan or Astra without looking back. What was there to say? All Saints Day and the wedding was approaching, and nothing had changed.

When they arrived at the manor, Lady Anne ran out with some others, and Cass felt her throat burn when she saw how she flushed with relief to see Gamelin safely returned. She offered him a cup of warmed wine, and Cass turned without waiting to see him take it and led Pebble away to the stables.

But there was no time to settle back into the pace of life at the manor, or to worry that Susan seemed pale and quiet since the battle. The very next day, the gate rang with the pounding of a spear butt and Sir Kay was ushered into the great hall, where he announced that the High King awaited Cass nearby.

Arthur's travelling tent was grander than all the rooms at the manor put together. The walls were hung with silk and the floor scattered with comfortable sheepskin rugs and warm blankets. There were wooden chairs and tables and flagons of spiced wine, though he did not offer her any, perhaps remembering the last toast they had drunk together, nor did he drink himself.

'You are a formidable fighter,' he said almost reluctantly. 'I can see why Lady Nimue felt the way she did about you.'

He fell silent then, and she realized that this was the closest he was going to get to thanking her or acknowledging that she had been right about the need to travel north, or accepting the part she and the other women had played in winning the battle. She did not want glory or appreciation for a thing she felt so conflicted about. But there was another part of her, perhaps the part that was beginning to feel like a twin, that was stubbornly furious Arthur could not properly apologize, or at the very least accept he had been wrong.

'It still feels like a dream sometimes. I cannot think of myself as the daughter of a king.' She shook her head. 'It is strange enough to think of myself as a knight. Any more than that seems too far out of the realm of reality to fully contemplate.'

'Yet you are a knight. And one of the best I have ever seen.' He watched her, and she knew he was experiencing the other-worldly sensation she sometimes had when she looked at him – the feeling of almost but not quite looking into a mirror.

'I have received word from King Ceredig,' he said quietly, holding up a piece of parchment with a broken wax seal. 'Our forces lay siege to Deva, but it is not enough. He writes to ask for further reinforcements.'

'So you will continue south?'

'Yes. We will pursue any who fled the River Glein on the way, and then join King Ceredig to lay siege to the rest at Deva until we have finished the job. But I have come to ask you to ride with me. And any of your number who would consider joining us.'

Cass did not immediately reply.

She had heard a story once of two dragons buried deep within a mountain, one white and one red. Every night the mountain shook and trembled as the dragons rose from the lake in which they slept and battled ferociously throughout the hours of darkness, only to fall dormant again at daybreak, ready to do battle again the following night.

She remembered the story now because she felt as if something similar was happening in her own breast: an endless and confusing tussle between the part of her that yearned to be a warrior, to explore the surging power within her to its limits and to follow the intriguing golden thread of her destiny and the part of her that still belonged on a farm in the sunshine, scratching the dog behind its ears and lying close to her sister at night. The part that longed always to stay here, near the white rocks where Lily was buried. The part of her that reeled in horror if she allowed herself to think about the number of lives she had taken, no matter how justified the reason.

'There would be rich compensation,' Arthur said, bringing her back to the tent and the offer. She looked at his messy curls and his blue-green eyes and thought how strange it was that two people could be so similar and at once so different. Or perhaps how differently they could be shaped by the situation in which they found themselves.

'I was not thinking about gold,' Cass said coldly, but then it occurred to her that perhaps Angharad, with so many new mouths to feed, might not thank her for dismissing his offer so quickly.

'But more importantly,' Arthur amended quickly, 'there will be peace. Lasting peace. If we rid Britain of the Saxons now, while they are so concentrated in Deva it will be an opportunity to prevent the constant raids and incursions for years to come.'

Cass sighed. 'I will speak to Angharad.'

She made to leave the tent, but Arthur spoke again.

'Do you miss them?'

She turned back to him.

'The people who raised you?'

'I miss my sister every day. I visited my parents.' She paused, thinking to correct herself, but did not. They remained her parents in almost every sense. 'I explained it to them, as far as I could. It was . . . bittersweet.'

'I have never been back.' His eyes clouded and he played with the parchment between his fingers. 'It was not a loving childhood.' She waited for him to elaborate, but he seemed reluctant to do so. 'There was a great focus on training and knighthood,' he said at last. 'I was fostered with other boys of similar ages and we were encouraged to see each other always as competitors, never as brothers. We were treated as squires-in-training, not as sons.'

'Do you blame them? For taking us away?'

'I do not think our mother would have wanted it any different. Not after . . .'

'What about Uther?'

'Perhaps he was more interested in an heir than a child.'

Cass saw the pain on his face and without really thinking she reached out and took his hand. It was warm and dry. She squeezed it and felt him squeeze back.

Chapter 35

They rode for Deva the next day.

'It is our best chance for peace,' Cass said, wanting desperately to believe that this was true and not just something Arthur had said to convince her to support him.

Angharad had sighed after they had looked at the manor's accounting of supplies and resources. 'It is necessary.'

'It is an adventure,' Rowan had replied, her eyes sparkling.

'It is an opportunity,' Astra said, and Cass knew she was calculating her chances of finding use for her various skills in a great war camp.

'It is too far,' Alys said very firmly, looking at Elaine, and for a moment it seemed as if Elaine might argue, but she had looked down at the baby sleeping on her lap and reluctantly agreed.

'We need you here, anyway, Elaine,' Angharad said soothingly. 'We cannot leave the manor undefended for so long. You must take charge in my absence. And with any luck we will return with full enough coffers to last us many months.'

She frowned into the fire. 'If we do not rout the Saxons entirely now, it will not be long before they harry our borders again, from the south next time perhaps, and we will forever be plagued with them, fending them off like flies over and over. Better to do the thing now and do it properly, than to regret later that we didn't take action when we had the chance.'

Sir Bale and a few of Mordaunt's men would stay too, along with most of the squires and some of the newly trained women, who did not feel ready to launch themselves into another fight so soon. But Martha proudly announced that she would ride with them, along with Agnes and a small band of the others, and Gamelin and a group of the other knights would join them as well.

Their arrival at Deva was very different from the stealthy approach to the previous battle, which, Cass thought, was lucky, as their numbers had swelled so greatly on the journey.

So many lords and lesser kings had now brought their fighting men to join Arthur that it would have been near impossible for them all to approach the enemy unnoticed.

Arthur, whose hand she could still feel in her own from the night before their departure, seemed gradually to become colder towards Cass the more their forces swelled.

As they had ridden through Northumbrian villages, it was not only Arthur's name that the people lining the streets shouted. They also called out to the women: to Angharad and sometimes to Cass. Arthur had stiffened upon hearing her name and later that day a reason had been found for her to ride further back, in amongst the wagons that carried their supplies.

Yet he had asked her to come, Cass thought, hurt and frustrated. And she had begun to think that perhaps he truly wanted to know her.

The site of the siege was clear from a great distance, with smoke rising into the sky, and, as they approached, they crossed flat, wide plains towards an awesome sight. Deva.

The fortress was square, with four sides of thickly reinforced sandstone walls, each lined with ramparts, sitting in the curve of a wide, slow-flowing river. There were towers built into the walls, rounded and large enough to provide shelter for numerous guards, and a ditch as wide as a horse's length and twice as deep surrounded the fortress.

Not far from it stood a grand Roman amphitheatre, its walls of white stone punctuated with huge archways. The plains surrounding the fortress were dotted with thatched wattle-and-daub huts, many of which seemed to have been taken over by fighting men, the locals long since having fled to safer areas. There were tents pitched among them, some bigger pavilions, others smaller and more ramshackle. Fires for cooking were surrounded by pots and plates and the charred remains of animal bones being picked over by stray dogs. Cass saw thick black smoke rise from a field forge, which rang with the noise of metal on metal, and makeshift fences used to pen warhorses as they grazed, apparently untroubled by the smell and the chaos.

King Ceredig had set up his headquarters in the imposing confines of the amphitheatre's circular walls, and when they rode in, Cass gasped audibly, along with several of the others.

It was the biggest structure she had ever seen. They rode along a sandy-floored passageway, between two high stone walls, before emerging into a vast circular arena, big enough to hold perhaps six or seven tournament fields. Rising up on all sides were imposing stone steps, steep and wide enough to comfortably seat thousands of spectators, though they were currently thronged with fighting men. Some nursed wounds or inspected weapons. Some ate and drank, others talked and laughed. Still others seemed to be fast asleep, despite the cacophony of noise, swords still in hand, using their shields as pillows.

A hush fell over them as Arthur swept in, and most of the men sank to their knees as Ceredig came forward to greet him.

He was a large man, tall and imposing, with a rounded belly protruding over a leather belt, which was fastened with a silver buckle in the shape of a griffin. He wore a circlet of dark grey metal and a cloak of red velvet, with a bushy black beard that reached halfway down his chest and straight black hair slicked back from his face with oil.

'My lord king,' he boomed in a deep unctuous voice, bowing to Arthur, though even bent at the waist he still dwarfed the young king. 'We are honoured by your presence here and grateful for your support.'

His eyes fell on Angharad and the other armoured women behind her and he raised his eyebrows. 'We had heard rumours, my lord, but—'

'Your faithful service has not gone unnoticed,' Arthur said, and if King Ceredig was stung by the supercilious tone, or the fact that Arthur was unceremoniously shutting down any questions he might have about the female knights, he did not show it, but simply bowed his head again to the much younger man.

'We are grateful Your Majesty was able to rout the enemy so quickly in the north, and to uncover the threat from the Scots before it was too late. We are all the safer for it.'

Cass looked at Arthur, waiting for him to explain that it had been Angharad and her women who had learned about the Scottish alliance with the Saxons, who had worked so hard to get word to him in time and fought bravely alongside him to defeat them. But Arthur kept his eyes focused firmly on Ceredig as he waved an airy hand and murmured: 'It is a High King's job to know when there is a threat to his country.'

Ceredig drew Arthur into one of several pavilions set up on the gravelly floor of the amphitheatre, and Cass noticed that Arthur, who had been glad to strategize with Angharad and her most senior knights when it had been just them at the manor, treating them as equal partners, barely spared them a glance here among other powerful men. *Angharad should be in that pavilion, should be part of the planning, just like any other leader who brought her fighters to put their lives on the line,* Cass thought angrily. But no invitation was extended and the flap of the tent was quickly lowered and secured, leaving them standing, forgotten, outside.

'They can piss into the wind the next time they need our help,' Rowan said, spitting into the gravel.

Angharad's voice was cold. 'Their failure to include us is

far more an indictment of their capability as leaders than ours as fighters.' Then she seemed to come to a sudden decision, and with a piercing whistle she summoned the sisterhood and began to lead them back out of the arena, their horses' hooves drumming up a cloud of dust.

They had not ridden for more than a furlong before a young scout caught up with them, panting and spurring on his horse.

'My lady,' he gasped out, when he had managed to catch up with Angharad, who paused calmly to listen. 'My lord king sends me to apologize for his thoughtless oversight and to invite you and your advisers to join him and King Ceredig in strategizing.'

Angharad seemed to consider for a few moments, making no rush to reply.

'My women and I are tired after the long ride. We will make camp and speak of strategy in the morning.'

The messenger stared at her, his mouth slightly open, and Cass wondered if he had ever had to carry such a message to the king before from even his most senior allies. Then he nodded weakly and disappeared back in the direction of the amphitheatre.

A small smile played around Angharad's lips as she directed the women to make camp.

*

Deva presented a steep learning curve. Cass and the others soon grasped that the challenges presented by a siege were completely different from those of open combat. The Saxons had completely sealed off every entrance to the Roman fortress, with guards posted at every tower and along the ramparts between, so it was near impossible to breach the walls. And with space inside for an entire settlement, including livestock and a running water supply diverted from the river, there was little chance of the Saxons being forced out in search of supplies. They might begin to run out of food when the winter set in, Ceredig's advisers estimated, but by that time the weather would present an even greater challenge for the men outside the walls anyway. Laying siege was not an easy task in the bitter cold.

One hot, still afternoon, Cass was walking to fetch water when a shadow fell over her shoulder, merging with her own. Arthur fell unexpectedly into step beside her, no guards or men accompanying him. It was the first time she had seen him since their arrival and yet he began with no pleasantries or greeting.

'They grow stronger by the day, ensconced in comfort behind thick walls, while we languish out here exposed to the elements and forced to rely on nearby villages and towns for supplies,' he burst out bitterly, as if looking to Cass for reassurance or some magical solution to the problem.

It was evident that the Saxons were confident they could outwait them, and Cass had to admit she could not see any other likely outcome. Each day it grew windier, and rain battered the tents that clustered miserably on the flat plains with little shelter. The leaves were beginning to turn on the few trees that lined the river's banks. Soon the weather would become so cold and supplies so limited that they would be forced to abandon the attempt, at least until the spring.

'Have you considered resuming the siege after the worst of the weather?' Cass asked directly.

He threw down the skein he was holding, splashing water across the rocks, and screamed at her. 'Have I considered it? Of course I have considered it. Do you think me a simpleton? You have a cunning and brilliant solution, I am sure, that you think I and my most senior advisers have simply overlooked? Because you've become so very worldly and experienced in matters of battle during your brief sojourn with women who play with swords in the woods?'

Cass withdrew then, hot bright sparks of light prickling the backs of her eyes as her whole body reeled with anger and hurt, and underneath it all Arthur's own white rage was laced with fear and uncertainty and blazed inside her like a star.

But he came to her tent that night and apologized in the cool sweet purple-grey light of the early evening. He looked at her sword, which was sheathed and stuffed into her pack because she still did not like to look openly at it, and he wrongly assumed she was preparing to leave. Then he took her hands in his and kissed them and he admitted his fear and begged her not to abandon him, begged her not to lead the sisterhood away, begged her to stay and fight alongside him as his sister. And his eyes were so imploring and his worries so real that she softened and reassured him and told him that he did not need to fear fighting without her by his side.

Chapter 36

The atmosphere at the camp was more tense than ever. The forces gathered in the amphitheatre and its surroundings grew increasingly despondent, and it seemed to Cass that they would not be contained much longer while their presence there seemed so futile. Small scuffles and fights began to break out, and one morning Cass woke to see a body being carried away on a stretcher fashioned from a cloth slung between two branches. The mood deepened and became as uneasy as the sky.

After a few initial jibes and some mockery at the outset, the women of the sisterhood had largely been ignored by the fighting men who thronged the plain; they kept to their own tents and never came into contact with the men from their own villages, who were quartered on the other side of the fortress. They took their cue from Arthur, who seemed publicly to accept the women as fighters, although he made little attempt to communicate with them. He seemed intent on being set apart, his kingship clearly defined. But as the men's restlessness grew, so did the reports of degrading experiences, from muttered comments to attempts to grab and paw at them, though their sword skills saw to it that none of these was successful.

Cass knew Angharad was worried because she doubled the night watch who stood guard outside their clustered tents and often crouched by the side of the campfire herself, sword at her belt, long after most of the men had gone to sleep, gazing into the flames, whether she was supposed to be on guard or not.

One evening, after another long day had dragged by, with her feet uncomfortably wet and nowhere to dry them, Cass felt so frustrated that she began to make her way towards Angharad's pavilion, with the idea of proposing that they cut their losses and return to Northumbria.

They would have to leave eventually anyway, when winter set in in earnest, and there seemed little point in exhausting the women who had ridden with them by forcing them to remain here much longer. Better to return in the spring, refreshed and ready to fight, especially given that the Saxons would not likely try to march far in the cold winter months.

She was rehearsing these arguments in her head as she passed a group playing dice, with Astra at the centre as usual. As she approached, the girl feinted, pretending to cast her coins into the bidding pot but palming them at the last moment, enabling her to tell, with a quick sharp glance at the reactions of the other players how they might have responded to such a bold bet. Cass shook her head and grinned as some of the men swore angrily, their faces having given away the strength of their hands.

Then she suddenly stopped stock still.

Moments later, she burst into Arthur's pavilion, after waiting impatiently for him to tell the guards to grant her entry.

'We feint,' she gasped out, panting to regain her breath.

'You're faint?' he asked, looking quite terrified at the idea, ushering her into a chair. 'Is it some kind of womanly complaint? Should I call—'

'Not "faint", "feint",' she spluttered, waving him away. 'We should withdraw,' she began, and he jumped in immediately to contradict her, listing all the strategic reasons it would be a mistake, but she silenced him with a raised hand, and for once he stopped and listened.

'We withdraw,' she repeated. 'Pack up our tents and our

supplies and leave. Most of our forces travel homewards. The Saxons will assume we've lifted the siege for the winter and will return in the spring. They wait. We do not return. Then they begin to venture out. Perhaps they turn out their animals to graze on the plain or make some supply runs. There must be some shortages, no matter how well their provisions have lasted.'

He raised an eyebrow at her, unconvinced. 'And?'

'And that is when those of us who have concealed ourselves and remained behind attack! We wait for them to let their guard down and then take advantage of any lapse in security to enter the fortress and force them out. And the rest of our forces can double back and engage them in battle at last.'

'And if the backup doesn't arrive in time? Or if we are foolishly outnumbered within the fort?'

'I didn't say it was a perfect plan,' Cass admitted with a slight smile. 'But I think it's the best one we've got.'

Arthur narrowed his eyes. 'So,' he said slowly, 'you would remain behind and claim the victory? Paint me as a turncoat who fled and left you to battle alone, the new great hope of Britain? This is just what Merlin warned me of when you arrived in Camelot.'

She gaped at him. 'I had not thought about how the victory would be perceived. Merely about how to secure it.'

He eyed her sceptically. 'What people think about a victory is ten times more important than the victory itself. Or it is if you hope to have a reign of any longevity at all.'

'Then it is lucky that I do not have a reign to think of,' she said lightly, and she could feel in her chest that his fear subsided a little.

Chapter 37

To Cass's surprise, Arthur eventually agreed. Ceredig was deeply reluctant, but he could not disobey the High King, and after a day in which three more of his men were seriously injured in drunken fights, he was forced to admit that there was little point in them continuing to sit outside the fortress walls any longer without success.

'But my lord,' he appealed to Arthur, 'are you sure it is not more prudent to withdraw altogether and return in the spring in earnest?'

'And allow them the time to grow stronger and plan their campaign of invasion?' Arthur asked scathingly. 'It is not a risk we can take.'

So the tents were struck and the stone fireplaces scattered, the amphitheatre emptied and the horses saddled and packed for their long journeys. It was agreed that the leaders of each fyrd would ride with their men in different directions, as if dispersing to their own towns and villages. They would ride long enough to convince any pursuing Saxon scouts that they really were returning home, before turning and hastening back to within a few hours' ride of the fortress. Then they would wait for a summons.

It was an ambitious proposal. If the fyrds turned back too soon, they would risk alerting the Saxons and spooking them back behind their thick impenetrable walls. If they turned too late, the small band of fighters who had been left behind would be horribly outnumbered and unlikely to survive without swift reinforcement.

'It has to be us,' Angharad said grimly the night before they were due to set their plan in motion. They had been talking in circles for hours, and everybody was exhausted and short-tempered. Arthur kept insisting he and his knights would somehow conceal themselves along the banks of the river, a plan Angharad repeatedly pointed out was extremely unlikely to work, and Ceredig continued to loudly proclaim that his knights were the bravest fighters in Britain and should be the ones to infiltrate the fortress.

'With the greatest of respect,' Angharad replied, her voice clipped with exhaustion, 'your formidable fighters have had weeks to infiltrate their stronghold with no success. We are the only ones who can approach without arousing suspicion.' She sighed, ignoring Ceredig and appealing directly to Arthur. 'We will wait a day or so after you have left and then approach the huts and hovels around the fortress dressed in women's clothing. It will appear to the Saxons that a group of the village women have returned to try to salvage what is left of their homes and possessions.'

'It will not occur to them that we might have anything to do with your forces,' Rowan chipped in drily. 'Trust us.'

And at last the men were forced to agree that there was no other viable option.

So they scattered, leaving the grass flattened and dry where their tents had been, and the earth scorched from the forge. And Angharad, Cass and all the other women peeled away after they had ridden for a few hours and withdrew to a nearby village to procure women's clothing and to wait.

'It will be dangerous,' Angharad told them, before they left the ranks of the other knights. 'Riskier than anything else we have attempted thus far. But we will be fighting for the life we have built for ourselves. Fighting to return to the manor and raise a new generation of girls there, strong and free. We are fighting to live peacefully, unthreatened by marauding bands of murderous men.'

Rowan raised an eyebrow. 'And if it means briefly allying ourselves with a band of murderous men to achieve that, then so be it,' she said sardonically.

Angharad suppressed a smile. 'Indeed. Our choices are never simple. But it is my hope that by driving out the Saxons we will rid Northumbria and the rest of Britain from the constant fear of invasion and conflict. How can any of us settle and build a home and a community and a way of life until the threat is extinguished?'

Nobody answered. Cass looked at the women's determined faces and knew that, like her, they were thinking of their families, of new babies wobbling their first steps, and of that sun-drenched field studded with wild flowers and full of free women, where her heart longed to return.

'There is no shame in choosing to return home instead of riding with us today,' Angharad continued. 'I do not ask this of any of you unless you truly choose to join us.'

Not one of the women moved. So they rode on together.

Five days passed, then ten. After the eleventh day they began to return cautiously to the settlements surrounding the fortress, their behaviour skittish and nervous as if they feared the besieging forces might have left some men behind. Truthfully, it was not much of an act. The idea of finding themselves inside the fortress, alone and dwarfed by the numbers of the Saxon forces was enough to make them all tense.

Once settled there, they waited, taking it in turns to keep close watch on the fortress and its entrances, each of them poised and alert, their bodies bristling, with weapons beneath their simple dresses.

Time dragged on, and as the nights began to draw in and the skies lowered and darkened, they began to wonder if the Saxons would choose caution and remain holed up without pause until the spring.

But it was not water that drew them out in the end, nor food or other supplies. It was women.

It happened so suddenly it took them completely by surprise. One morning after they had just rotated the watch, Astra, who was crouching below the small window of the hut hissed, 'Men! Around a dozen of them. Heading directly this way.'

They passed the message from hut to hut and waited, hearts hammering, palms sweating. Urgently, Angharad dispatched two messengers to summon the fyrds, their horses taking them swiftly out of the reach of the oncoming men. To the remaining women she spoke fiercely and fast. Her message was very simple: 'Do not wait too long to fight back. I will not see any one of our number sacrificed for the sake of extending the moment of surprise.'

The men did not speak as they entered the huts and seized the women. They did not stop to search them but laughed and shouted loudly to one another in tones as casual as if they were bringing in the harvest. Some of the younger women screamed, but none resisted, though Cass could see it took every ounce of Martha's self-restraint to lie limp and wide-eyed in her captor's arms instead of boxing him around the ears. Cass saw Angharad's eyes blazing as she was taken, and then she herself was seized roughly by the upper arm and marched towards the fortress.

Groups of men stared, leering and shouting insults as the women were pulled inside the gates. The first thing that hit them was the smell. Hundreds of men had been confined in these walls for months and Cass was almost knocked off her feet by the stench of it. She gagged, as the shouting intensified.

Cass did not understand the language they used, but she did not need to. The tone was clear enough. She was half dragged, half carried towards a row of low-roofed stone buildings, casting wildly around as she stumbled forward, attempting to gauge how many men there were and how the fortress was laid out. Beside her, eyes scanning frantically back and forth, she could see that Angharad was doing the same. But before she could get more than a general sense of dozens of leering faces and heavily armed bodies, they reached the stone building, which looked a bit like a long low stable, and each of the women was thrust unceremoniously into a separate locked cell, the floors heaped with fresh straw.

It was far worse and far better than they had imagined. The Saxons had hauled them directly into the very walls they had spent weeks deliberating how to penetrate. But as Cass sat on the straw, feeling it prickle the backs of her legs, and working desperately at the thin rope that bound her hands behind her back, she thought grimly that it was not difficult to predict what the men garrisoned here had planned for them.

She heard Angharad's voice, muffled and hoarse, through the gaps in the stone wall. 'It will not be long before the fyrds arrive. We will not sacrifice ourselves to wait for them, not like this. The moment they enter, we fight. Fight like hell, and do not let them take you alive.'

Cass heard the hard edge of fear and fury in the older woman's voice and knew that Angharad had been in a situation not unlike this before. She would never allow any of the other women to suffer the same fate.

Clumsily, Cass shuffled towards the opposite wall, still working at her ropes, and passed the message through the stones to Rowan, who was in the next cell.

'Really?' Rowan's voice drifted back, as dry and sarcastic as ever. 'Because I'd been planning to sacrifice myself for the sake of the country to distract them and win the men outside some time to arrive unnoticed. You know me, Cass. I was just planning to give up and not to fight back at all.'

Cass gave a tremulous laugh as she pictured Rowan's slow grin and she hissed, 'Shut up and pass it on, you idiot, before they come back,' and began to rub the ropes against a sharp stone that was sticking out from one of the walls.

She felt it begin to fray and redoubled her efforts, as her ears pricked up. There was a subtle but unmistakable shift in the noise within the fortress. Outside the door, the bustle and shouting of the men had quieted a little, and there was a new excitement and hunger to the buzz of low conversation she could hear. Almost, she thought grimly, as she felt the rope snap at last and rubbed her sore wrists in relief, as if dozens of men who had been starved all summer had just seen a rich meal being carried into their fortress and were deciding who was about to take the first taste.

As the sound of boots on stone approached, Cass unstrapped her sword from the bandages she had used to bind it to her waist and down her leg, thanking every lucky star that it had not occurred to the men to search these peasant women for weapons before kidnapping them. She allowed herself a grim smile. They would soon regret that.

She concealed herself directly behind the door and clutched her sword tightly, hands in front of her waist, the blade resting against her cheek, hoping against hope that the others had also managed to free and arm themselves in time.

Then there was a screeching of bolts and a scraping of wood on stone as the doors to the cells were opened, and all hell broke loose.

Chapter 38

The first man through the door had already undone the button at the top of his breeches, and the sight of it filled Cass with such rage that she swung the hilt of her sword up furiously, with a crack that split open his chin, spraying blood into the eyes of the shocked Saxons close on his heels.

'*Thought – you – would – watch – did – you?*' she panted, punctuating each word with a battering from her fists and the handle of her sword, until all three of them lay dazed and bloodied in the straw.

Then she exploded out of the door, sword held high, and took in the scene before her.

To her left and right, Angharad and Rowan were panting

as they wielded the weapons they had drawn out from concealment under their clothes. Over her shoulder, Cass could see several men tangled in a bruised heap inside the cell Rowan had recently vacated. The room behind Angharad was eerily silent, and blood was dripping from a fresh scratch on her cheek.

The doors to the other cells all stood open, and Cass could hear struggling and swearing, and the clattering of weapons against stone, suggesting that the other women were in various stages of combat with their attackers. As she watched, a large Saxon stumbled out of the door on the other side of Rowan, his face mottled, gasping for breath. Martha was clinging to his back like a limpet, her knees digging into his ribs, her hands clasped tightly round his throat as his eyes popped.

'Need a hand?' Rowan asked casually. She jabbed sideways with a dagger, and the man crashed to the ground.

Martha sprang up, unsheathing a short sword from inside her dress. 'Couldn't quite get to it in time,' she muttered, and she dashed immediately into the next cell along and came out with her blade dripping and Astra behind her.

Standing at a distance, open-mouthed, was a stunned group of Saxons in a semi-circle. Evidently they had been waiting their turn to follow the other men into the building and had been completely taken aback by this unexpected turn of events.

Rowan, Angharad and Cass moved quickly, taking advantage of the fact that the men were unarmed and apparently so shocked that they simply stood there for a few precious moments, dumbfounded. The women raced swiftly from cell to cell, helping the others to release their hands and neutralize their attackers. Cass darted into the last cell, where she found a heavy-set Saxon crushing Susan against the wall and stabbed him in the back without hesitation so he slumped into the straw, and Susan let out a long shaking breath and kicked him hard.

But now the men outside had recovered from their shock and begun to raise the alarm. Loud angry shouts echoed around the fortress as the women gathered in a tight knot, backs pressed together, swords raised. Saxon fighters who had rushed to grab swords, axes and shields began to advance on them, pressing in on all sides, teeth clenched, weapons ready.

There was a long, unbearable moment of tension as sweat dripped down the back of Cass's neck and each side seemed to wait for the other to make the first move, then a huge Saxon fighter with blonde hair and a ruddy face swung his axe above his head with a furious yell and brought it whistling down towards Rowan, who brought up her sword to protect herself, holding it fast at both ends, though she cried out and buckled to her knees at the force of the blow.

Then Astra flicked a deadly knife through the air to lodge in the side of the man's neck and suddenly the air was filled with blades and screams, sweat and blood.

Cass plunged into the sea of Saxon men without hesitation. The sheer mass of their bodies was so densely packed that it was impossible to find the space to swing her sword and she stabbed instead, over and over again, finding soft bellies and unprotected thighs. Few of the Saxons were wearing armour, and she took full advantage of it, letting her rage at the way these men had intended to treat her and the other women drive her blindly forward.

Rowan was at her back, responding to the lack of space with hard punches to faces and elbows to the gut, hardly bothering with her sword, leaving a trail of men winded and doubled over in her wake. Angharad was engaged in a violent clash of swords a little way to the left, and the other women seemed to be clustered in groups, targeting one Saxon at a time between them and dispatching them efficiently.

Cass panted, her vision blurring for a moment, and when she wiped her hand across her eyes, she felt it leave behind a warm smear of blood. She dodged the driving point of a spear, lashing out with her foot and tripping up the man who had aimed it, then ducked as a double-sided axe swung above her head so that it bit dully into the skull of another Saxon instead.

But there were too many of them. The Saxons were massive, well rested and eager to do battle after many long months cooped up inside these walls. And it was clear that they were half crazed with fury at being attacked by a band of women.

Cass moved like lightning, her sword buzzing in her hand, but she could feel herself tiring, feel her lungs screaming for air and her biceps protesting as she repeatedly and relentlessly forced her sword forward. Glancing sideways, she could see exhaustion setting in amongst the others, too. Martha looked as if she could barely stand, and some of the other women seemed to be trembling at the wrist when their swords made contact.

They only had to last until the reinforcements arrived, Cass reminded herself. They just had to hold out a little bit longer.

Briefly the crowd in front of her shifted, allowing Cass to see through the throng of lashing furious bodies to the outer wall of the fortress, and her heart sank like a stone. The enormous reinforced wooden gates they'd been dragged through had been closed again. Arthur's men would have no way in, even if they did arrive in time.

Cass knew she had only one option. They were all as

good as dead unless she somehow reached that gate and opened it. She seized her chance, taking off at a run before she even knew she had made the decision, streaking down the pathway that had momentarily opened in front of her through the heaving, roiling bodies. Men gaped at her as she passed, some swinging wildly at her with their blades, but she swerved and ducked, her terror lending wings to her feet, and suddenly she was behind them, with only open flagstones between her and the gate. She was going to make it. And, better still, she thought that over the din of the battle behind her she could hear another noise coming from outside. The regular thudding beat of hooves.

Cass looked up. The ramparts were practically empty. The men who had been on guard had all leaped down to join the fray below. Even as she watched, a solitary guard seemed to be screaming up there, waving his arms frantically, trying to get the attention of his fellows in the melee below, but nobody could hear him. Then an arrow appeared between his eyes, and he fell slowly backwards to land with a sickening crack on the stone floor, his eyes staring blankly at Cass.

They were outside. Help had arrived. All she had to do was open the gate and let them in. Cass scrabbled wildly at the thick wooden slab that rested horizontally in metal brackets, barring the door from any outside pressure. It was enormous, she would never be able to lift it alone, but then her eyes fell on a metal handle connected to cogs and pulleys and she realized she only had to pull it to lift the bar and open the gates. She reached out towards it, brushing the cool metal with her fingertips, and stopped dead.

A sudden silence had fallen over the fortress. Everyone was looking at Cass. But none of the Saxons were near enough to reach her before she pulled the handle. Then a man who appeared to be one of their leaders was screaming at the top of his voice. He wore a conical helmet of beaten iron, with a flat nose guard, and he was holding the point of his enormous sword directly to Martha's neck.

Cass did not understand the words he was yelling and yet his meaning was crystal clear. Move and she dies. Pull the handle and she dies. Do anything at all and she dies.

Cass froze. Martha's chest was heaving, and one of her eyes was swollen and bloodied, giving her familiar wrinkled face a strangely lopsided appearance. She was looking directly at Cass, a hard blazing look that said: 'Pull it.'

But Cass couldn't. As the Saxon chief kept his sword point pressed firmly into the soft hollow at the base of Martha's throat, he nodded to one of his men, who started to walk swiftly towards Cass. He was perhaps fifty paces away. If he reached her, it would all be over. There would be no second chance to open the gates.

Sacrifice one to save the rest. Cass knew it made sense and

yet still she stood motionless, as the stocky scowling Saxon ate up the ground between them, swinging an ugly wooden club studded with metal spikes.

Thirty strides. Twenty strides. Ten. He was almost upon her.

She heard Martha's cry and screamed helplessly to stop her, suddenly knowing what was about to happen but powerless to prevent it.

'*Do it!*' Martha screeched in her high wavering voice, and she threw herself forward so that the sword slid deep into her throat.

Chapter 39

Cass dropped her sword, seized the smooth metal handle with both hands and heaved with all her might. Even as she heard the groaning and screeching of metal and saw the enormous piece of wood begin to lift, a Saxon shield smashed into the side of her head and stars exploded in front of her eyes.

Everything was pain and relentless high-pitched ringing. Cass found herself on the floor without knowing how she had come to be there and peered up, confused, through swirling colours and flashing lights to see a blurred object that she somehow knew to be a spiked wooden club rush high into the air and pause for a moment before beginning to make its lethal descent.

Cass closed her eyes. She had let them in. She had done her part. The sisterhood would survive.

Then there was an almighty smash and she felt splinters of wood raining down on her face but strangely felt no pain.

She opened her eyes. Sir Gamelin was standing over her, wild-eyed, his sword bent out of shape, and what remained of the Saxon and his shattered club lay motionless on the ground beside her.

Things happened very quickly after that.

Cass sat propped against the stone outer walls of the fortress, struggling to keep her eyes open, while the battle in front of her slipped in and out of focus.

She saw Arthur and his knights streaming in through the open doors, a great wave of red and white that swept away the hordes of men in their path. Arthur's Excalibur flashed as if lit from within, moving as fast as lightning as it struck down man after man, none of them seeming to stand a chance against the High King's wrath.

Though she could not hear her over the din of the weapons clashing and hooves ringing, she saw Rowan, her mouth open wide in a scream, staring down at Martha's body. Then she hurled herself furiously into the fray and Cass lost sight of her, though she saw several men topple and lay still in her wake.

She watched Susan hacking away alongside the other

squires, her face white with terror but set and determined. Together, three of them felled a Saxon who was double their height then ran on to the next.

Arthur and Angharad's knights fought side by side as one united front. She saw Galahad come racing to stand beside Angharad, cutting off one Saxon who threatened to take her unawares with a spear from the side as she fiercely clashed swords with another. Then Rowan appeared out of nowhere to strike down a gigantic brute who had just disarmed Sir Bedivere and was bearing down on him to strike a final deadly blow. In front of her Sir Gamelin battled steadfastly, blocking the enemy from reaching Cass, his useless sword thrown aside and a dead Saxon's weapon grabbed in its place.

Suddenly a body in a scarlet cloak came tumbling towards Cass, staggering backwards from a great blow struck by the butt of an axe. Arthur stumbled and fell backwards onto the flagstones beside her, his sword tangled in his cloak. As he fought to free it, a long-haired Saxon with blood dripping down his plaited beard came barrelling towards him, his blade raised to strike.

There was a single terrifying moment when Arthur's eyes met hers and their terror merged into a single high-pitched keening note, then Cass twisted to the side, ignoring the wrenching pain that seemed to explode through her body, and reached her sword with her fingertips, swinging it upwards in a single smooth motion so that the man who was about to kill her brother slid slickly down her blade instead and was still.

Arthur's fingers found hers just before the pain became too great and soft blackness took her from herself.

Later, she hardly remembered waking to the news of their victory, or the ride home, or the parting with Arthur. Snatched moments resurfaced sometimes and then seemed to sink away again. How they buried Martha's body outside the fortress walls with the rest of the fallen Britons. How King Ceredig grudgingly acknowledged the women's bravery before he and his forces rode off to pursue the last straggling band of Saxons who had fled towards the sea. How Arthur held her tight and promised they would see each other again. How Angharad insisted Cass ride home in a wagon, with Pebble trotting along beside, and she reluctantly agreed after realizing she could not stand up, let alone keep her seat in a saddle.

She longed for the calm and quiet of the manor, for long slow days foraging in the forest with Elaine and sparring with Rowan. For soft weak autumn sunlight to warm her face as her body healed and she tried to teach her mind to sleep again without seeing the blade slipping easily into Martha's throat.

But their arrival was not to be the salve Cass had hoped for.

Elaine greeted them at the gates, her face white, her eyes marked with deep dark circles as if she had not slept in days.

'Hugh?' Rowan cried, jumping down from her mount and racing to her.

'He is safe,' Elaine reassured her, and Cass felt a weight lift from her chest.

'But—' Elaine bit her lip, as if she did not know where to begin. It was Sir Gamelin she seemed to look to first, her eyes full of guilt and sympathy.

'What is it?' he asked sharply, also dismounting, so that Cass had to strain and heave to prop herself higher against the side of the cart in order to see.

'We were attacked,' Elaine told them, and as she spoke Alys came out of the manor into the courtyard to stand beside her, limping heavily and walking with the aid of a thick stick. 'By a small band of Saxons. They came at night – we had guards posted at the gates, but they were too quick and too strong.'

'How many?' Angharad asked in a low voice, and Cass knew she was not asking how many Saxons there had been.

'We lost twelve,' Elaine said heavily, and Cass saw Angharad's face fall.

'Three of our own squires, including Elizabeth –' Cass

heard Susan let out a low, awful sob – 'one of Mordaunt's men, some of the women from the villages, and –' Elaine paused again, then seemed to steel herself – 'Lady Anne.'

Sir Gamelin gasped. 'But she did not fight,' he said weakly. 'She was gentle; she did not even have a sword.'

'She was taking a hot drink to the women posted at the gates,' Elaine explained. 'She was simply in the wrong place at the wrong time.'

'How did you repel them?' Angharad asked, putting a hand on Sir Gamelin's shoulder as he stood there looking dazed.

Alys took up the tale. 'Iona and Blyth were still awake when they came, working on a fresh supply of weapons—' Her voice cracked a little. 'If they had not raised the alarm, we might have lost far more that night. They held them off until Elaine and the rest of the women arrived. We outnumbered them but they were brutal. Several of them were already injured, yet they fought like wildcats. We heard them say something about heading to Deva after taking the manor, but they never had the chance in the end.' She smiled with grim satisfaction.

'I am sorry, Alys,' Angharad said, her voice hollow with grief and guilt. 'I should have left more knights behind.'

Alys shook her head, her eyes swimming with tears. 'You were not to know, my lady. And I am glad of the forces you took with you, because they have enabled your safe return.'

Then they abandoned formality, as Angharad swept the short plump older woman into her arms and held her tight, stick and all, burying her face for a moment in her frizzy grey-streaked hair.

Cass felt dazed and winded. It had been difficult enough to breathe anyway, with her bruised and battered ribs, but it seemed suddenly quite impossible to force any air into her lungs. She watched as Sir Gamelin drifted inside, and her heart ached with grief and guilt. For Elizabeth and the others she had not been here to protect. For the version of herself she seemed to have left behind, because returning to the manor now felt strange and different, as if she brought the ghosts of the men she had killed back with her. And for Lady Anne, who had been quiet and kind and had neither deserved this violent fate nor the betrayal Cass had subjected her to.

Chapter 40

For months there was peace. Cass wrapped the ruby-hilted sword in rags and left it under her bed to gather dust. The sisterhood thrived, with many of the women who had joined them remaining at the manor even after the men of the Northumbrian fyrd returned to their villages. And though some went home to husbands and families, the occasional story of a local woman whipping out a dagger unexpectedly when a trader tried to charge her too much or a suitor treated her roughly was the source of much mirth and pride for Cass, Angharad and the others round the hearth in the evenings.

Winter passed and spring came, bringing with it a thaw that gradually seemed to melt the frozen numbness Cass had felt since she returned from Deva, as well as the ice that had crystallized in the puddles at the edges of the meadow. She watched, delighted, as little Hugh took his first, unsteady steps in the long grass, clapping his chubby hands in delight as his mother laughed and scooped him up in her arms.

Cass and Sir Gamelin had retreated to a stiff, awkwardly polite distance after Lady Anne's death and there seemed to be a chasm between them that they simply couldn't cross. Neither of them could seem to move past their guilt, and every time he drew near to her she felt that she was somehow betraying the poor woman all over again and she made excuses and swiftly withdrew.

Eventually, along with most of Mordaunt's other men, Sir Gamelin left the manor, and Cass could not find it in her aching heart to ask him if he would join another lord's court or whether he would return home to his family farm. She liked to think of him sometimes, as she lay awake in the dark, too afraid of the spectres that haunted her dreams to allow herself to fall asleep. She pictured him on a windswept hillside at sunset, sitting among a vast flock of sheep, watching the colours of the sky slowly changing. She liked to imagine him at peace.

So the manor was the sole domain of women again, and Cass was not the only one who was glad of it. Slowly, as word of their exploits at Deva spread, more and more girls joined them, coming to learn or to escape, seeking adventure or running away from it. Angharad welcomed them all.

Cass found purpose and satisfaction in the long days she spent teaching the young women to ride and joust or training them in swordswomanship. It was hard rewarding work, with plenty of opportunity to joke and spar with Rowan and Elaine, and occasionally Astra, when she was there teaching the new girls to throw daggers and not off earning dubiously sourced coins to add to the manor's coffers. Most of all, the longer Cass spent pushing her body to the limit in the meadow in the daytime, the fewer nightmares awoke her, screaming and drenched in sweat, at night.

She knew Alys worried about her, but she avoided time alone with her, always sending one of the younger squires if some poultice or medicine needed fetching, retiring abruptly in the evenings if they seemed at risk of becoming the last two left sitting beside the dying fire. Though her physical bruises had healed, there were others that were not so quick to fade, and she did not want to hear any more about 'destiny'.

'Sir Galahad' stopped by from time to time, bringing them news of Arthur's court and his campaigns against the sea wolves and the small bands of Saxons who continued to arrive on their shores.

And gradually, though Cass felt anchored in time, never moving, as if Lily's death and Lady Anne's and Martha's and Gamelin's departure and the blood that dripped from her sword in her dreams all kept her trapped like amber sealing her in place, things changed.

Blyth proudly welcomed a new batch of foals, who staggered around the courtyard on wobbling legs and slept curled into their mother's ribcages.

Little Nell grew tall enough for her first sword and started her training at last.

Susan, who had seemed to become paler and thinner each day after Elizabeth's death, left the manor and married a farmer in Mercia. She did not write or visit.

Slowly the Saxons' numbers began to creep back up, as autumn and winter passed, and spring came again. News filtered through to the manor from travelling musicians and scouts of skirmishes at the coast, of villages ransacked, of the High King's forces on the move again. That was when the messengers began to arrive. It was always the same. A lengthy missive to Cass detailing Arthur's woes, his difficulty in persuading the lesser kings to leave their homes and mobilize their fyrds to help him, his fears for Britain, and the crushing sense of responsibility to make the right decisions. And every letter ended with a plea. If Cass would come, if she would just bring her sword and some of her fellow knights, he knew it could make the difference between victory and defeat.

The first letter she answered by return messenger. Explaining that she could not pick up her sword. Telling him she was needed here. She could not come. The second and third she ignored. But then Arthur arrived.

The king came under cover of nightfall with an entourage of only a few knights, Sir Galahad among them. Angharad greeted him warmly, but Cass watched warily as they supped the following night, and her suspicions were confirmed when he sought her out in the late evening and begged her to ride with him to rout the Saxons at Linnuis once and for all.

But it was not to be the end. They rode for Linnuis the next morning and the ruby sword sprang gladly into Cass's hand. She and Arthur rode together this time, and on the journey they talked about his hopes for a united Britain, about how conflicted he felt about Uther and replacing him as king, about what their father had been like and what it would have been like if they had had the chance to know their mother. He spoke of his loneliness and his desire to be a great king, and Cass knew, feeling the truth of it in her heart, that he meant what he said.

'I just want to live up to my birthright,' he said quietly, as the horses slowed and the sky glowed blood red before the sun sank below the horizon.

Cass wondered what it was like to be a man, to have a birthright that was not contested or questioned or hidden but simply stated and celebrated. How different her life might be. And she knew that it did not occur to Arthur even for a moment.

They stood side by side in the battle this time, and each wielded the sword they had drawn from a stone with such power and strength that they struck awe into the hearts of those who beheld them. When she was near Arthur she felt somehow connected to him, as if they were part of the same being, his feelings alive in her body. And as they took on the Saxons shoulder to shoulder it was as if their weapons shared the same affinity. Her sword flew like lightning to mirror his, to thrust when he thrust and to sweep when he swept. Or perhaps it was his sword that followed hers, like a reflection or a faithful shadow. She only knew that together they seemed unstoppable. Fighting alongside him was like dreaming; she only seemed to awake afterwards, aching, a little dazed, and often surprised by the acts they had wrought together.

Afterwards they sat together a long time in Arthur's tent, not saying much to each other. The magic drained slowly from Cass's body, from her fingers and her muscles, and she could see and feel Arthur coming back to himself as well. And he looked into her eyes and told her they were meant to do this, destined, together, to be a point of light amid the darkness.

They defeated the Saxons that day, so thoroughly and terribly that Cass felt certain there would at least be a few seasons of peace to enjoy before they dared to invade again.

But it was not to be. It was the beginning of a long and weary pattern. Cass always capitulated in the end. He would hug her and thank her and kiss her hands, and she would ride the next day, usually with Angharad and Rowan, Elaine and some of the others, to join Arthur's men on hillside or coastline, wherever the newest battle lines had been drawn up.

Linnuis, Bassus, Guinnion: the High King would call and Cass and the other women knights would answer, lending their swords, their strategy and their strength to his campaigns as Arthur's star burned brighter and brighter for the people of Britain. And each time she grew closer to her brother, as they fought alongside each other and talked late into the night, won battles together, lost friends together and triumphed together over the Saxons.

Cass grew to know Arthur, and, in spite of his flaws, to love him. Sometimes she wondered what their lives would have been like if they had been allowed to grow up together as children, as twins, far away from Uther's court, Merlin's controlling influence and any idea of destiny or kingship or glory. If neither had ever touched a sword.

The two dragons in Cass's chest fought day and night.

There was part of her that relished the feeling of being needed, the sense that she could use her skill for a purpose and that she was in some way fulfilling the prophecy that had been made about her. And when she was engaged in campaigns and battles, exhausted physically and mentally, there was less time to sit, gazing into the fire, and remember all the dead.

It was obvious to Cass, then to Arthur, and perhaps to more of their knights than would dare to admit it, that it was not Arthur's sword but Cass's that heralded the turning point in their battles. Arthur was a formidable fighter, and when he rode into battle with his knights alongside him there was no more glorious sight to be seen in all the land, but it was the slight figure beside him, her untidy curls sometimes spilling out of the bottom of her helmet, her sword blinking with a red eye that seemed to see all, who radiated power and turned the tide of the conflict more often than not.

Arthur struggled with this. He seemed trapped between his love and admiration for Cass and his jealousy and bitterness when her sword shone brighter than his. And it was jealousy, she realized with a heavy heart, when the flaps of his tent remained firmly closed to her the night after the battle at Bassus had ended. She had fought like a demon that day, destroying every man who approached her, and she had seen the gratitude and awe on her brother's dirt-streaked face when he had turned to her in the worst heat of the fighting. And yet that night, as she sat wrapping bandages round a long deep cut in her forearm, waiting for her brother to come to her and talk as they always did, as the sky blackened and the cold became more bitter, she realized he was not coming. And she sat through the night alone.

The longer this went on, the longer the other dragon began to beat its wings and stoke the furnace in her chest. It roared that she was a monster, that she had become something unrecognizable, that this was not the reason she had learned to fight. And she wondered if her affection and loyalty for her brother was blinding her to the reality of what she had been drawn into.

And there was Merlin, who had crept imperceptibly back into Arthur's life and court. The first Cass knew of his return was when Arthur began making casual mentions of his counsel and plans, eyeing Cass sideways as if to gauge her response. Later he began to reappear at Arthur's side, towering over the battlefields on his huge grey charger and occupying Arthur in his pavilion with maps and strange texts long into the night. And the more Merlin was present, the more Cass felt Arthur beginning to slip away.

She understood his conflict. Merlin had been kind to him as a lonely boy and Arthur, with the weight of a kingdom on his shoulders, had been grateful for any care he had been shown. But it was *she* who had saved Arthur on the battlefield, ridden into danger with him time and time again. And yet Merlin was regaining his control with every passing day.

Suddenly Arthur began to talk less about the security of the borders or the unity of the different regions and more about his kingship, about blazing a trail of glory to unite his people. She saw how his face shone when travelling bards sang songs of his victories and how it darkened into a scowl if the singer referred to Cass or to the other women whose names were increasingly widely known, even if just in passing.

The conquests became bloodier and more desperate. Arthur would write to Cass, begging her to come to his side to help protect villages from marauding groups of Saxon warriors, but when she arrived, the supposed pillagers would be straggling bands of wounded men, pursued as they ran away and stamped out without mercy. And Cass, who already felt so uneasy about the ruby sword that slept beneath her bed, began to fear that it might stain her very soul.

Arthur began to be plagued with black moods that descended upon him for days at a time and could not be shaken. He would greet her with almost hysterical gratitude when she arrived but then seem to resent her deeply after the battle had been won, particularly if it had been her sword that had played the decisive role in winning it. And all the while Merlin was at his side, always whispering, whispering in his ear, and Cass began to fear that he was dripping a kind of dark magic into her brother's heart.

So when at last her fears and doubts and sickening horror at the endless violence that she cradled in her chest all poured out of her one night, as she and Arthur surveyed the carnage together while the sun set on yet another battlefield, it was an outburst that had been a very long time coming.

'It is necessary,' he replied slowly, after her fears and her self-disgust had rushed out of her, and he did not look at her but at the horizon. 'It is necessary for unity, for the future of Britain.'

Cass gave a heavy sigh and felt as if every bone in her body was old and tired and longed to rest. 'But there is another way forward. A path to peace that doesn't rely on slaughter. A way to live alongside newcomers, instead of spending our whole lives repelling them.'

'That is weak and fanciful talk,' he said dismissively. 'Women's talk.'

'Don't you *dare*.' She faced him, her teeth gritted and eyes flashing. 'Don't you dare suggest that my sex has anything to do with the validity of my opinions or I will draw my sword here and now and we will see the difference between a woman's blade and a man's, and you know as well as me what the outcome will be. It was me who saved your life at Deva. I who continue to save you, over and over again.'

'I am the High King,' he roared furiously, and she felt suddenly that overwhelming sense of pity for him that surfaced now and then, when he seemed to prefer to cling to an idea of himself, of his kingship or of his marriage, rather than have the courage to confront the truth.

'Who am I talking to?' she demanded, exasperated. 'Arthur my king, Arthur my brother, or Merlin speaking through Arthur his puppet?'

He flushed a deep angry red. 'It is I, Arthur, who will unite all Britain, who will hold back the darkness and lead it into the light.'

'I have heard that phrase so many times, Arthur. I never really questioned what it meant. But how do we know that *we ourselves* are not the darkness?'

Chapter 41

They had never parted on such cold terms. He did not emerge from his pavilion as they rode away the next morning, and she did not look back.

But it was only a few short months before the next letter came. And this one was different. The tone was conciliatory and openly acknowledged her doubts. Often, he admitted, though he had not been able to say it in person, he was haunted by the same fears as her. He did not have the answers. He would not have sent for her now, he wrote, if there had been any other choice. This would be the last time. He promised.

The situation sounded very grave. The remaining Saxon forces massed at Badon, Arthur wrote, and they were preparing for one last great battle. They had gathered every one of their men in Britain to an area of flat marshland, and intended to stage a last stand, risking everything for the chance to destroy Arthur's forces. It was a moment of great peril, Arthur wrote, but also of great opportunity. If they defeated the Saxons now, there would be peace. Real, lasting peace, for years, not weeks. And wasn't that what Cass wanted most of all?

He had always been persuasive.

And he wrote that there was a chance to avoid bloodshed: a way to take the Saxons unawares without sacrificing hundreds of their own. A strategy that could only work with Cass's help.

She frowned and read the part of the letter containing Arthur's plan three times. Then she hastened to Angharad's chambers.

There were new silver threads in Angharad's hair, Cass noticed, with a jolt, as they saddled their horses together in companionable silence early the next morning. She thought that it was as if a small part of Vivian, whose long silver hair had shone brightly as she galloped down the lists, had attached itself to the woman she had loved. The thought gave her comfort.

Every year, Cass knew Angharad was giving more and more responsibility for the running of the manor to

Rowan, preparing her to take over some day, though none of them ever discussed it explicitly. Rowan was always uncharacteristically delicate when they veered close to the topic, as if she feared Cass would feel slighted or overlooked, but Cass understood. It was better this way. Rowan, who had always been searching for a home, belonged to the manor as completely as it belonged to her. And she wondered if Angharad suspected, as she sometimes did herself, that Cass would never be completely free to remain in one place or to make her own choices, not for as long as the ruby sword held its magnetic power over her.

'So Arthur wants to use us as bait?' Rowan clarified, as they rode south. She did not sound impressed. The most senior knights rode in a tight cluster, led by Angharad, and three dozen or so of the other women, mostly knights and a few squires, followed behind.

'Not bait exactly,' Cass replied, irked at how quick she was to defend him. 'A distraction.'

'We draw them into the marsh, they get bogged down, Arthur and his forces surprise them from behind and cut them down before they can get out,' Elaine summarized succinctly, throwing her head back and closing her eyes to enjoy the morning sun on her face.

'Exactly. And if we succeed, it should end the struggles with the Saxons for good,' Cass said, allowing the blazing brightness of the blue sky and the cheerful twittering of birds in the hedgerows to fill her with fragile hope.

'We've heard that before,' Astra muttered, but Cass chose to ignore her, and they did not mention Arthur again for the rest of the journey.

It was an eerie site for a battle. The weather had become increasingly changeable as they rode, and the skies hung grey and uneasy over the flat, boggy terrain. There was an insipid mist curling in from the west, in the direction of the coast, and it lent an other-worldly strangeness to the marshland. Shadows and figures seemed to move just out of reach, and trees and rocks loomed suddenly and unexpectedly out of the mist, startling the horses.

'There.' Cass pointed to the landmark Arthur had described: a group of three dead trees, their skeletons reaching up towards the sky, next to the ruins of a small building. Behind them the terrain rose slightly, forming a long ridge lined with alder trees. 'The Saxons are camped just beyond that ridge. We attack at midday, draw them over the ridge towards the marsh, and Arthur will arrive soon afterwards.'

'What could possibly go wrong?' Rowan asked, cracking her knuckles and grinning.

'We are outnumbered,' Cass admitted. 'Arthur wrote that there are at least two hundred of them. But his forces will dwarf theirs. We only have to distract them long enough to lead them into the boggier ground. He will do the rest.'

She carefully read and reread Arthur's missive, making sure all the women knew the lie of the land. There was a strip of firmer ground, he had written, marked by a line of willow trees. If they stayed close to those, their horses would retain their footing while the Saxons floundered.

When she looked back on that day, Cass would realize that she knew, before they even crested the ridge, that something was terribly wrong. Deep in the pit of her stomach there was an aching, groaning sense of foreboding. But she would wonder later if she refused to allow herself to feel it because she knew that if she did she would have to face the reality of her brother's betrayal.

The forty or so women burst over the top of the incline, swords and spears and bows raised, poised to capitalize on the element of surprise. If they could fell a few dozen of the Saxons before they engaged them in combat, it would help to offset the disadvantage of their smaller numbers.

For a moment, Cass could not make sense of what she was looking at. She had expected an encampment of two hundred tents. There would be some men on guard inevitably, but others, with any luck, would be at leisure and be easier targets for the women's arrows.

She stopped, as the others galloped over the ridgeline

behind her and wheeled about, checking their horses in shock.

Below them on the marshy plain was massed an army of Saxon warriors, at least eight hundred of them. There were no tents, no off-duty men slumbering and ready to be picked off. They stood in formation, fully armed, shields interlocked in neat impenetrable rows. They faced the ridge, poised and waiting. And as the last of the women appeared, they released their arrows and spears.

Chapter 42

'*Retreat!*' Angharad screamed, and the horses whinnied in horror as the air around them exploded with the hot sting of flying arrows.

At least half a dozen of the women dropped instantly, some sliding out of their saddles and leaving their terrified horses to career riderless down the slope, others tangled and bloodied amongst thrashing hooves on the ground.

Cass wrenched Pebble's reins round and fled, back through the alder trees and down the other side of the ridge, back towards the marsh, as the awful vibrations of eight hundred men marching in step shuddered the ground beneath her.

'They knew we were coming!' Rowan shouted furiously, leaning down flat to her horse's neck to urge it forward.

'Scouts?' Cass panted, doing the same.

'Perhaps,' Rowan threw back, and Cass knew what she was thinking.

But Arthur surely could not have betrayed them. Not like this. He was coming; he must be. And as they streamed back towards the safety of the willows, she tried to ignore the voice in her head that asked why, if that were true, he had given her such a massive underestimate of the enemy's numbers.

There was worse to come.

As the first of the women reached the trees, their horses began to struggle, slowing and stumbling, picking their hooves up strangely as if they were being sucked into the ground. Too late Cass realized that nothing in Arthur's letter should have been trusted. Too late she yanked at Pebble's reins.

The bog was as deceptive and malevolent as quicksand. Within moments most of the horses were thrashing in panic, sending up sprays of dank foul-smelling mud as they struggled to regain their footing. Only Elaine and Angharad, bringing up the rear, had seen the danger in time to avoid it, stopping their horses before they entered the bog. But they were now marooned, trapped between the unsafe ground and the rapidly advancing might of the Saxon lines.

Cass felt adrenaline exploding in her veins as she

struggled to calm Pebble. She pulled an arrow from her quiver and fitted it to her bow, shooting in the direction of the oncoming army. It struck harmlessly into a wooden shield. She drew back the bowstring again and again, releasing a volley of arrows, and the other women did the same, forcing the Saxons to slow as they lifted their shields in a defensive formation, crouching beneath them like a protective shell, but the arrows bounced off the shield wall and the men continued to advance.

Cass's hand scrabbled frantically for her quiver again and found it empty. She began to urge Pebble back towards Angharad, but the little horse was sinking frantically in the spongy ground, seemingly unable to find firm footing.

Cass watched, her heart in her mouth, as Angharad and Elaine sat tall and still on their mounts, shields and swords firm in the face of certain death. She felt her eyes sting with the burn of furious tears and wanted to scream at the unfairness of it all. That this should be how it ended. After everything. How dare he discard her like this, after she had made his kingship everything he had wanted?

The Saxons halted their advance, and two of them stepped forward out of the front line towards Elaine and Angharad. They knew the victory was theirs. They were going to take their time and savour it. Cass felt sick. She did not want to watch, but she could not tear her eyes away.

Angharad and Elaine dismounted lightly, stepping forward to meet the Saxon men, who towered above them. Cass's heart swelled in her chest. They would die with honour, facing their enemies in single combat.

They raised their swords.

She braced herself for the clash of metal, but a different noise came instead: the whistling of spears and arrows, quickly followed by howls of pain. At the back of the Saxon lines, something was happening. The two enormous Saxons who had been advancing swiftly towards Angharad and Elaine paused, turning to look behind them.

Cass looked too, and for a moment she thought the sky had darkened in a sudden storm rolling in over the ridge. Then she saw that it was not dark clouds, but a great mass of bodies on horseback, pouring past the elder trees and racing down the slope to crash explosively into the rear of the enemy formation.

The Saxons were unprepared for this. They had been entirely focused on protecting the front of their ranks with their shield walls, leaving their backs dangerously exposed. The onslaught of new fighters toppled the back few rows of their formation as swiftly as dominos, sending the rest stumbling forward in panic, the neat rows bending and buckling as men lurched and crashed into one another.

Cass saw Angharad and Elaine exploit the confusion to

remount their horses, as the two Saxons they had been poised to fight turned and lumbered back towards this new threat instead.

She felt relief and gratitude explode inside her chest. Arthur had come after all. But in the same moment, she realized that there were no red tunics or white shields among the bloody frenzy of the battle in front of her.

Cass redoubled her efforts, slipping down out of her saddle to land with a freezing splash thigh deep in the marsh water, and attempting to lead Pebble back to dry land by the reins. Around her others were doing the same, taking full advantage of the distraction.

But Pebble was confused and scared, her eyes rolling to the whites, and Cass gave up, patting her gently on the neck before dropping the reins and beginning to wade back towards Angharad and Elaine on foot instead.

By the time she reached them, the melee was at a fever pitch. The noise was almost unbearable. Men grunting, screams and cries of pain and the endless grating crash and screech of metal on metal. Most of the Saxons had turned towards the enemy behind them, and Cass, Angharad and Elaine sprang forward to attack while their backs were exposed.

The fighting was furious and frenzied, unlike anything Cass had ever experienced. As they attacked from one side, the knights who had come to their rescue pressed relentlessly from the opposite direction, squeezing the Saxons between them in a confused tumult of blood and noise. Some of the knights on the other side broke away and rode round the side to attack the Saxons' flank, led by a rider who seemed to be in charge, raining down spear thrusts and sword strokes like some kind of avenging demon.

Closer and closer they came, men falling in their wake, and it was not until the leader was almost upon her that Cass suddenly knew the familiar coat of the horse and could see the details of the leather breastplate that she had polished so often she knew it better than her own.

'You looked like you could use a hand,' Sigrid shouted over the din of the battle.

Chapter 43

Cass had fought alongside Sigrid so many times in her dreams that it was difficult to be sure she was truly awake. But even in her dreams, Sigrid had not fought so courageously or led her forces with such relentless and brilliant focus.

She and Cass stood back to back, their swords flashing and wheeling as they steadily took down one man after another, sometimes turning to switch opponents, each instinctively knowing the other's patterns of attack like a well-trodden dance. The battlefield faded around them and Cass was back in the practice room at the manor where Sigrid had drilled her relentlessly throughout the freezing nights of that first winter, cajoling and praising and goading her until the golden thread of power that had tentatively started to bud inside Cass was drawn out into her sword and did her bidding.

And it emerged again now, pouring out of her like lightning, striking the men around her down as if in some terrible storm. She let everything flow out through her fingers like liquid fire: her fury and grief at Arthur's betrayal, her heartsick repulsion at the massacres she had played a role in, her terror that her legacy might not be light but death and destruction. The light seemed to grow until it almost blinded her, bathing the whole battlefield in a brilliant spectral light that glowed on the women's heads, crowning them with gold.

It seemed to Cass later that perhaps there had been golden eyes on the battlefield that day, not staring passively at her but standing alongside her, amplifying her power, fighting by her side. But she could never be sure. And nobody else seemed to have seen a thing.

The heat and the light seemed to spread, as it had never done before, as if it could no longer be contained by Cass's body and her sword alone, and she saw the wonder and the fear on the other women's faces as it seemed to flow into their weapons too. They began to move faster, impossibly fast, their spears seemed always to find their targets and their swords struck true and bit deep, even through thick leather armour. Cass saw Elaine's eyes widen, saw Angharad and Rowan glance towards her and did not know if it was awe or terror on their faces, but she could not speak or explain or even question what was happening because it had taken over her so completely that every cell in her body seemed to be singing and vibrating with the sound and the fury of it and it was all she could do to stay on her feet and allow it to flow through her without burning her alive.

Slowly but surely, almost imperceptibly at first, the advantage began to shift towards the Britons. It seemed impossible – they were outnumbered two to one, even with the arrival of Sigrid's forces – yet men were falling, falling, their bodies piling up in the cloudy water at the edges of the marsh, their blood running in rivulets to merge with the darkness of the bog.

Even as the tumult around her lessened a little, as the other women began to slow and seemed to take back control of their swords, Cass could not calm the chattering of her teeth or the molten burn of the energy that still rushed through her and out of her, singeing her skin until it felt like it crackled and steamed in the misty air.

And the looks that had been filled with admiration and wonder began to change, as the direction of the battle swung in the women's favour, as the remaining Saxons began to grunt in pain and panic, and some began to break away and try to flee. They were winning, they were slowing down, some of the women were even pausing to rest, their hands on their knees, or removing helmets to wipe sweating brows, and yet Cass could not pause, could not relent, could not stop. Her sword was moving of its own accord, so fast it was almost a blur, slashing and slicing relentlessly, leaving no man standing at the edge of the marsh.

She felt herself beginning to shake, first her hands, which seemed almost fused to the handle of her sword, then her forearms and soon her whole body, as if the vibrations passing through her had become overwhelming, too powerful to bear. She heard Angharad cry out and knew that the women were closing in around her, and then she felt a hand on hers, wrapping round the handle of her sword. A cool strong hand, both gentle and commanding, and she looked up into the eyes of the woman who had changed her life. Then the sword seemed to jerk in her hands without her bidding, as if it would shake Sigrid off, as if it would bury itself in her torso, to regain its own control over Cass, but Sigrid was there, both arms round her, their foreheads meeting, her eyes never leaving hers, and her connection with her mentor was even greater than her connection with the power and the sword. With a wrenching effort that felt almost too great to bear, Cass broke the bond with the weapon and allowed it to drop to the ground at her feet with a splash.

At once she felt her whole body weaken as if a flame had been blown out, and she staggered and swayed, and knew that Sigrid had caught her in her arms before the world turned black.

Chapter 44

The sky was black when Cass arrived at Camelot. The day was stiflingly hot. There was no breeze to give relief from the stuffy humidity and the air seemed to crackle with pent-up power that longed to release itself from the threatening clouds.

By the time she had climbed the steep and winding path to the gates of the castle, sweat was running into her eyes, but she kept the visor of her helmet closed and did not slacken her pace.

She was ready, this time, for the questions of the gatekeepers, and presented them wordlessly, with the papers Angharad had secured for her. The gates opened and she strode forward, grimly gripping the handle of her sword through her gauntlet. She had not touched it with her bare hands since the battle.

Her feet carried her faultlessly in the direction of Arthur's chambers, remembering every staircase and corridor, the beautiful tapestries and treasures blurring brightly together as she passed.

When the two guards at the door leaped forward to stop her, she ducked, allowing the blow one had aimed at her head to stun the other instead, then cracked him sharply on the side of the helmet with the hilt of her sword so that he, too, slid down the wall to rest, motionless, beside his partner.

Arthur and Merlin were sitting in front of the fireplace on the same chairs Cass and her brother had sat on, side by side, the night they had first met. Before she had revealed herself to him. Before she had propped up his campaigns and his kingship. Before he had tried to kill her.

His face paled even before she wrenched off her helmet to stand, breathless and flushed, before him, her eyes aflame with fury and hurt.

'My lord,' she said, her tone deferential and ice cold, and she bowed to him.

'You are not—' Arthur half leaped from his seat, though Merlin did not stir.

'Dead? No. Sorry if you're disappointed.'

Arthur stumbled a few steps towards her, as if he wanted to embrace her, and then stopped abruptly at the expression on Cass's face. He half turned to Merlin, and Cass could see genuine regret and guilt on his face. Guilt but also fear. And still he looked to Merlin for guidance.

Merlin stood, his lips curling in that thin gruesome smile that made the hairs stand up all along Cass's arms. 'So you were victorious, Cassandra Pendragon.'

'No thanks to you,' she said, her voice tight with fury. She turned away from him and looked directly into her brother's eyes – *her* eyes. 'You left me to die, Arthur, alongside all the women who have fought so bravely for you. How could you do it? How could you let this monster into your mind and your heart?'

Arthur seemed dazed; he glanced between Cass and Merlin and took a step back, falling weakly into his chair. 'I never meant . . . He did not tell me until afterwards,' he stammered. 'When I sent the letter, I believed it all to be true. I thought we would come to support you. But Merlin told me our initial reports had been inaccurate. The enemy's number had increased. There was no possible way we could win – it would be a massacre, leading more men to die. I was trying to do the right thing, Cass. I did not think we could save you.'

'And you believed him?' She snorted derisively. 'You did

not even try? I would never have left you to die like that. Never. We were completely outnumbered, overwhelmed by the Saxons, but we still fought. We did not give up and run away like cowards.'

'And yet it was not your victory, Cassandra,' Merlin purred, and his self-satisfied tone made her seethe with anger. Suddenly she noticed that the gauntlet holding her sword seemed to be warming; was it her imagination or was the metal becoming hotter to the touch?

'The Battle of Badon will go down in history as the day that Arthur alone defeated the Saxons. The once and future king, wreathed in glory for ever more.'

'He was not even there—'

'It does not matter. Those peasants who chant your name, they cannot write, Cassandra. History will not remember you; it will crown him with glory. You will be forgotten, and the other women with you. Nobody will know your name. Nobody will even know you existed.'

Cass smiled at him, and the sword burned so hot that she thought she would not be able to bear to hold it much longer. It seemed to her that light was glimmering all along the blade, shining out of it, flooding the room with a brightness that was almost unbearable, and yet neither Arthur nor Merlin seemed to have noticed.

'It does not matter,' she said quietly, as she took a step

closer to Merlin. 'It does not matter if my name is not remembered. I will still have fulfilled my destiny. To enable the light to push out the darkness.'

And before anybody could move, before Merlin had time to react or Arthur to stop her, she allowed the burning sword to bury itself deep in Merlin's heart.

The metal turned cold almost at once. She looked down at the hilt of the sword, buried in his chest, and it seemed that the ruby that had once burned and flickered was cold and lifeless at last.

Arthur gasped helplessly, gaping at her in horror as his adviser's blood spread across the floor and began to pool around the soles of his boots.

'Cass.'

'You will survive this, brother,' she said, 'and both you and Britain will be far stronger for it. I was never meant to take the throne. I was meant to protect it from this evil.'

And as she turned and left the room, she thought that she heard a faint hiss as the first drops of Merlin's blood reached the hot stones at the edge of the fire.

Chapter 45

She found the farm as the day was dying. Golden light set fire to the seas of wheat that swayed gently around it. The air was warm but it smelled like rain.

He was bringing the cows in from the field, speaking to them gently as he ushered the last of the herd through the gate and closed it behind them.

Their soft lowing was like music as he looked across the bright green grass and saw her waiting.

'Hello, Cassandra Pendragon.'

Sir Gamelin leaned on the splintered wooden gate and watched her as she walked closer.

'Are you free?' he asked at last.

The hazel eyes met the green and blue, and she nodded.

'What about Arthur? And Merlin?'

She told him.

So he took her to the orchard, where the last of the overripe apples lay thick on the ground, spilling their pulpy sweetness onto the sun-baked earth, reminding her of another orchard so long ago. And she dug a hole, wide and deep, beneath the tallest tree, and wrapped the ruby sword in a cloth and buried it there. Then she replaced it in her sword belt with a weapon of Iona's making, light and sharp.

'You came', he said, his hand in hers. 'But wasn't this everything you were running away from? He gestured to the farm, the fields and to himself. 'Marriage, domesticity . . .'

She kissed him, hard, and swung herself back up onto her waiting horse.

'It wasn't exactly marriage or domesticity I had in mind.'

And he led his own charger out of the stable, mounted, and followed her.

Angharad never explicitly pardoned Sigrid, but there was great celebration at her return to the manor, bringing her late brother Jonathan's squire, who had become a formidable knight, and the fighting force they had assembled together in the time since her departure.

It had been chance that she had been near to hand that

day at Badon, when her scouts had alerted her to a Saxon force nearby and she had arrived to find Cass and the other women outnumbered and close to defeat. Though Alys scoffed at the notion and told Cass it was no more chance than her initial meeting with Sigrid in the orchard had been.

Suddenly the manor was bursting with new arrivals. There were seasoned knights, glad to gather to Angharad and swear fealty to her after the story of her sensational victory at Badon spread like wildfire. And eager young recruits, keen to learn and to be part of Northumbria's new fyrd.

'You could use the space,' Cass laughed, though her voice broke, as she sat round the fire with Angharad and Rowan, Elaine and Alys, the night before she and Gamelin were due to leave on their first quest. 'You'll need my chambers for the sheer number who are vying to become Rowan's new squire.'

Rowan grinned, running a cloth along the blade of her sword and eyeing it critically. 'My reputation precedes me. And it's about time I had someone else to polish my weapons, I'm terrible at doing it myself.'

'You will be missed,' Alys said quietly, and Cass took her weathered hands between her own.

'I will be back. From time to time. I can't leave Astra to her own devices for too long.'

Astra threw a shoe at her and continued to whittle at the piece of wood she was was shaping into a new die. 'Shave it just the slightest bit on this side,' she muttered, 'and it will fall more often than not on the number two.'

They all laughed.

'Where will you go first?' Elaine asked.

'West,' Cass replied, simply. 'Lady Nimue has work for us to do there. A town where the women are ill-treated by their menfolk under a bullying lord who needs to learn the meaning of fairness.' She tested the blade of her sword with her thumb, and for a moment it was a cold winter night, years earlier, and she and Lily were gossiping together beside the embers as they sharpened their mistress's weapons.

She recalled the hunger she had felt then, for an unknown destiny, for the chance to prove herself, and, above all, for adventure. And the ever-present fear and doubt about who she was and whether she could live up to all she was supposed to be.

Cass sighed, contentedly. There was a calm certainty within her now. And she would not swap it for anything.

'And if Arthur comes looking for you again?'

She stirred, coming back to the present. 'I do not think he will. I have done everything I can for him. The rest is up to him now. I can be more useful elsewhere.'

'And if we need you?' Angharad's voice was soft, and her

throat worked as her eyes met Cass's across the flickering fireplace.

'With Sigrid and Rowan at your side and the fiercest fyrd in Britain at your disposal?" She shook her head. 'You have Astra and Elaine to train the new recruits and Alys to heal them. Northumbria is in safe hands.'

'I did not mean if Northumbria needs you. I meant if we do.'

Cass swallowed hard against the lump that had risen in her throat. 'Then I will come back. I will come *home*.'

'Go then,' Alys said quietly, as Cass rose to take her leave. 'Britain is lucky to have you, Cassandra Pendragon, daughter of Uther.' And Cass knew that the soft crack in her voice was not sadness, but pride.

'And remember that there has always been more than one way to be a queen.'

Acknowledgements

Working on this book has been a dream come true. I'm so grateful to all the wonderful and passionate readers I have met who have taken Cass and her sisterhood to heart.

I am so lucky to work with the most wonderful team of people who contribute a huge amount to each book I write – none of it would be possible without them.

A heartfelt thank you to my wonderful and supportive editor Lucy Pearse, who is the greatest cheerleader, and to Arub Ahmed, for her brilliant editing. I am so lucky to work with the peerless team at Simon & Schuster, including Jess Dean, Laura Hough, Sarah Macmillan, Olivia Horrox, Ellen Abernethy, Lizzie Irwin, Olive Childs, Lilli Bagnall, and all the rest of their colleagues as well as Laura Smythe and Nic Wilkinson, who have worked so hard to help my books find their readers. Thank you to Jennie Roman and Kathy Webb for their eagle-eyed copy editing and proofreading. And a huge thank you to the brilliant Micaela Alcaino (archer and artist extraordinaire) and Sean Williams for creating a cover that surpassed all my hopes and dreams!

I couldn't be more grateful to Abigail Bergstrom, my wonderful agent, and everyone at Bergstrom Studio, as well as Alexandra Cliff and everyone at Rachel Mills Literary, who do such an excellent job of finding foreign homes for my books. I'm hugely grateful to all my wonderful editors and translators in other languages and territories who bring Cass and her adventures to new readers.

Training with the Knights of Middle England at the Warwick International School of Riding was an absolute highlight of the research process for this book, and I'd like to say a big thank you to Tanya, whose expert instruction in horseback archery resulted in many of the training and fight sequences in the book, as well as fearless jousting instructors Joe, Jon and Chelsea, who were the most supportive and encouraging team to work with.

Finally, I'd like to say thank you to my readers, many of whom I know have followed and supported me from non-fiction to YA fiction, to fantasy and beyond. I feel so lucky and grateful to have such a dedicated and supportive readership and meeting you at book events is the highlight of my career. I hope this book created the same escapism and feminist joy for you as it did for me!

Photograph © Siggi Holm

About the Author

Laura Bates is a feminist activist and bestselling author. She writes regularly for the *Guardian, New York Times* and others. Her Everyday Sexism Project has collected over 250,000 testimonies of gender inequality and has helped to put sexual consent on the school curriculum, change Facebook's policies on sexual violence and transform the British Transport Police's approach to sexual offences. Laura works closely with bodies like the United Nations, the Council of Europe, MPs, police forces, schools and businesses to tackle misogyny. She is a Fellow of the Royal Society of Literature, an Honorary Fellow of St John's College, Cambridge and recipient of a British Empire Medal for services to gender equality.